There was a reckless voice [...]
[...]en care. He'd killed another monster. He only
[...]ished he could get them all..."

WHAT IF IT WAS YOUR DAUGHTER HE DESTROYED?
WHAT IF IT WAS YOUR LIFE HE SHATTERED?
WHAT WOULD YOU DO?

"A REVENGE TALE WITH HEFT."—*People*

"HEART-WRENCHING, CONTROVERSIAL,
AND PROVOCATIVE."—*Orlando Sentinel*

"TIM GREEN IS A MASTER."
—Nelson DeMille

THE·TRUE·ADMINISTR[...]

6.99
3.50

PRAISE FOR
TIM GREEN'S *THE FIFTH ANGEL*

"Green has a great ear for dialogue [and he] writes with admirable economy."
—*Kirkus Reviews*

"Briskly paced...compelling."
—*Publishers Weekly*

"Dark, gritty, and engrossing. A provocative story of a lawyer who brews his own justice."
—Robert K. Tannenbaum, author of *Absolute Rage*

"GRIPPING...THOUGHT-PROVOKING...A SOLID THRILLER."
—*Booklist*

...AND FOR HIS PREVIOUS NOVELS
THE FOURTH PERIMETER

"A page-turner of the week...deftly braids two strands of suspense." —*People*

"Full of twists and surprises...a delightful thriller.... Green is a craftsman of the written word."
—*Winston-Salem Journal*

more...

"Green keeps the suspense building and the reader continually off guard."
                                    —*Chicago Tribune*

THE LETTER OF THE LAW

"Taut…page-turning…Green's best novel to date, and that's saying a lot."
                                    —*USA Today*

"A top-notch writer….This book moves fast and hits harder."
                                    —*Tampa Tribune-Times*

"Green scores big!…Highly recommended."
                                    —*Library Journal*

"A fun read….Green keeps the pages turning."
                                    —*Booklist*

"Interesting characters…an intelligent plot…a page-turning legal thriller."
                                    —*Tulsa World*

"Entertaining…suspenseful, and exciting."
                                    —*Wichita Falls Times Record News*

DOUBLE REVERSE

"Over-the-top...absorbing."
— *Entertainment Weekly*

"Green keeps the suspense building and the reader continually off guard throughout the book...explosive...a quick and entertaining read."
— *Chicago Tribune*

"Plot twists as complicated as a double reverse play....Green, whose writing is ever more polished, scores a touchdown in this one."
— *Atlanta Journal-Constitution*

"Fast paced....Green knows the territory and leads us briskly right through the bloody, satisfying climax."
— *Publishers Weekly*

"A highly entertaining novel....Green is at his best."
— *BookPage*

"Green delivers another gritty story of violence and greed...great action."
— *Library Journal*

Also by Tim Green

Fiction

Ruffians
Titans
Outlaws
The Red Zone
Double Reverse
The Letter of the Law
The Fourth Perimeter
The First 48

Nonfiction

The Dark Side of the Game
A Man and His Mother: An Adopted Son's Search

ATTENTION: CORPORATIONS AND ORGANIZATIONS:
Most WARNER books are available at quantity discounts
with bulk purchase for educational, business, or sales
promotional use. For information, please call or write:

Special Markets Department, Warner Books, Inc.,
135 W. 50th Street, New York, NY. 10020-1393
Telephone: 1-800-222-6747 Fax: 1-800-477-5925

THE
FIFTH
ANGEL

TIM
GREEN

WARNER
VISION
BOOKS

An AOL Time Warner Company

This book is a work of fiction. Names, characters, places, and incidents are the product of the author's imagination or are used fictitiously. Any resemblance to actual events, locales, or persons, living or dead, is coincidental.

If you purchase this book without a cover you should be aware that this book may have been stolen property and reported as "unsold and destroyed" to the publisher. In such case neither the author nor the publisher has received any payment for this "stripped book."

WARNER BOOKS EDITION

Copyright © 2003 by Tim Green
Excerpt from *The First 48* copyright © 2004 by Tim Green
All rights reserved. No part of this book may be reproduced in any form or by any electronic or mechanical means, including information storage and retrieval systems, without permission in writing from the publisher, except by a reviewer who may quote brief passages in a review.

Cover design and art by Tony Greco

Warner Vision is a registered trademark of Warner Books, Inc.

Warner Books, Inc.
1271 Avenue of the Americas
New York, NY 10020

Visit our Web site at www.twbookmark.com

W An AOL Time Warner Company

Printed in the United States of America

Originally published in hardcover by Warner Books

First Paperback Printing: January 2004

10 9 8 7 6 5 4 3 2 1

For my beginning and my end,
my beautiful wife with her radiant smile.
Illyssa, you complete me.

ACKNOWLEDGMENTS

Some of the best things in this book, and the book itself, couldn't have been done without the help of others: my agent, Esther Newberg; my editor, Rick Wolff; the careful reading and constructive criticism of Sara Ann Freed, as well as my parents, Richard and Judy Green; for the tireless questions answered by my friends in the Syracuse Police Department, Inspector Michael Kerwin, Detectives Pete O'Brien, Pete Patnode, and Vernon Thomson; and also all the people at Warner Books, including Larry Kirshbaum, Maureen Egen, Jamie Raab, Dan Ambrosio, Mari Okuda, Chris Barba, and Tina Andreadis.

In addition, a very special thanks to my brother in words and my particular friend Ace Atkins.

I thank you all.

THE
FIFTH
ANGEL

And the fifth angel poured out his vial upon the seat of the beast and his kingdom was full of darkness; and they gnawed their tongues for pain.
Revelation 16:10

CHAPTER 1

Despite the horror of his crime, there was a chance that Eugene Tupp might go free. The legal system was a board game. Right didn't always prevail. Chance could supersede justice. That's what Jack Ruskin was afraid of.

A mist hung in the night air, muting the light. Fluorescent street lamps glowed pale blue. The scent of damp concrete and pavement floated up, mixing with the smell of cooked onions blown outside by an unseen kitchen fan somewhere down the side alley. Jack Ruskin lifted a ream of paper from the passenger seat of his Saab convertible. He tucked the bulky package beneath his long raincoat and, with his briefcase in the other hand, stumbled into the Brick Alley Café.

He stepped up onto the dining room floor and surveyed the tables, looking past the inquisitive hostess. Gavin Donohue was in the back, beyond the old wood bar and its high leather chairs, back near the emergency exit. Gavin sat upright beneath a copied Monet. He faced the quiet crowd, a big dark Irishman with the stoic expression of an elected official. He was the D.A. of Nassau County. When he reached for his wineglass, a silver Rolex Submariner flashed on his wrist.

Jack made his way through the mill of waiters and

waitresses. They were dressed in white shirts and black bow ties and moved with expedient politeness. When Jack bumped one he turned to excuse himself, jostling a second, tangling his legs, and losing his balance. His papers spilled in a gusher on the hardwood floor.

Jack cursed quietly and knelt down. He thanked the staff and even the other diners who bent down to help him collect his things. Gavin got up and came halfway across the room to help.

"Not the best place for this," Jack said, rising, his face feeling warm. He adjusted his glasses, looking through the steam and up into Gavin's face.

"I thought you'd like some dinner," Gavin said, handing him a transcript sheet from the floor. "Come on, let's sit down."

Gavin tucked himself back in the corner, still upright. He was tall and thick, and his thinning dark hair matched his eyes. His cherry face was made serious by a concrete smile. Even years ago, when they'd been young assistants together in the D.A.'s office in Brooklyn, people had been afraid of Gavin.

Jack set his briefcase on the floor beside his chair, then thumped his stack of papers down on the linen tablecloth. He took off his coat, tossed it over the back of his chair, and sat down, loosening his tie.

Jack knew Gavin had something to say to him and he didn't like the precipitous angle of his old friend's eyebrows. He felt short of breath. His heart pumped faster. He moved the brass lamp on the table and the flowers to one side. Yellow stick'um flags sprouted from the ream. Jack reached for the one closest to the top, pulling out the page. He wanted to talk, to keep Gavin from talking.

"I'm not telling you what to do," he said, "but I just don't think this Unger woman is the right one to be doing the cross on a witness, any witness. Listen to this: 'Mr. Billings, do you—'"

"Jack."

"—'do you think that you might have been mistaken wh—'"

"Jack."

"You don't ask someone if they 'might' be mistaken on a cross, Gavin," Jack said. "I don't want to sound peevish, but goddamn."

"Jack, stop."

"What?"

"Just stop." Gavin's face turned to stone. He said flatly, "The judge ruled to exclude the van."

The quiet din of the busy restaurant suddenly sounded to Jack as if it came through a long tube. He saw the rest of the evidence falling like dominoes. The van. The blood. The chloroform. The duct tape. Without them, they couldn't hope to prove that Eugene Tupp was the monster who had abducted his daughter. It was the kidnapping charge that would put that piece of human scum away until he was either harmless or dead. His stomach gave a violent heave.

"I'm sorry," Gavin was saying. "I wanted to tell you in person."

"You're serious," Jack heard himself say.

"Jack, you of all people knew this was a problem from the start. The cop busted into his garage with a crowbar, for God's sake," Gavin said.

"The garage was attached to the house," Jack said, accenting the point of law.

The search warrant was for Eugene Tupp's house. In New York State that meant just the house. If the garage was separate, then anything found inside couldn't be used as evidence. The police should have gone back and gotten another warrant for the garage. They were too anxious.

"Not in the traditional sense maybe," Jack said, "but the covered walkway, that could be construed—"

"Jack," Gavin said. "He ruled the van inadmissible. He's not going to change. You know that."

Jack stood. He looked around for something. Then he lifted the massive transcript off the table and slammed it down to the floor, where it burst into a flurry of paper. The restaurant went quiet. Heads turned. Gavin backed them all down with his darkest scowl.

"Please," he said to Jack. "Sit down."

Jack dug into his pocket and took out a wallet-sized photo of his little girl: Janet. She stared back at him with his own glass blue eyes, her long radiant blond hair—also his—tucked back behind her ears, a small smile on her pretty face. She was only fifteen when it was taken. Only fifteen when Tupp snatched her, and left her with a shattered mind.

"This is my little girl," Jack said in a husky voice. He slapped the picture down on the table in front of his old friend, rattling the silverware and the ice in the water glasses. A messy purple stain began to spread from the base of Gavin's wineglass.

Gavin didn't look.

"I'm going to get the max on the rape charge," he said. "He'll do time."

"Time? How much?" Jack said, his voice rising. Heads

began to turn again. "Four years? Five? Six? He did time before. Do you know what he did to her? He shouldn't do *time*. He should be strapped to the fucking chair!"

Gavin removed one hand from the edge of the table and grasped the knot of his tie, shaking it loose like a dog tugging on a sock. His face was scarlet now. Beads of sweat broke out on his forehead.

"It's not a perfect system, Jack." He looked around and lowered his voice into a raspy plea. "This is not my fault."

Jack felt his anger and disgust peak and then begin to wane. His face drooped. His shoulders sagged. He felt weary, but not weary from being run too hard. He felt instead like a man who had been tied up and beaten with a pipe.

He took a deep tired breath and exhaled his words. They sounded hollow, empty. "I know that, Gavin," he said, pocketing the photo. "Did I ever tell you why Angela left?"

Gavin cleared his throat and shook his head no.

"She found this rich fat bastard from the club, but that wasn't really it," Jack said. "I was supposed to pick Janet up the day he got her.

"This whole thing . . ." Jack said. "It's not your fault. It's my fault."

Jack turned and stumbled back through the crowded tables like a bum. Instead of going straight for the entrance, he turned and banged his way outside through the emergency exit door and into a garbage-strewn alley. An alarm howled after him. Jack didn't care. He felt Gavin's hand on his shoulder.

"I'll get him, Jack," Gavin said. He handed Jack his

briefcase. "I'll get him for everything I can . . . I wish it were more. I do."

Jack said nothing. They reached the end of the alley. Gavin stopped. Jack kept going, plodding slowly up the sidewalk through the mist and to his car. The melancholy glow of the streetlight illuminated a parking ticket on his windshield. Jack didn't bother with it. He drove home with it flapping in protest. It stopped when he reached the assembly of barren trees that lined his cobblestone driveway.

His vast home was illuminated in a haphazard, uneven manner. More than half the exterior lights buried in the yard had burned out months ago. Still, there were enough random beams of light to make out the rich orange brick and the tangled gray tendrils of dormant ivy as they snaked their way delicately across the intricate white trim. The tall mullioned windows were dark and empty. Many of them hid behind ornate wrought-iron balconies. After Jack turned off the car, he sat for a moment in the garage listening to the tick of the engine as it cooled.

Inside the house he found the big handgun he had recently purchased. It lay at the bottom of his underwear drawer under a mess of unfolded clothes. Behind the purchase of the gun was a wild scheme that hadn't fully taken hold, a rage building up inside him that needed a vent, but now it seemed to him that the gun's true purpose was more horrible than what he had originally imagined. Or had he known all along in the back of his mind that this was the fate that awaited him?

He descended the long curving staircase with the cool black Glock 9mm in his hand. He found a bottle of

Chivas Regal in the kitchen. A pizza box lay open on the table, exposing greasy stains, crumbs, and three chewed-over crusts. In the corner of the sticky floor was a haphazard stack of newspapers. Without thinking Jack filled a tall glass with ice from the machine and then poured in the Scotch until it nearly overflowed. He sat at the kitchen table and began to sip. The ice jiggled noisily in its bath of liquor. Jack's hands were quivering.

He thought again of Eugene Tupp and what he had done. Without the van and the evidence inside it, the man would spend no more than six years in jail, and given the crowding of New York's penal system, he was likely to be free in much less. It was so wrong. Tupp would be out and free to attack someone else's little girl and that ate away at Jack's insides.

He had taken to drinking Maalox to get him through the day. But Jack believed that he deserved to suffer. After all, this was his fault. Like his wife—his ex-wife—everyone else seemed to know that, too.

The Scotch was nearly gone when he lifted the gun from the tabletop. He brought the barrel to his lips. Tears spilled down Jack's cheeks. The gun barrel slipped effortlessly into his mouth. He wasn't bothered by the tangy taste of metal against his tongue. But when the end of the barrel tickled the back of his throat, he had to fight the urge to gag.

Jack felt himself unravel like an industrial spring. His tears were now accompanied by heaving sobs that grew in strength, sobs for Janet, sobs for himself, sobs for the injustice and the futility of life.

He squeezed his eyes shut tight, wondering what it would feel like to die.

Then he pulled the gun from his mouth and slammed it down on the table. If he was mad enough to kill himself, then fine. He could always do that. But he would be damned if he weren't going to kill someone else first.

CHAPTER 2

Amanda Lee's eyes burst open at the sound of the radio and she thought of oatmeal. She read in *People* magazine that Demi Moore cooked oatmeal for her kids. Amanda couldn't shake the notion that it sounded like a very motherly thing to do, and today she was going to stop thinking about it—whether it was silly or not to do something because Demi Moore did it—and just do it. She flipped the clock radio off and slipped quietly out of bed.

Parker, her husband, moaned and rolled away from her. The ring of faded brown hair that circled his balding head was a wild tangle. Amanda sighed to herself, then kissed her fingertips and placed them gently on the back of his naked head.

She wanted to love him.

She dressed herself in running shorts and a faded Georgetown University soccer T-shirt, crept past the kids' rooms, and tiptoed downstairs. Six at six. Six miles at six o'clock. That was the resolution she had come up with about a month ago after she'd had to get into a bathing suit at Hershey Park. A small boy had mistaken her for his own mother, and when Amanda had seen the size of the real mother's rump, she'd decided to get serious. She'd been wanting to get back in shape anyway. In college she was a whip. That all faded after the kids, but she was determined.

At the Bureau women didn't worry about their looks. It was a man's world and femininity had no place. That was fine. Amanda didn't need her looks to compete. Still, there was no reason that with some effort she couldn't have both. It was like her home life. There was no reason she couldn't be a successful agent and a good mother. It was like a dual major. It just took effort.

She laced up her shoes on the front steps and stretched a little in the chill morning air. She put on her headset and tuned into Bob Edwards on NPR. Although she'd never met him, she loved Bob. She felt like he could relate. He was understated but smart, and she knew she could count on him to always be up and talking at this ungodly hour.

She ran the streets, passing row after row of squat shingled suburban homes. The sky grew brighter. Finally the day began. The sun came up and she washed away the sweat in the shower. The rest of her family was still asleep, and now she felt good. She looked in the mirror and decided to put on some makeup, not for Parker, but because she was going to see the other mothers today. She wasn't entirely comfortable with them.

There was never anything to say and she hadn't had the chance to go to lunch or out for coffee, as so many of them seemed to do. Some of them didn't work at all. Those who did had nine-to-five jobs. In her family it was Parker who did most of the driving around and the pick-ups and drop-offs at school. He was the one with the nine-to-five job. He sold heavy equipment for Virginia Supply and when times were good, he could come and go as he pleased.

She pulled on a black Donna Karan sweat suit. She wanted to look good without appearing to have tried. She was neither tall nor short. And while no one would call her ravishing, she knew from the woman at Lord & Taylor that a little makeup applied in the right places brought out the green in her big almond-shaped eyes, the best of her otherwise plain features. Her red hair, too, cut shoulder length, straight and styled, had become an asset—although her more inflexible friends sometimes grew annoyed at the way a certain lock always seemed to curve back across her cheek, sometimes infringing on her eye and begging to be pushed back into place. Occasionally she would wear bright red lipstick to better define her small thin lips, but only on the rare occasions that she and Parker had someplace special to go.

Finished, Amanda smiled doubtfully at herself in the mirror and went back downstairs to cook her oatmeal. The rich aroma of the cereal mixed pleasantly with the smells of spring that drifted in through the kitchen window on a warm breeze. Amanda breathed deep and sighed, considering the next three days. This was exactly what she needed, no travel, no late nights. Instead she would live the life of a normal suburban mother. It was a reprieve from the grind of her latest case.

The children stirred upstairs.

She heard Parker thump his way to the bathroom and flick on the screeching shower. Just as the cereal was ready, they all began to appear. Her nine-year-old son, Teddy, wandered into the kitchen. Teddy had the round red face of his father with Amanda's hair. He was oblivious to her, tousle-headed, wearing just his pajama bottoms and playing an electronic Gameboy. His little sister,

Glenda, wasn't far behind him. She, on the other hand, was already dressed in a pink jumper. She had pulled her own brown hair into pigtails and tied them off with two pink hairbands.

"Hi, Mommy," she said, her voice nearly chirping. "You're going to come with me to Brownies today after school, right?"

"Good morning, sweetheart," Amanda said, kissing her daughter. "Yes I am.

"And what about you?" she asked her son. "Don't I get a *good morning* from you?"

"Oh, hi, Mom," Teddy said without lifting his head.

"Did you do your homework last night?" Amanda asked.

"Maybe," he said. Not even looking her in the eye.

She watched his face.

"Why does it matter?" he asked.

A thick lump grew in her throat. "You have to do well in school," she said.

"What was I supposed to do last night?" he asked.

She didn't know. "Wasn't it that science project?" she said. "That thing you were doing with worms and electricity?"

"Electricity kills worms, Mom. That was two different assignments and about four months ago."

"What's this about electric worms?" Parker said in his booming southern drawl. He had burst into the kitchen still working on his necktie. He was flush with the raw cheerfulness that had attracted Amanda to him so many years ago. Now it grated on her, but she let him kiss her cheek and hug her from behind.

Amanda even leaned back into him. Parker was a big

man, heavyset and solid like a bear despite a stomach that was beginning to get away from him. She thought it would be good for the kids to see them that way, and she squeezed his thick hand while she stirred the pot. It troubled her to show him affection for appearance's sake. She wanted to mean it. She wanted this moment to touch her deep down. She concentrated on the sun's warmth, the smells of the kitchen, and the comfortable sound of a family.

But before she could really feel it, the phone rang.

Amanda turned and looked at it on the wall. She looked questioningly at Parker, who scowled in turn. It kept ringing until he finally said, "Well, aren't you going to answer it? It's not for me."

"Me neither," Teddy piped in.

Glenda grinned and stuck out her tongue at her older brother as Amanda finally picked up the phone.

"He got another one."

It was Marco Rivolaggio, assistant special agent in charge, her nominal boss and sometimes partner.

"Where?" she asked.

"Just outside Atlanta," he said. "Fourteen years old."

CHAPTER 3

Amanda looked involuntarily at her own little girl. Her stomach plunged and she swallowed the wash of bile. The bubble was burst.

"This time the body is fresh," Marco said. "Some guy pulled over on the side of the highway last night into one of those rest areas. He wandered into the bushes to do his business and found her. From what they're saying, it sounds like it might have happened late yesterday."

"Then he's still close by."

"According to your theory," Marco said, "he shouldn't be far. There's a flight from National at eight-fifteen . . ."

Amanda looked at the clock on the wall, trying not to let Parker's scowl rattle her. Sometimes he acted like he were ten.

"I'll be on it," she said. "Let me get a bag together and I'll call you from the car."

She hung up and braced herself before turning to face her family.

"I've got to go," she said. "I'm sorry."

"But what about Brownies?" Glenda said.

Amanda felt desperate. She looked at Parker. He

pursed his lips and shook his head as if he wouldn't help.

"Parker?" she said, trying not to let it sound like she was pleading.

"Oh, I know," he said, his features softening. "Drink water on the flight. Helps with the headache."

Glenda absently twisted her spoon in the cereal, her head down like her brother's.

Parker watched her, took a breath, and said, "Your mother is an important lady. She'll be back soon."

Amanda heard her daughter's soft acceptance as she bounded up the stairs. Minutes later, Amanda was dressed in a navy blue linen skirt and jacket with an eggshell blouse and flat shoes. She kissed Teddy on the head, then stopped in front of Glenda and knelt down.

"Honey, I'm really sorry about Brownies." She looked up into her daughter's eyes. "Are you okay?"

Glenda lifted her head toward her father. He nodded. Her lower lip curled a little and she nodded, too.

"I'm the star of the week," she said. Her little voice was quiet. "I get to go first in everything we do."

"Well," Amanda said, "you'll be a great star."

She kissed Glenda again, then stood up to kiss Parker.

"Here," he said gently, handing her a napkin off the table.

"For what?" she asked.

"You've . . ." he said. "There's something in your eye."

Amanda took the napkin, looked at the clock, and rushed out the door. She called ahead to the airport to arrange clearance with the airline for her gun then dialed up Marco, who said he needed to call her back. That was fine. It gave her time to think. She forced her mind away from the spoiled plans at home.

There was nothing she could do. She thought of Parker's words about her being important. It wasn't that. It was her job. Her job was important. Her plans with the kids were a cool fog, forgotten in the midday heat. She was fully focused now on the case she'd been working for the past ten months.

During the last five years, since Glenda had turned two, Amanda had established herself as one of the FBI's preeminent investigators of serial killers. Her colleagues were almost exclusively male, mostly in their forties and fifties. Amanda knew why she was part of that elite group. She wasn't conceited, but it was an objective fact that her IQ had enabled her to go through college with a double major in just three years at the top of her class. She'd finished her master's in one. But beyond being highly intelligent, she soon found as an agent that she had something you couldn't learn from books, something she was more proud of than her intellect. She had instincts.

To date every case she'd been assigned she had also solved. It had gotten so that it was no longer an embarrassment for even her male chauvinistic counterparts to call her in for an opinion. She was quickly developing a reputation. This case, however, was proving to be her most difficult. It was also the most horrifying.

The victims were young. Amanda couldn't even think to herself about what happened to them. She had to block that out. With other killers, she had been able to consider the victims with the detachment of a medical examiner. But not these. These were too young, too mutilated. Oh, she had seen the bodies and the detailed autopsy reports. But she'd take the information and plug it into her mental profile formula, then never think about them again. She just couldn't, not if she wanted to stop him. The hatred would be too much of a distraction.

Her cell phone rang. It was Marco. He was busy helping coordinate with the Georgia Bureau of Investigation as well as the state police. They were covering every hotel, motel, and campground within a twenty-mile radius. It was no small task, but absolutely essential.

"And they all know to be low-key?" Amanda asked.

"Of course," Marco said impatiently.

She couldn't help herself. This was the break they'd been waiting for. Usually they didn't find his victims for weeks. But the pattern of gruesome details, reminiscent of a horror film, had given Amanda the impression that the killer was watching the stories unfold on television. That meant, in order to glean the full impact of the media sensation, he had to remain local.

Although the crimes were being documented superficially on the national level, the morbid details, the hysterical interviews with family and friends, were available in their entirety only on the local news. The other thing that supported her theory was the fact that each new body was being found closer and closer to civilization, as if their man was becoming more and more impatient to see his work stirring up horror in the news.

Based on that theory, Amanda had every hotel, motel, and campground in the vicinity of the last crime scene outside Nashville heavily canvassed for clues. The maneuver had paid off at a roadside motel just seven miles from the place the body was found. Although the killer was gone by then, they had a record of a man who'd stayed in the hotel from around the time of the crime until just three days after the body was discovered. The room had been curiously soiled by the stench of cats, whose fur and excrement were everywhere. More important, they then found minute traces of the victim's blood on the mirror over the bathroom sink, presumably from when he'd washed up after the crime, and Amanda's theory was elevated one step closer to fact.

The killer had registered at the motel in the name of Bob Oswald, but no one believed that was his name. He'd paid for the room with cash. No one had yet found a witness who could even give them a description of the car he'd driven, let alone a plate number. For that matter, none of the motel employees or guests could be quite sure he'd even had a car, although Amanda knew he must've. Descriptions of the man were vague. He had straight blond hair, a beard and mustache. He was so slick in the commission of his crimes that it sometimes seemed he must have an accomplice. But that was impossible. Serial killers by definition were loners.

Oswald had been killing at an alarming clip. The trail stretched back almost three years. In the first year there were only three murders; in the second, six. During the last twelve months he had doubled his efforts. It was an exponential pattern that wasn't unheard of with serial killers. Often this kind of spiral pattern ended in the killer's own suicide.

Amanda bit her lip. That couldn't come too soon. In the meantime this deranged monster was snapping up children at random, destroying lives, families, and communities. Amanda knew that he was close and, if they were careful, they just might be able to catch him before he could strike again.

But in her mind, mashed with the details of autopsies and police reports, was her daughter's smiling face. And the smell of oatmeal.

CHAPTER 4

After a long ride on the airport's underground tram and searching for her bag, Amanda emerged into the burning Georgia sun. Marco was waiting curbside in a dark Crown Vic. His hands were on the wheel.

His thin dark hair, wavy and slick with gel, was plastered flat on his tan head. He had the nose and chin of a predatory bird. His small dark eyes were now covered by a pair of Ray•Ban sunglasses. He wore a sedate blue tie and gray pin-striped single-breasted suit. His wife had left him five years ago, ran off with his brother of all things. He never talked about it.

Amanda looked at him and smiled despite the implacable look of disgust that had been stamped on his face. She liked Marco. He seemed to understand her more than most. She tossed her bag in back and slid onto the front seat. Marco put the car in gear and bolted from the curb before he even began to speak.

"They've got him," he said.

Amanda let out a long stream of air.

Marco shot her a glance and swerved crazily around a rental car shuttle bus before punching the accelerator. He raced up the median of the freeway ramp past a long line of crawling cars. One frustrated driver who saw what they were up to pulled out so they couldn't pass. Marco leaned on the horn and began to flash his headlights on and off. But instead of moving out of the way, the man braked to a stop, got out of his little foreign car, and flipped them his middle finger.

Marco threw the Crown Vic into park and jumped out. He had his badge out and in the man's face in less than two seconds.

"Get your ass out of the way or you'll spend the next week in jail, you dumb son-of-a-bitch!" Marco screamed, waving his badge. His tan face was now a shade of purple.

The man's eyes widened and he jumped back in his car to move aside.

Once they were on their way, Marco said calmly, "It's only about twenty minutes from here, in a little roadside motel just off I-Seventy-five outside a little town called Jackson."

"Does he know we're onto him?"

Marco shook his head and replied, "I don't think so. A plainclothes detective from the GBI was the one who found him, a blond-haired man with a beard, average height and build, and check this . . .

"Yesterday the woman at the desk remembered seeing a pornographic magazine sticking out of his bag. Then she saw him dragging a young girl kicking and screaming like a wet cat into his unit sometime in the afternoon. She called the room, but everything was quiet and the man said the girl was his daughter, so the woman at the desk didn't think anything of it."

Marco glanced at Amanda again.

Her skin began to tingle and her stomach, which had nothing in it, gave a little roll.

They rode mostly in silence after that. Occasionally Marco would get an update over the radio as to the various personnel that began to arrive. The GBI had a Tactical Response Team in Atlanta. They were the first to get there and quickly surrounded the motel. Marco talked with their commanding officer and instructed him to have everyone stand by until they got there.

Doing just over a hundred miles an hour, they reached the exit in eighteen minutes. After that, they fell into a speeding convoy of state police, all racing toward the scene with their lights flashing, but no sirens on. They raced right through the little town of Jackson, and soon after they saw the 1950s-style motel. It was a long low row of rooms set off the road in a cluster of tall straight pines. The place had been painted turquoise years ago. The clapboard siding was now chipped and faded. The hand-painted wooden sign hanging from a rusted post out by the road was pink and orange.

Amanda and Marco had just hopped out of their car when a TV truck from Atlanta mounted with a satellite dish raced up behind everything and swerved to a stop in the dusty gravel lot, almost tipping over.

"Get them back!" Marco yelled to a cluster of troopers.

The GBI captain turned to Marco and Amanda and said, "We've got every corner covered. We think he's sleeping in there. There hasn't been a sign of any kind of movement. We're ready to go in."

CHAPTER 5

Amanda surveyed the scene. Snipers with flak jackets were everywhere. Some rested flat black high-powered rifles across the hoods of police cars. Others braced automatic weapons—MP-5s with glossy hundred-round clips—against tree trunks or tires. Each gun was trained on the last unit of the run-down motel.

The sun beat down through the dust, and Amanda dabbed at the thin line of sweat on her upper lip with the back of her hand. The look in the captain's eyes disturbed her. He had the wide-eyed rolling glaze of a racehorse about to burst from the gates. They all did. Someone was going to get killed.

Amanda knew that word of a crime like this, the abominable details, would spread quickly through a unit of cops. Every man with a gun had in his mind the image of the mutilated body of the girl that had been found only hours before on the side of the road. This motel was now surrounded by a platoon of men looking for even the hint of an excuse.

"I want these men to put their weapons down," she said.

The captain, a big corpulent man in his midforties with

a dark brush cut and a tall gray hat, sneered, then chuckled and said, "I can't see us doing that, ma'am."

"I'm not your ma'am," Amanda said with her eyes trained on the motel. "You get these men's fingers off their triggers or you're going to find yourself handing out parking tickets in Dunwoody."

The captain's mouth fell open and he narrowed his eyes.

"Do what she says," Marco said with quiet authority. "We don't want this man killed."

The captain's face was now contorted with rage. "This man," he hissed through gritted teeth, "just dismembered a little girl who was on her way to the church choir. This man is armed and dangerous, and doesn't deserve to take another goddamn breath of life."

Amanda drew her gun and turned to Marco. "If one of these men shoots me, I want you to make sure you prosecute this good old boy for murder." With that, she left the two men standing behind the captain's car and walked across the dusty lot toward the hotel with her compact Heckler & Koch USP 40 in both hands. She felt she knew this man, Oswald, for lack of a better name. She had studied him for ten months now. She had been right about where he would be and she felt confident she was right about everything else, too.

He wouldn't have a gun. He used knives and work tools to commit his crimes. And even in light of the atrocities he had committed, she didn't want him gunned down, although she certainly understood why others might. No matter what he'd done, Amanda wanted him to have a trial. That's what separated her and the officers and agents she worked with from the men she hunted. That's what held her together.

"Get that stupid bitch back here!" Amanda heard the police captain yell from halfway across the lot. But it was too late now. She was at the door and pressed herself tightly against the rough faded siding beside the room's entrance before reaching over and gently knocking.

Nothing happened.

Amanda knocked again and heard movement inside the room. Her heart was sprinting. She crouched. The door rattled and swung open.

CHAPTER 6

Amanda sprang at the man with her gun in his face. He fell backward inside the room and she quickly pinned him down to the floor with her knees, screaming, "Don't move! Don't move a goddamn muscle!"

The man's eyes were wide and darting back and forth. He held his hands up over his head and splayed the backs of his fingers against the musty carpet. The girl who looked to be no more than ten began to scream in a heavy southern accent.

"Daddy! Daddy! Daddy!"

In the confusion three strike team officers spilled into the room training their automatic weapons everywhere and kicking down the bathroom door. On the nightstand between two sagging double beds was a fitness magazine with a half-naked man and woman on the cover. On the TV, Bugs Bunny rolled a boulder into the path of Elmer Fudd and then crunched on a carrot. Amanda closed her eyes briefly and shook her head until the shouting of the officers who had followed her inside subsided. The girl continued to cry for her father.

"Ehhhhh, what's up, Doc?"

Amanda slowly got up off the man's chest and sighed as the other officers flipped him roughly onto his stomach, stepping on his hands and feet before they cuffed him. Amanda walked to the frail-looking young girl, who was sobbing loudly, and took her quietly in her arms.

"It's all right," she said, stroking the girl's long blond hair. "Your daddy's going to be all right. He didn't do anything wrong, honey, and neither did you. These men won't hurt him. They're the police, honey. They won't hurt him. We made a mistake."

"We got him!" one of the officers shouted out into the parking lot. "All clear. We got him. All clear."

Amanda pushed through the officers and past the trembling man with the girl in her arms. Marco rushed up to her.

"We got the wrong man," she said in a dying voice to Marco.

"How do you know?" he asked. "How can you say that?"

"Because I know who I'm looking for," she said over the top of the girl's quivering head.

"You want to explain yourself, Annie Oakley?" the captain asked.

Marco pursed his lips in frustration and turned to the captain. "She's been after this man for almost a year," he said, "and seen what you saw this morning more times than you want to know."

"Terrific," the captain said.

Amanda made her way toward a female trooper, a big woman with close-cropped hair but a round, matronly face.

"Will you take care of this young lady?" she said. The woman's taut features went soft. "That's her daddy and this whole thing is a mistake. They thought she was the one that . . . the other girl . . ."

The woman officer gave Amanda a knowing look and began to fuss over the girl. From the TV inside the room came the sound of Bugs pounding Fudd over the head with a mallet. The girl shook in the cop's arms.

Amanda turned away and got into the passenger side of Marco's Crown Vic. She sat staring straight ahead without bothering to watch the Georgia police stuffing the young girl's innocent father into the back of a cruiser. There really was no one to blame. Things like this happened. An innocent man in the wrong place at the wrong time.

After a few minutes Marco got in beside her.

"Well," he said, exhaling with exasperation, "that was different."

He looked at her and said it again. "That was different."

"What do you want me to say?" Amanda said, staring back at him.

"Nothing," Marco said. "I don't want you to say anything."

"I was right," she said.

"I think you probably were."

"I know I am. That's not the man. That woman at the desk said he had a pornographic magazine. Do you know what magazine he had?"

"What?" he asked.

"A muscle magazine. He wasn't a pervert. Just wanted to lose his gut."

Marco shook his head. "This is the Deep South, you know. You can't make a local police captain look like an ass."

"Can you get them to keep looking?" she asked.

Amanda still knew she was right about their killer. She was certain that somewhere close by he was waiting to feast his eyes on the evening news, maybe to even go back to the crime scene and watch the excitement, to press his fingertips into the yellow crime scene tape.

The problem was that Amanda was thinking two or three steps ahead of everyone else. She knew the man they'd just taken into custody wasn't the right one. But the GBI wasn't going to be that easily convinced. Just because some crazy redheaded FBI agent said her instincts were telling her the man was innocent didn't mean they weren't going to follow through with the thoroughness that defined them as police.

"It's going to be tough. I'm sure you ain't on Barney Fife's favorite people list," Marco said. He didn't say *ain't* so it sounded funny coming out of his mouth.

"But I was right," she said. "Can you imagine if one of the cops killed that father? Can you imagine the stink of that mess? Where would we be then? The whole thing would be out, and even if we did get this kind of chance—a fresh crime scene, I mean—he'd know that we were going to search every motel in the area and he'd change his pattern."

"That may happen now anyway," Marco said. "There was a TV truck there, you know."

They rode for a while in silence. Amanda looked at her watch.

"Damn," she said. She dialed information back in Virginia and got the phone number of Glenda's Brownie leader.

"Hi, Allison? This is Amanda," she said. She could

hear the chatter of young girls in the background. They were giggling, talking, and even shrieking. It was a happy sound and it made Amanda strongly aware that she was hundreds of miles away.

"Who?"

"Amanda," she said. "Amanda Lee."

"Oh. Oh, yes, I'm sorry. Do you want to talk to your husband?"

"My . . . yes. Please."

Amanda bit into her lower lip.

"Hi," Parker said.

"Hi," she said. "I just was checking. How's the star?"

"She's shining pretty bright," he said. "How's it there?"

"Fine."

"You want to say hi?"

"I'd like that," Amanda said. She stole a glance at Marco. His eyes were fixed on the country road. His mouth shut tight.

The sound over the phone was muffled as Parker covered the receiver. She could just make out his voice, asking Glenda to come and talk. Marco started to whistle quietly. Parker took his hand off the phone.

"Can we give you a call back?" he said. "She's right in the middle of these felt stars that we're cutting out to go on her vest. She's . . . I . . ."

"That's fine," Amanda said. "I just wanted to let her know I'm thinking of her. I'm glad one of us could go. I love you."

"Love you, too. Bye."

"Bye."

She hung up and bit into her lip again.

"Everything okay?" Marco asked.

"Yeah," she said. She lifted her chin. "I'm fine."

As they pulled into the small town of Jackson, the road turned into four lanes. Its center was bisected by two sets of railroad tracks. On either side was a handful of three- or four-story brick buildings—rows of freestanding store-fronts standing shoulder to shoulder along a sun-bleached sidewalk. American flags hung limply from many of the buildings. With the car windows down, Amanda could smell the pungent aroma of creosote from the train tracks baking in the noontime heat.

Amanda suddenly said, "I think we should pull every-body we've got out of the Atlanta office. Right now. I think we should get our own people down here in force and keep up the search ourselves."

Marco winced at the suggestion.

"What?" she asked.

"Rand," he said. "I'm not too high on his list."

"Why? Because you left him in Atlanta?"

"We never got along," Marco said. "It was a personal thing. One night we were all out in Buckhead. We had a few. He said some things and I popped him."

"This is bigger than some pissing match between boys," she said.

"I know. I know," he said, holding up his hand. "I'll do it. I just want you to feel the pain in my ass, that's all."

"Okay," she said. "I feel your— Stop!"

"What?"

"Stop the car!"

Chapter 7

Before Marco could brake, Amanda had the door open, and as he slowed she jumped out. A battered red pickup driven by a young farmer passing them on the right swerved and screeched to a halt. The truck just clipped Amanda, and she spun a full circle before she fell to the pavement. She was up in an instant, as if she'd done nothing more than trip on her own feet.

"Are you crazy?" the driver said out of his rolled-down window.

Amanda ignored him, drawing her gun and beginning to run now for the street corner. A bearded blond man had just come out of a coffee shop across the street and disappeared behind that corner.

"It's him, Marco!" Amanda yelled back over her shoulder.

Marco swung the car around amid the blaring horns and started after her. When Amanda got to the coffee shop, she passed its broad front window and peeked furtively around the brick corner. She saw him. He was wearing a pair of jeans, cowboy boots, and a black leather vest without a shirt. His arms were crawling with tattoos; a cigarette hung from his lips. He looked both ways for traffic down the side street and jogged across. He slipped between two parked cars and proceeded briskly down the opposite sidewalk, but without any apparent awareness of being followed.

Amanda started after him at a fast walk, trying to keep her excitement in check. Just then Marco took the corner with a shrill little yip from his tires and pulled up alongside her. Amanda scowled his way then looked back down the street just as her man dipped into an alley between a hardware store and a pool hall. She had no idea if he'd noticed the car and that's what made him bolt, or if that was simply his chosen route. Without a word to Marco, she dashed across the street and peeked around the second corner.

Halfway down the alley, the man quickly glanced her way. She thought she'd been seen, but he then mounted a rickety set of stairs and disappeared into the back of a building without hurrying. She presumed the building must have its front entrance on the main street. Marco had stopped the car and was out of it now and beside her.

"You see those wooden stairs just this side of that red Dumpster?" she asked him, pointing.

"Yes."

"He went in there," she said. "You go around to the front and I'll go in from the back."

"What the hell are you talking about? What did you see?"

"He fits the description," she said.

"So do about a million people," he said.

She looked at him and said, "Marco, you know me. Right?"

"Yeah, I know you . . ."

"Well, trust me, it's him," she said. "I can't tell you

why I know, maybe the way he was dressed, I don't know, but let's go get him and we can sort it out later."

Marco shook his head but drew his gun anyway and checked the action. As he started back up the sidewalk toward the main street, she heard him say, "This can't be any more of a disaster than what happened back at the motel . . ."

Amanda waited a few minutes to give Marco time to get to the front of the building, then stepped cautiously down the alley. It was cooler than the street but still close and quiet and strangely peaceful. She didn't know for certain if the man had seen her, but she had to proceed as if he did. When she got to the stairs her nose wrinkled at the smell of kitchen garbage mingling with the hint of raw sewage that drifted up from a shadowy grate beneath her feet. She mounted the steps cautiously with her gun in one hand and the other on the railing.

She pulled open a flimsy wooden screen door whose springs squeaked in protest as she entered a dim hallway. To her right was the abandoned kitchen of a restaurant, and to the left a filthy laundry room. The linoleum floor was dirt-stained, with banks of built-up dust and grime next to the wall and in the corners. A bare bulb hung from a corroded pair of wires in the ceiling, revealing a dark set of stairs that climbed steeply in front of her and off to the right. She wondered if Marco was already inside.

Then she heard him yell, "FBI!"

Amanda launched herself up the stairs. Halfway up, she heard more shouting then the crash of a door slamming shut. By the time she got to the top of the steps, all was quiet except for the steady hammering of her heart in her ears.

The second floor was lined with doors, and down at the far end of the hall she could see the front stairwell in the light of a dusty window that looked out onto the main street. The long narrow building was a dreary flophouse, the kind of transient hotel that probably rented rooms by the week.

Amanda breathed deeply and tried to steady her hands, which still shook in the wake of the adrenaline wave.

Part of her wanted to cry out to Marco, but something told her to keep still. Slowly she proceeded down the hall, stopping to listen at each door and test their handles. Halfway down, she grasped the old brown ceramic knob of a door on the right side and twisted. Like the others, it wouldn't budge. She ran her eyes up and down the faded oak door and wondered, if she did hear something behind one of these doors, whether or not she could kick it in.

Suddenly the door on the opposite side of the narrow hall sprang open.

Amanda leveled her gun and there was a shriek.

In the doorway was the shocked and haggard face of a heavy middle-aged woman with a cheap blond wig. Her sagging eyes were red and bleary, and she wore a ratty pink terry-cloth robe. At the sight of a gun she dropped her cigarette to the floor and swatted at the air with both hands as if bugs were attacking her, then slammed the door shut.

Amanda breathed deep again and shuddered. She had nearly fired a round into the woman's face.

Three-quarters of the way to the front of the building she came to a door whose handle turned. She readied her gun and opened it slowly. She was struck immediately by the pungent aroma of cats. Her heart leapt into her throat.

It was the same stench she'd smelled in the motel room outside Nashville where Oswald had tortured and killed his last victim. She swung the door wide and the scene flooded into her mind.

On almost every flat surface above the floor was a cat, dozens of them of all different breeds and colors bathed in the yellow light of a single floor lamp in the corner. When she stepped inside, they began to move, flowing away from her like ripples on a pond, hopping from a couch to a windowsill or from a chair to the floor. The stench of their excrement was overpowering. Beyond the couch, through a doorway that led into a small kitchen, Amanda could see a man busily working on the floor. It was the blond, bearded man from the street. He was intent on whatever it was he was doing.

Amanda moved across the room, spilling cats in her wake.

She was halfway to the kitchen before the man they knew as Oswald looked up into the barrel of her gun.

He jumped off Marco's body and yanked her partner up in front of him as a shield. Marco was semiconscious and bleeding from the temple. He had already been hastily bound and gagged by Oswald with duct tape. Oswald had one arm around Marco's chest, holding him up with amazing strength.

In his other hand an enormous bowie knife was pressed tight to Marco's throat and already drawing blood.

"Freeze!" Amanda heard herself shout. It was nearly a scream.

Behind Marco and Oswald she saw the flash of another face, black eyes, short dark hair, and a goatee. A second man. So brief was the image that she wondered if it was the devil or if she'd seen it at all.

Her USP 40 was leveled at Oswald's head. She was only fifteen feet away. Her accuracy within that range was deadly, her marksmanship unparalleled, but she wavered. It was a decisive moment, one she'd never be able to take back as hard as she might wish. A malevolent white-toothed grin bloomed in slow motion on Oswald's face as he drew the gleaming blade across Marco's throat, opening it with a thin scarlet gash. The wound split open with meat-red lips, then in a blink it yawned wide, roaring blood.

Amanda fired her gun, striking Oswald squarely in the face. Both men fell to the floor and she felt an instinctive scream erupt from her throat. She leapt toward Marco's body and in a bath of blood tried desperately to keep him alive.

CHAPTER 8

Nearly two months after his dinner with Gavin Donohue, Jack gazed at the wallet-size school picture of his ruined little girl. The sight of her small round innocent face with its trusting smile left him floating in a dizzy haze. It felt like nitrous oxide in the dentist's chair. Only a slim tether kept him connected to reality, maybe even consciousness itself. But soon the moment passed and he felt his feet on the floor of the rented Ford Taurus, his hands tightly gripping the vinyl wheel. His heavy breath had painted a patch of fog on the cold windshield and even steamed up the lower half of his round gold-rimmed glasses.

The fear was back, dressed in uncertainty and revulsion for what he was about to do. He beat it back with raw hatred and rock-hard logic. He needed a purpose. He needed to do something about what went on every day. It wasn't only his daughter. There were others. An old newspaper clipping he'd taken from the library rattled between his fingers. The headline read: CHILD RAPIST GETS TWO YEARS. Every day Jack could read about the violation of some young girl in the newspaper, each act more horrible than the next.

His daughter's photo now lay facedown in his lap

with the date marked in pen on the back by his wife, Angela. His ex-wife. He stuffed the picture into his pants pocket and got out of the car. It was good that no one was on the street. They might have remembered a straw-haired man with pale skin dressed all in black. His slick leather coat and ribbed turtleneck looked like the uniform of some dark foreign agent. Or they might have remembered the nervous way in which he fumbled with his keys, glancing all the while at his surroundings as if he expected someone to jump out at him from one of the blackened storefronts.

Despite the late hour, there were other cars on the street, mostly belonging to patrons of two clapboard bars separated by a bankrupt rental center. This was the side of town where windows stayed broken and sidewalks were allowed to buck and heave without repair. Dim lights hid behind shaded windows on the second and third floors above the empty storefronts. Dandelions sprang from the cracks and broken bottles grinned up at him, their dirty jagged teeth gleaming beneath the street lamps. Old litter lay lifeless in the fetid gutter, waiting for fresh rain to wash it into the rusty sewer grate. Rain was a long way off. The sky beyond the halogen haze of the small city was dark, clear but for the stars and a sickle moon.

Jack walked to the corner and then three blocks into the tangle of old homes, once grand, now multifamily slums. Many of the drooping porches bore the rotting furniture that migrated outside every spring and stayed until fall. The nights were still too brisk even for the stir-crazy inhabitants of the North Country to think of being out this late. Nevertheless, Jack continued an almost panicked surveillance as he plunged even deeper into the neighborhood.

Soon he came to the corner where he had spent hours, just sitting in the back of a rented van, hidden from the world but acutely aware of everything that went on around him. Between the yellow fire hydrant and a massive locust tree was the crumbling asphalt driveway and the battered aluminum door on the side of the house. The driveway hugged the massive but aging Georgian Revival and led to the garage out back. The enormous front columns were crooked like bad teeth, stained by rot. Hans Strauss, the man from the news story, lived in the basement apartment behind the cheap aluminum door.

Jack began to feel lightheaded again, and his breathing became a staccato rhythm of short heavy bursts. His heart seemed to be expanding in his chest, tightening his throat. He pulled on a skintight pair of leather driving gloves and reached inside his coat to grip the handle of his 9mm Glock. The long cool cylinder of the silencer pressed awkwardly into the back of his ribs. He remembered the long-bearded hillbilly who'd sold him this gun from the back of a van outside a gun show in Albany, Georgia.

There was no perfect crime. But there were thousands that went unsolved. Jack's former life as an assistant district attorney had taught him that. And the hardest ones to solve were the ones that simply possessed no obvious connection between the victim and the killer.

Jack had never spoken to Hans Strauss. He had never written to him or been seen with him. He didn't live in this small town of Oswego, New York, nor had he ever even crossed paths with the man whose life he hoped to now end. Strauss had never done anything to harm Jack Ruskin or anyone he knew.

Jack crossed the street, skirting the cone of light from the street lamp above, and walked up the driveway. The lights in the apartments above Strauss's were dark, as were the windows in the house next door. Only Strauss's window, a rectangle cut into the house's foundation at ankle height, glowed red in the night. A blanket had been hung over it from inside the subterranean hole. Strauss was awake. He stayed up late and went to work each day at eleven.

The screen from the outer aluminum door hung limp, a casualty of anger or stupidity, possibly both. Jack took out his wallet from the breast pocket of his leather coat. He held it in his left hand and, as it fell open, a silver badge glowed pink in the faint red light from the basement window. With his other hand Jack removed the pistol and pressed it as inconspicuously as he could against his leg. With the back of his knuckles he knocked softly on the metal door frame and waited. He scanned the neighborhood, then knocked again, this time louder.

Jack heard movement inside the apartment below and then the *clump clump* of Strauss ascending his wooden stairs. Jack's heart raced; each breath now seemed pitifully short and bereft of oxygen. A globe of light beside the door suddenly burned up his cloak of darkness. Jack shifted from foot to foot, the gun now naked in the light. He hugged the weapon to his side and did a half turn to hide it. The lock on the wooden door rattled. The handle turned and Hans Strauss opened it a crack.

CHAPTER 9

W ho are you?" Strauss asked. His voice was gruff, and he peered suspiciously over the chain. He was a tall man, big and sloppy. His strangely wide forehead was crowned by curly brown hair. He looked ten years younger than the photo in the newspaper, and for a brief moment Jack wondered if he was the right man.

Jack held his badge up to the crack in the door.

"Police," he said, trying to disguise the quaver with gruffness. "Are you Hans Strauss?"

Strauss's eyes widened at the sight of the badge.

"Go away," he said, slamming the door.

Jack felt his nostrils flare.

"You haven't done anything wrong, Mr. Strauss," he said. He wondered if his voice sounded calm through the door. "I just need to ask you a few questions about—"

"About what!" Strauss said. He yanked open the door with a scowl. In a voice now laced with growing anger he said, "I won't let you in. I don't have to. I haven't done anything. I have a lawyer, you know. You can't talk to me without a lawyer! I have a lawyer . . ."

Strauss examined Jack's face, as if to read the effect of his words.

"I know," Jack said. He dug hard and fast into his brain

for the name of the man who ran the ice rink where Strauss emptied trash cans.

"That's okay," he said. "You don't need your lawyer . . . I'm sorry it's so late. You haven't done anything. I promise . . . This isn't about you, Mr. Strauss. It's about Mr. Sempleton; he's in some trouble. Frank Sempleton . . ."

Strauss's eyes widened, and Jack saw the flicker of satisfaction. Strauss was the kind of criminal who believed in his paranoid heart that the world was pitched against him. People like him took pleasure in seeing someone else twist under the law. And this wasn't just anyone, but the man who ordered him to empty other people's garbage day after day.

"Sempleton?" he asked.

"Yes."

The chain rattled and the door opened, revealing the inside of an apartment whose walls were covered with nude pictures of young girls.

To make room on the small landing, Strauss had taken two steps down the stairs. As Jack entered, he drew the gun up from his leg and moved toward Strauss.

Strauss saw the gun. He lunged at Jack with a growl.

Jack stepped back, banging the door shut.

He pulled the trigger, ripping off several shots in succession before Strauss got his hand on the gun and yanked Jack toward him and down the stairs.

The two of them crashed through the flimsy banister and down to the carpet. Jack grasped the gun with both hands, letting his head, shoulders, and back take the brunt of the fall, but still holding the gun.

"I'll kill you!" Strauss yelled, kicking, biting, and scratching.

The gun fired over and over and things around the filthy apartment began to erupt from the impact of the 9mm slugs—a plastic lamp, a smoky mirror, a box of cereal on the table spraying cornflakes across the kitchen.

As Jack began to rise, he slipped on something like jelly and struck his head against the staircase. Strauss was on top of him now wrestling for the gun. He came up with a shoe. He began to beat the side of Jack's head with its wooden heel, screaming as he swung the makeshift weapon in vicious wide arcs.

Jack inched the gun, trembling, toward Strauss's face, and the moment he thought it was close enough he took a deliberate shot, punching a hole into Strauss's neck and knocking him backward.

Jack jumped to his feet and emptied what was left of the gun into the man's chest and head until the metallic clicking of the trigger told him the gun was empty.

Everything was quiet, but only for a moment. Jack heard the pounding of feet and the shout of voices from the floor above. They were coming for him.

CHAPTER 10

Jack froze. He was helpless. He heard a door in some upper part of the house open and slam shut. He heard footsteps on the blacktop outside as they came from the back of the house toward the front. He stared in alarm as the faint shadow of legs appeared and then disappeared in the basement window that was hung with the red blanket.

The neighbor began to pound loudly on the frame of the outer aluminum screen door.

"Strauss!" the man screamed. "Strauss! What's all that damn noise? I told you, Strauss!"

Jack didn't move. He looked down at the gun with its silencer hanging uselessly in his hand. He lifted it. It seemed to have the weight of a respectable stone. Blood covered his shirt, and the floor beneath Strauss was a pool of deep red. He stuffed the gun back into the holster under his jacket.

"Strauss! Come out!"

Jack looked down at Strauss's bloody corpse. His eyes were still open, the mouth hanging loose on its hinges. Blood still ran in little brooks from the black holes in his chest. The son-of-a-bitch was dead. That's what he deserved. Still, Jack felt the stirrings of nausea.

Jack thought about one of Strauss's victims: a girl like

his own daughter when she was violated, fifteen. Fifteen years old. Strauss was a piece of shit. Jack looked down at the dead man's face and smiled.

He put his hands up over his mouth to muffle his voice and yelled, "Fuck you!"

There was silence for a time and then, "Fuck you, too! If you don't quit making fucking noise, I'm calling the police."

The neighbor struck the frame of the screen door with his fist once more in frustration and walked away. Jack's blood surged through his head. He heard the neighbor slam his own door and then begin to stomp around above his head. The toilet above flushed. There was some more stomping and then it got quiet. Jack's pulse began to settle.

The refrigerator kicked on, humming. The blood that had splattered Jack's face was growing sticky. He stood still for another twenty minutes before he began picking the shell casings up off the floor with his gloved fingertips. Because the Glock's polygonal barrel left no traceable marks on the slugs, the only ballistics evidence he had to worry about were the shell casings. Without them and without any fingerprints or DNA, there wasn't a shred of physical evidence that could link him to the crime. He felt his own head; it was bumped and bruised from the shoe, but there was no blood.

He picked up the shoe that Strauss had used to strike him and tiptoed toward the steps. He climbed them slowly and searched the entryway until he found the first few casings he'd fired. He counted the casings, pocketed them with the rest, and opened the door without a noise.

The screen door he opened a millimeter at a time, minimizing the anxious squeaking of the hinges.

Jack ran for six blocks down the dark and broken sidewalk. His feet seemed to float above the concrete. They were numb. He ran until his lungs burned in his chest and then he stopped and spun wildly around, searching for any sign of another human being who might have seen him.

He exhaled great gusts of steam that glowed faintly in the light of a nearby street lamp. He spun around again, half expecting to hear sirens or the shouts of a mob coming after him on the street. With effort he was able to walk, not run, turning this way and that through a maze of streets, keeping his bearings by the sickle moon.

When he reached the corner where he'd parked his car, he looked the street over before walking up to the Taurus and getting in. He searched the street again, then started the engine and pulled away from the curb. He fought the urge to smash the accelerator to the floor. That wouldn't help him. That would get him caught. He was still covered with blood.

CHAPTER 11

Jack arrived at the Motel 6 near the airport at three-thirty in the morning. He let himself into the room and closed the door. He took a deep breath and let it out in a slow steady stream.

On the floor a plastic tarp was waiting. Jack stood in the middle of it and stripped off his clothes, every stitch. Barefoot, he walked into the bathroom and turned on the shower. He got wet, then shut off the water. For ten minutes he scrubbed. White lather covered him from head to toe. Then he rinsed off.

When he was finished, he got out and dried off. His face stared back at him in the mirror, his hair a wild thatch of straw, and circles under his glassy blue eyes. Around the edges of his scalp the welts from Strauss's shoe were beginning to swell and darken. He still felt dirty. He brushed his teeth, then got in the shower and washed off again.

Afterward he got down on his hands and knees and used a washcloth to clean the tub. When the tub began to squeak, he stopped and looked at the cloth. He remembered watching Sesame Street with Janet when she was about five. The count's hands were dirty. He washed his hands. The soap was dirty. He washed the soap with a cloth. The cloth was dirty. He could never get rid of it.

Jack filled the sink, then rinsed out the cloth, draining the water several times. He walked naked back into the room and tossed the washcloth onto the pile of things on top of the plastic. He put on a new set of clothes then carefully wrapped everything he'd been wearing, as well as the shell casings and the washcloth, into the plastic tarp and stuffed it all into a green garbage bag.

The only exceptions were his gun and holster. Those he locked inside a trim metal briefcase that he removed from his travel bag. He packed the metal container into a UPS box, stuffed it with newspaper, and sealed it up. He put on a fresh coat and, with the bag in his hand and the box under his arm, went back out to his car.

He knew right where he was going. The garbage bag went into a Dumpster in back of a nearby shopping center, and the package went into a UPS drop-off box. He returned to his motel and lay down on the bed in his clothes. He felt as though a giant hand was pressing him down, squeezing him. His breath came in short gasps. His mind scrambled over the jagged details of the crime, scouring for some small overlooked shred of evidence that could lead to his arrest.

He didn't know when exhaustion finally overtook him, but he soon found himself trapped in a dream. He tried to tear himself from his sleep, but it was no use. This was part of his punishment, the price he paid for failing to protect his little girl. He was forced to watch, caught in the nightmare that had haunted him since they'd found her . . .

It was a windy autumn day, the kind where leaves

swirled down from the sky cutting through broad bands of sunlight like snowflakes. The rickety sound of their sprint across the sidewalk concealed the deadly squeal of car brakes. A van had stopped short halfway up the block, but she never noticed. She was concentrating on the cracks in the sidewalk, careful not to step on one.

In her mind she heard the singsong children's rhyme, *"Don't step on the crack or you'll break your mama's back."*

Her hair was a brilliant blond and it fell in a sheet over the hood of her sweatshirt and straight to the middle of her back. It was a striking feature—her best. Why did she hesitate? Why? She should have run at the sight of the stranger with the balding head and the odd smile when he sprang from the van.

It happened so fast. All she was able to do at the last second was to throw her book bag in his direction. The man—he was so much stronger than he appeared— grasped her by the throat and snatched her into the open side panel of the van. She gasped. The air soiled by the pungent damp cloth that had been jammed into her mouth filled her lungs.

Everything went black.

When she awoke, she begged God that it was all a horrible dream.

The room was dark. She was bound down to a bed, alone in the small room. Crickets and frogs hummed peacefully outside. The sudden scream of a jet's engine made her start. She had no idea where she was. She didn't know how long she'd been there.

Two leather straps bound her down. Her right wrist was handcuffed to the headboard of a sagging bed.

Slowly she wormed her way out from underneath the leather straps. She yanked frantically at the handcuffs to no avail. She groped with her fingertips along the borders of the spindly wooden headboard. Panic flooded her insides. She tore at everything within her grasp. She knocked over a small table, and its lamp shattered. She ripped wads of stuffing out of the mildewed mattress.

She stopped only when her breath was reduced to short painful gasps. Then she began to work in earnest. For a long time she plied the headboard back and forth until finally the rusty screws holding it to the rest of the frame snapped. Dragging it behind her, she felt her way through a small doorway into a larger room. The quarter moon spilled in through a small square window. A rotting net hung from the wall next to curling photographs of old men proudly holding up their dead fish.

The door, warped from moisture and mold, was locked from the outside. She kicked at it until her feet were sore and bleeding. Finally it gave way and she was able to drag the headboard behind her out onto a rickety porch. Reeds sprang up from below, concealing the black pool of water beyond except for a gap where a small boat might be run up to the cabin. Another jet roared past overhead. She watched its lights flash through a filter of tears. She still didn't know where she was.

"Daddy," she said. It was no more than a whimper.

After a moment, she dragged the headboard to the edge of the porch and jumped in. The black water was cold, but the night air was not. She clambered up onto the headboard, keeping clear of the water as best she could.

She paddled and steered blindly and madly until the horizon began to lighten in the east. She moved toward shore, and her toes soon sank into the muck. Up on the soft shore amid the tangle of cattails she burrowed as best she could into the warm dark mud and then fell into a shivering exhausted sleep.

The sun was high and burning when she awoke to the sound of a small outboard motor. She closed her eyes and curled up into a ball. The muddy headboard lay beside her, half in and half out of the dark water. Her heart raced frantically as the engine came closer; still she remained motionless. She was praying. The chugging grew louder. She shut her eyes tight. Her raw wounds began to burn anew. Then she heard a voice.

"What's that?"

She opened her eyes. Two men in fishing gear stared in bewilderment down at her from their boat.

"It's a girl," one of them said.

"Is she alive?"

Her eyes spilled hot tears. She covered herself as best she could with her hands and nodded frantically that she was . . .

Jack bolted up from the sheets. They were twisted and damp. He wiped the sweat from his brow and looked around, blinking. His heart hammered against the inside of his chest.

After a deep breath he got up and drove to the airport. Inside the terminal he got a newspaper and sat down near his gate. He hid his face behind the paper, dropping it only to catch quick glimpses of the people who began to surround him. He felt naked sitting there and wondered if the sickness inside him would ever stop.

CHAPTER 12

Three days after the news of Strauss's murder appeared in the upstate papers, Jack was able to see his daughter again. It had been exactly a month since they had allowed him his last visit. It was a cruel month and possibly the thing that had given him the final resolve to randomly choose and destroy Strauss. Since her admission into Crestwood, Jack had grown accustomed to seeing Janet every Sunday. His last visit, however, ended in a horrible scene of hysterical screaming. He was asked by the doctor to give Janet a month's reprieve.

Crestwood was a gray stone mansion with dark green shutters and a slate roof. The hospital rested on a hilltop overlooking a spacious tree-covered lawn, shrouded on the other three sides by a stand of ancient and majestic spruce trees. Crestwood had been converted into an asylum shortly after the Second World War, when two wings were added, one on either side, that blended seamlessly with the original architecture. Then more recently, in the early 1980s, it had taken on the sole mission of treating children who were mentally ill.

Jack turned off the highway and wound his way up the private road leading to the old stone edifice. Halfway up, he slowed at the sight of a jogger. As he pulled alongside, he realized that it was Beth Phillips, Crestwood's elementary education teacher. Her long dark hair was pulled back into a ponytail that bounced with her gait. Frumpy gray sweats covered her small athletic frame, but the expression on her face was anything but drab. Her high round cheeks were apple red, and she wore the indefatigable smile of a child winning a race. She waved and burst out in a happy hello as he passed. Jack felt compelled to lightly tap his horn.

He parked his car in the visitors' lot and assessed the sky. The warm afternoon sun was now weighing battle with a collection of heavy clouds. He took a deep breath and strode up the walk through the tall green front doors and into the reception area. He stood for a moment in the towering marble foyer of the old mansion and looked around at the somber antique furniture and the grand heavily framed oil paintings that lined the walls. It smelled old and musty.

Anne Steinberg, Janet's doctor, smiled warmly at Jack and buzzed the electric lock that allowed him to enter into the inner sanctum of Crestwood.

"It's good to see you," she said. Then her pleasant face took on a worried look.

"I don't want you to have any expectations, Mr. Ruskin," she said.

Jack swallowed hard. His stomach was already in knots. Dr. Steinberg stopped halfway down the hall and looked up at him through her silver-rimmed glasses with penetrating pale green eyes.

"As I told you before," she said, "you were not to blame for what happened the last time . . ."

It was too late for that. Jack blamed himself for that

and everything. It was he, after all, who was to have picked her up from soccer practice after school. That's when Tupp got her. It was ten days before anyone else saw her again. His nightmare had filled in the details.

"Actually," Dr. Steinberg said, "her reaction, to anything, I think gives us reason to hope.

"Please," she said before continuing down the hallway, "be patient with her and be patient with yourself."

Janet hadn't spoken a word since her abduction. Dr. Steinberg said it was her mind's way of insulating itself from the pain that she'd experienced. She had, in effect, shut down. The only difference between Janet and the victim of a traumatic head injury was that her injury had been psychological and not physical.

Dr. Steinberg turned to the door on her right and slowly swung it open. It was a small sitting room that looked out over a koi pond. Jack stepped inside. Despite the warm yellow walls, it was barren. Absent was any artwork or knickknacks, anything that could be remotely harmful.

Janet was on the couch, facing the glass doors. The white-and-orange-spotted fish writhed just beneath the water's surface, gulping for food.

Janet sat motionless in the soft blue flowery material of the couch. Her pale legs stuck out like bare matchsticks from her lifeless cotton gown. Her feet were tucked inside pink terry-cloth Peds with dirty white nubs across their bottoms. Her beautiful hair had been cropped close and hung in blunt little blond bangs. Under her eyes were the dark puffy circles that came with heavy medication. On her rail-thin arm were the faded pink scars burned into her flesh by Eugene Tupp's smoldering cigarette.

Jack's stomach tightened and rolled. He felt his nails digging into the palms of his hands. Janet stared absently out the window. Then she blinked, just once, and turned her head his way.

CHAPTER 13

Jack took a step toward his daughter, just a step. He wanted to cross the small room, scoop her up, and press her whole body to his chest. His heart ached, and tears filled his eyes. Hold her tight. That was what he'd always done. He couldn't think of any specific incident, only vague but powerful images of Janet in her room, sullen or wounded and needing love, needing him. Even as a teenager she would let him hug her.

Janet's mother wasn't like that. The nice word for Angela was *reserved*. And when there were problems—as there are with every high school girl, a boy calling too late, a poor mark on a test, a broken curfew—it would be his presence, his touch that would make everything right. That's what he begged God he could do at this moment, to make everything right again.

He took another step closer and the pupils of her eyes seemed to widen. Then Janet emitted a low wailing sound. It was a single plaintive note, but it struck a chord so deep inside Jack that he swayed backward, sickened. It was the grievous sound of a small animal, trapped and helpless. Jack felt it somehow accused him. No, it convicted him of causing all this. A father too busy to remember his little girl.

Jack felt Dr. Steinberg's birdlike hand lock onto his upper arm. She pulled him back toward the door. He felt his strength wither, helpless in her firm little grip. She was whispering some consolation to him, but the sound came to him as if through a tube. It didn't matter. As he moved away, he could see the anxiety in his little girl's face begin to diminish. He thought that nothing could have injured him more than her hysteria a month ago, but he'd been wrong. He took a deep breath and broke free from Dr. Steinberg. He followed the long, bleak hallway to the reception area and out the front door.

The sky was now a tumultuous charcoal gray, and the wind above had begun to howl through the treetops. Jack started for his car but saw two staff members emerge from the thick cluster of pines that surrounded the lot. They were talking and heading straight for him up the brick walkway. Jack dipped his chin and headed in the opposite direction, ducking down one of the brick paths that led into the garden. He kept going until he came to a stone bench inside a decorative hedge. He collapsed there and buried his face in his hands.

The tide of agony came rushing back from some hidden place within and Jack cried like a child. There he sat, sobbing and shuddering for some time until he felt the touch of a hand, warm and tentative, on his shoulder.

"Mr. Ruskin, are you all right?"

Startled, Jack turned toward the voice. It was Beth Phillips. She spoke in a soft whisper that was barely audible over the sweeping wind.

Jack put his hand on hers and pivoted his whole body toward her. He clung to her desperately, soaking the large front pocket of her sweatshirt with his tears. She didn't shrink from him. Instead she put her arms around his shoulders and rubbed the back of his head and neck with her open palm.

"It'll be all right," she said, whispering. "Mr. Ruskin, it'll be all right."

"I'm so alone," he heard himself say. He knew he should be embarrassed, but somehow he wasn't. "My God, I'm so alone."

Jack didn't know how long he held on to her. He was emotionally spent and his sense of time had come undone. The sky grew darker and fat drops of rain began to strike them intermittently.

"Mr. Ruskin? I'm sorry," Beth said, "but I have to go. Mr. Ruskin? Are you all right?"

Jack shut his eyes and nodded.

After a moment, he looked up at her. She had let her hair down out of the ponytail, and as she turned her head it slowly revealed her face. Her blue-gray eyes were luminous and full of pity; he realized that it was a slight upturn at the end of her nose that gave her a youthful appearance. Instead of blushing, she smiled warmly and took his hand, giving it a gentle squeeze. Between her two front teeth was a small gap.

Her hand was so warm, he hated to let go, but he did. He watched longingly as she disappeared around the corner of the hedge. She had some kind of inner light and strength that surged into him like electricity. The warmth was startling.

Angela never had that. Angela loved Jack the hard-working lawyer. Jack the successful husband. She loved the masks, the costumes of suits and jewelry. By the time it was over—when she'd moved on to an ex-fraternity boy with a double chin and thicker wallet than Jack had ever dreamed of—Jack realized she'd always been just an empty shadow in his life.

He wiped his face on his sleeve and stood up to go. The drops were less frequent now, and the air was filled with the musty scent of the warm rain. He stopped in front of the old mansion on his way to the parking lot. The vastness of the place was enhanced by the knowledge that inside its towering three-story stone walls was his little girl, drawn and thin and pale. Jack winced.

CHAPTER 14

The drive home in the rain seemed longer than the drive out. Jack's mind was mostly blank. When he did emerge from his mental fog, he thought of Beth Phillips. His mind groped for not just the image, but the sensation of her holding him. He had no idea where she was in her life. She didn't wear a wedding band or an engagement ring. Since his divorce, Jack found himself noticing those kinds of things automatically when he saw an attractive woman. Maybe that was a survival instinct as well.

At home Jack found a big blue can of Foster's Ale in the refrigerator. He poured some into a glass, took the can as well as a backup, and planted himself in front of the television. Jack usually found some consolation in old black-and-white movies, and he found one starring Gregory Peck that had only just begun. He was halfway through the movie—Peck was a missionary in China—when Jack realized he'd forgotten to eat. Instead of doing anything about it, he reloaded with two more of the big blue cans of beer. At one fifty-two in the morning, he awoke long enough to shut off the television and find his bed.

It took Jack three cups of coffee but less than half an hour to drive to his office in the morning. The commute would take him three times that if he didn't arrive every morning at six-thirty A.M., long before the traffic from Long Island into Midtown Manhattan became a disaster. He was working on a power-plant acquisition just outside Pittsburgh for an international power company called U.S. Fuel.

Some of the work had to be done in Pittsburgh. That aspect of these transactions was what allowed Jack to slip in and out of a community over a three- or four-month period without notice. After a morning of document review and conference calls Jack got back into his car and headed for LaGuardia. The gray gloom was beginning to break up, and the rain had stopped. As he crossed the Triborough Bridge, a beam of sunlight fell from the sky and illuminated part of Manhattan in a golden glow. It was enough to give Jack's spirits a slight lift, which didn't mean an awful lot since they were starting from the bottom.

The cell phone rang at his side. It was Dr. Steinberg, Janet's doctor.

She was soft-voiced and hesitant and Jack knew something was wrong. He asked.

"We want you to take a break from your visits," Dr. Steinberg said. "Janet had convulsions after you left."

Jack remained silent. He heard the hum of the uneven asphalt drift past beneath his car.

"What did I do?"

"It's all men," she said. "She is the most frightened little girl I've ever treated."

Jack spoke to her for another ten minutes. She tried to console him. She urged him to be patient. But in the end what Dr. Steinberg really wanted was to put some distance and time between his next visit. She wouldn't say how long.

He numbly agreed with the doctor's wishes.

Her words stayed with him to the airport. He bought a sandwich and forced himself to chew it down during the flight while he worked on the U.S. Fuel file. He counted each swallow. There were fourteen.

In Pittsburgh he rented a car, got some directions at the desk, and went straight to police headquarters. On the fourth floor in an obscure office at the end of a long hall, Jack asked a frizzy-haired receptionist for Sergeant Tidwell. Moments later an enormous black man with a dark flat face emerged from the labyrinth of desks and cubicles behind her. He had bags under his big round eyes, giving him the sad expression of a basset hound.

"I'm Sergeant Tidwell," he said in a soft but deep voice. "Can I help you?"

Jack extended his hand. Stepping around the receptionist's battered gray desk, he began his well-rehearsed tale: "I'm Mark Kane."

Jack had actually gone to the trouble of having business cards and a fake driver's license made up in the name of Mark Kane in the event that these were ever needed.

"I spoke to you last Thursday," he continued, ". . . about the subdirectory."

"Oh, that's right, that's right, that's right," Tidwell said, the scowl of concentration suddenly disappearing into an uncomfortable smile.

"Trisha," he said to the receptionist, who had busied herself with a Judith Krantz paperback novel, "number three is open, isn't it?"

"Mmmm-huh," she said without looking up.

"We can go right in here," Tidwell said.

He led Jack into a small interview room whose faded wood door was marked with a brass 3. The number was missing one of the two small nails that held it in place so that it now hung upside down and backward. Jack sat down at the small decrepit table whose surface had been marred by years of use. Tidwell excused himself momentarily, returning with a large three-ring binder that he dumped down onto the table with a thud.

Jack looked at the sergeant apprehensively. Even though he had a right by law to examine the subdirectory, he felt the need to repeat his fabricated story.

"We had a problem in the neighborhood where we lived," he said. "Nothing happened to our daughter, but our neighbors had a high school girl . . . I just promised myself and my wife."

"Well," Tidwell said, shifting his massive weight from one foot to the other, "there it is. Everything is in there. I don't have to be here with you, but would you make sure you tell Trisha when you're done? You can write down any information you like, you just can't take anything with you and you can't use a photocopy machine. That's all."

"Fine," Jack said, forcing a smile.

When Tidwell had gone Jack stared at the binder for a minute. It was innocuous enough looking, a dark blue plastic-covered binder with a small white label that read LEVEL 3 SUBDIRECTORY. But inside, Jack knew, was a cache of horrors that most people would find unthinkable. Inside was a collection of the most dangerous, violent, predatory criminals in the city of Pittsburgh. They were out there, roaming free, only biding their time until they committed their next crime. Jack didn't believe in redemption for these people. Statistics proved that the rate of recidivism was nearly 100 percent. He was aware that many of them had also been the victims of sexual abuse. Jack felt badly about that, but it didn't change his determination to put an end to the cycle. In his mind these people were better off dead than being allowed to destroy more lives.

His mouth turned down into a nasty frown. His face transformed into a mask of hatred. Jack opened the binder and began to leaf through the names, the faces, and the addresses of these real-life monsters and a chronicle of the crimes they had committed: unlawful imprisonment, kidnapping, sodomy, sexual assault, and rape. One crime was worse than the next. He flipped through the pages and looked at the victims: young women, occasionally boys, torn from their homes or the streets, taken to some hidden spot and violated.

The perpetrators came from all walks of life: bus drivers, clergymen, doctors, camp counselors, lawyers, teachers, accountants, salesclerks. Some looked like ordinary people, and Jack knew the stories of the guy next door, wolves in sheep's clothing. He shook his head in disgust and felt his hands begin to tremble. Others were more conspicuous, deviant in their appearance, human trash inside and out.

These monsters never got the death penalty. They never served life sentences for the things they did. Instead they were turned free to prey on the innocent again and again. The only chance society had was when they finally killed one of their victims. But even then, there were no guarantees they would be caught or put away forever.

Jack found a criminal whose victim was the same age as his own daughter and felt a charge of fury and repugnance surge through his core. As he studied the black-and-white photo of the man named Roland Lincoln, Jack ground his teeth. His hands tingled with a film of hot sweat. His eyes widened and he took in the face, memorizing its features: the thick fishy lips, the broad pale forehead; the thin wispy light-colored hair, the small flat ears and scrawny neck. And the glasses—large black plastic frames with thick lenses that magnified the man's dark faraway eyes.

Jack took a yellow pad from his briefcase and ground the ball of his pen into the paper, scribing out the name and the address. He put the pad away and returned the book to the indifferent receptionist on his way out. Tidwell was nowhere to be seen.

CHAPTER 15

Jack spent the rest of his afternoon with the local lawyers from Karlston & Banky going over the staffing details of the U.S. Fuel transaction. When they invited him to dinner afterward, Jack declined, saying he had work to do back at his hotel.

After checking in Jack changed out of his blue windowpane suit, strapped on his gun, and slipped into a black nylon sweat suit and running shoes. He pulled on a worn Yankees cap over his hair and walked out onto the street. In the fading orange sunlight he found a sandwich shop around the corner. He bought a bottle of water and a turkey sandwich. He wasn't hungry, but he knew he should eat. That was part of his plan. With the water bottle sticking out of his pocket, Jack walked down the sidewalk studying a map until he came to a trash can on the corner.

He glanced at his watch and tossed the sandwich in the can. His stomach couldn't handle it. The map went back in his pocket. He located a pharmacy and bought a bottle of Maalox, his second that day. He chugged it down as if he were gassing up a car then wiped the chalky fluid from his lips. He tossed the empty bottle along with the water into another trash can, then set off at a steady jog down

Fifth Street, out of the city center and toward the university area.

Within several blocks the buildings and streets began to decay, until Jack was running alongside decrepit graffiti-stained homes with boarded windows, crumbling grimy brick storefronts, and vacant lots of rubble peopled with rusted junk cars. The setting sun, crimson now, cast long purple shadows that softened the squalor. The residents of this neighborhood clustered like fungus in dark nooks, porch steps, or inside menacing vehicles parked along the curb. They drank from brown bags and smoked and murmured among themselves until Jack passed by them, a strange specter. They stared, sullen and silent.

Sometimes a young man or two with sagging elephant pants would step boldly and belligerently into his path; Jack would have to trade his sidewalk for the street. At one point a young woman, either drunk or on crack, began to trail him on a bicycle, pestering him with an incessant banter about what a pretty white boy he was. Jack kept his face set sternly and staring straight ahead, determined to run through them without a sign of fear.

After a couple of miles the black sky extinguished the last glow of the sun. Jack turned off Fifth Street and began to climb a hill. The decay began to lessen, but only a bit. It was still a rough neighborhood when Jack passed the cove of three-story apartment buildings where Lincoln lived. He ran a block farther then crossed the street and jogged slowly back, reconnoitering. Across the street from the apartment building was an old abandoned clapboard home whose gaping black windows and door frames as well as a terrific hole in the roof were charred around the edges. On one side was a tangle of overgrown bushes. Jack looked around, saw no one, and darted into the unlit crevice between the bushes and the house.

For nearly two hours he stood leaning against the burned-out house, absorbing the pulse of the neighborhood. Dogs barked. Mixed races of people drifted in and out of apartments. Cars patched with duct tape and fiberglass came and went like beetles belching blue fumes from broken muffler pipes. An old house across the street trembled from within with the throb of hate-filled rap music. It wasn't until around ten that the pulse of the neighborhood began to ebb.

This was his penance for failing as a father. This was the only way he could make good on what had happened. He felt an almost biblical conviction that he had been cast into a pit of misery for a reason. That reason was to save others from the same fate. The only way he could do that was to follow through on his carefully laid plan.

At ten-thirty he took a deep breath and crossed the street. Building A was the one on the left, and Jack went up the steps and into the open-air alcove in the center of the building. On the wall by the stairs was a scarred directory of mostly handwritten names. Number 16-A was blank. Jack stepped over a brown smear of dog crap and mounted the crumbling concrete steps with his heart thumping madly. Number 16-A was on the third floor and all the way to the back of the building, not far from an iron railing that overlooked the house still shaking from the rap music's bass. Between the house and the apartments was some additional parking lit by a single streetlight and bordered by a chain-link fence.

The hidden spot behind the Dumpster in the parking lot would be the perfect place for him to sit and watch

Lincoln's movements. He turned to go, then jumped back with a cry of surprise. Roland Lincoln had silently emerged from his apartment and stood staring at Jack, blocking his path.

Lincoln was dressed in a white open-collared dress shirt, dark pants, and sneakers. He seemed to float, standing ghostlike in the eerie blue hue cast by the glow of the street lamp. He blinked at Jack, but otherwise his face was expressionless.

"I'm a police detective," Jack said. The words rushed out before he even thought about them. His chest was pounding with fear. Then, pointing toward the noisy house below, he said, "I'm watching that house. Drugs."

Lincoln stared for another moment. Then his enormous eyes seemed to shift their focus past Jack out at the rumbling house whose windows vibrated like the wings of an angry insect. Nodding abruptly, he turned and disappeared back inside his apartment without a word. Jack inhaled sharply and hurried away, shaking. As he jogged back down the hill and through the dark and relatively quiet streets, his face underwent a change. His tight mask of anxiety and fear slowly transformed into a determined frown. The incident with Lincoln had shaken him. But as he jogged down into the civilized section of the city, he realized its importance. His victim believed he was a cop. Knocking on his door and gaining entrance late at night would now be easier. A perfect prelude to the execution he was about to carry out.

CHAPTER 16

When Jack arrived home on Long Island the following day, his spirits were higher than they'd been in some time. The luck he'd had while reconnoitering Lincoln's apartment had spawned a new idea. Lincoln could be taken care of on his very next trip to Pittsburgh. With so many days left before the transaction was complete he could go and get a second name from the directory, something he should have considered before now. Who knew? If things went smoothly he could eliminate several predators in each city. By the time anyone linked them together, if they did at all, Jack would be on to his next transaction and his next place. Brilliant.

When he touched down in New York, there was still enough of the workday left to prompt him to go into Manhattan and his office. On the way he directed his secretary to make his travel plans for the following week. After that he considered the things he would need: a set of disposable clothes, a large piece of plastic, a garbage bag, and, of course, his Glock. The gun he would ship to himself at the hotel. Then, as he did after the Oswego job, he'd ship the gun back home when he was finished. Jack combed through the details as he drove and found nothing lacking. Satisfied, he was able to focus on just legal work when he reached his office.

It was late in the afternoon, and he was reviewing a batch of SEC documents when Arthur Wells, the firm's managing partner, summoned him to his corner office overlooking the Chrysler Building. Wells was a large man in his sixties. He was remarkably fit, with waves of white hair that made people overlook his homely features and crooked Irish teeth. Wells was on the phone when Jack entered, but the older man smiled and motioned for him to have a seat. Jack did and listened in silence as Wells debated with his personal broker whether or not to buy IBM at 61.

As he hung up, Wells said, "That guy couldn't find his ass with both hands and a flashlight but he's luckier than a horseshoe."

The two of them sat there for a moment with Wells smiling and Jack waiting.

Wells leaned back into his chair and crossed his arms in front of him in a satisfied way. Then he said, "Sometimes, Jack, the best tribute to leadership is the progress of those in the ranks. Now, I'm not going to bullshit you. When I took over this firm four years ago, the word on you was that the best you could hope for was a window . . . if you outlived twenty percent of your peers."

Wells's smile turned into a painful grin, and his blue eyes were nearly lost in a sea of mirthful wrinkles. Jack, on the other hand, wasn't amused, and he was beyond bothering to pretend he was.

"Well, you're all business," Wells said, "I know that Jack, all business, and that's what I like. Have you seen the numbers from the first quarter? I'm sure you have."

"No," Jack said candidly, "I haven't."

Most lawyers worshiped the quarterly performance spreadsheet. Attorneys were listed and ranked by the hours they billed and the revenues they brought in. Partners were also given credit for leveraging associates by involving them in projects. When he first joined the firm, Jack had followed the performance numbers as assiduously as the rest. For the last two years, however, he hadn't paid the slightest attention, and it didn't matter much to him even under the circumstances.

Wells chuckled and waved his hand in the air to disperse what was surely a jest.

"You left us all in the dust, Jack," he said, his gaze not wavering. "Those Deerfield Academy boys Kincaid and Westmoreland can't even keep up. You jumped from one fifty-seven to six. Damn, boy. You're number three in the firm. Jack?"

He looked into the younger man's face.

Jack returned his stare. He'd been watching pigeons on the concrete sill.

"You're going to get the M and A chair. Right?" he said, his voice trailing off. "What's wrong? If I'd been your age and heard that, I'd have crapped my drawers."

Carlton Obermeyer IV was old money. He was Yale. He was a workhorse. He was also a brilliant man, revered by the other five hundred members of the firm. To be given his office, his corner office overlooking the East River, was a plum worthy of champagne. But when Jack's mouth twisted up into a small smile, it wasn't from self-congratulation, but from irony.

Funny how he'd taken the work that was in his path and gobbled it up, not so much to make money for the firm, but to provide a medium for his plan to kill and distract his mind from its ongoing self-torment. He now commandeered work without regard to previous client relationships and meted out assignments to associates and fellow partners with the dispassion of a Hun warlord.

"I appreciate it, Arthur," he said, not wanting to be outright rude. "Is that all?"

"Is that all? Damn that's good!" Wells said with a chortle and another slap at the desk. "I'd say that thing about all work making Jack dull. But my accountant wouldn't let me. Dull is rich."

The intercom on Wells's desk came to life and his secretary announced that Rob Blumenthal from Deutsche Bank was on the line.

"Tell him I'm with Jack Ruskin, but I'll be right with him," Wells said. His face then turned serious and he said to Jack, "Everything all right at home?"

"Fine," Jack said, wondering if Wells had even the slightest clue as to what he'd been through. People seemed to think that what had happened to him had somehow gotten better over the last two years, but in fact it was worse.

"Good," Wells said with a slap. "Congratulations."

"Thank you," Jack said.

Jack returned to his own claw-footed mahogany desk and got to work immediately without another thought about his elevation in status at the firm.

Leather-bound books stared down at him from their shelves. Outside his tenth-floor window the city revved up for rush hour, but Jack never noticed. The slow grind of words and terms had the narcotic ability to deaden his other thoughts and feelings. After a time, the noise outside began to wind down and it grew dark. Jack worked until his stomach rumbled audibly. He knew he should eat something even if he had no appetite.

CHAPTER 17

It was after ten P.M. when he pulled into the driveway. He took his briefcase from the front seat and removed his overnight bag from the trunk. A gentle breeze whispered through the new leaves of the trees overhead. The sky was dark, but his eyes soon adjusted and he could clearly see the large unfriendly house that used to be a home. Now it was just a place for him to sleep.

Jack walked down to the end of the driveway and emptied his mailbox. A neighbor strolled down the sidewalk on the opposite side of the street, walking her dog in the darkness and talking into a cell phone. Jack silently watched her pass, then retraced his steps up the driveway. As he opened the front door into the dark maw of the empty house, he felt the urge to go find a warmly lit bar, drink himself into oblivion, then return only when he was in a respectable stupor. But he had already abandoned himself several times to that yearning and he knew it would bring him no real satisfaction. Even the dull throb of loneliness was better than the piercing agony of a massive hangover the next day.

With a sigh, he flipped on the lights and walked into the kitchen. The sink stared back at him, a smooth flow of white porcelain set in a pink sea of granite. It wasn't a particularly special sink, but next to the faucet was the spray nozzle that he used to wash Janet's hair when she was a baby. He remembered the first time he had done that. She was only about ten days old. It was during the night when he let Angela get some sleep. Janet had gotten sick all over everything and Jack had taken that bold move: her first bath.

Like every baby, Janet had cried. The unusual thing was that Jack had cried along with her. It was a moment burned into his memory, and not just because his little helpless infant daughter was crying. Rather, it was in that moment that he realized there were things in the world that he could not protect her from, and that notion had torn into him. All he ever wanted, from the moment Janet had been born, was to protect her as much as possible from the hurts of the world. And yet . . .

Jack tossed the mail down on the table and went to the refrigerator for his usual can of Foster's. He owed himself that much at least. As he poured the beer into a glass he noticed from the corner of his eye the flashing red light of the answering machine. Since his wife's departure many months ago, the machine had fallen into disuse.

The last time he'd checked, more than a week ago, the message on it was someone with the wrong number asking for a person named Kate. Jack's parents were both dead and his sister had married the full-bearded priest of a strange religious cult out in Oregon. He hadn't heard from her in three years. Now that Angela was gone, Jack had no social life. He sat his beer down on the table and dropped into a chair, musing.

Out of habit, he played the message. This time it was for him. The inflection of the voice, not just the words, filled him with a surge of adrenaline. It was Beth. She wanted to know how he was doing. All the feelings he'd experienced in the garden at Crestwood came rushing back.

Jack played it again, and then again.

She had actually called him, at home. And left him her number. He went to the cupboard above his sink. Looking down on him was a regiment of blue bottles: Maalox. He took one down and cracked the cap, gulping it hungrily. It seemed to be the only thing that would quell the feeling that beleaguered his stomach. He tossed the bottle into the garbage and picked up the phone, trembling as he dialed.

"Beth?" he said, in a strangled voice.

"Yes?"

"This is Jack Ruskin."

Silence ensued, and Jack wondered in an irrational instant of panic if he'd made some mistake.

"I . . . I didn't know if I should call you at home," she said. "I'm sorry."

In his mind, he could see her face, the small nose and the deep caring eyes slowly revealed from behind a dark luxuriant curtain of hair. He could feel the warm touch of her hand against his bare neck.

"No, please," he said, pinning the phone against his shoulder with the side of his head and taking up his glass to steal a quick mouthful of beer. "I'm glad you called. I appreciate it."

"Because, I guess, technically," she said, "I shouldn't . . . I guess . . ."

"Well . . ."

"Well, you're the lawyer," she said, "I thought you might know . . ."

"There's no law against calling someone. I know that," he said. "Even if there was, the rules of ethics in mental health are for the counselors and doctors. And even if Crestwood has any policies about the staff, that's for your privacy. You know, to keep people from bothering you or something. I mean, not the other way around. I'm sorry, I'm babbling."

"Well, I didn't want to do anything wrong, but I was worried about you," she said. "Even though I don't work with the older girls, I know you're in a . . . that you're going through a difficult time. I don't know, though. I still feel funny calling."

"I know how you can make it up to me," Jack said.

"How's that?"

"How about having dinner?"

There was silence for quite some time. Jack felt a jet of humiliation beginning to flood the cavity in his chest. She was obviously fumbling for a comforting way to reject him.

Finally, she spoke.

In almost a whisper she said, "I'd like that."

CHAPTER 18

Amanda shaded her eyes from the white afternoon sun and watched Teddy run to first base through a flurry of insects in the golden haze. The cluster of other parents beside the bench sitting on lawn chairs erupted in cheers. Amanda clapped as well. She didn't cry out her son's name even though she had swelled at the sight of him running like a colt breaking into his first gallop.

As a former athlete herself, Amanda despised the overdone enthusiasm that she felt spoiled so many children's sports contests. Little League was supposed to be for fun, a replacement for the days of a safer world when kids simply chose up sides for a game in someone's backyard. Unfortunately, most youth league sports had turned into farm systems for high school sports teams. It was ludicrous.

Still, Amanda was thankful that Teddy was a capable player. She had no delusions of grandeur, but she did harbor that common maternal hope that Teddy would always find acceptance among his peers. She knew from her own childhood that sports was the great leveler. Her own red hair—carrotlike as a girl—buckteeth, and glasses were cause for crucifixion as a young teen. But on the soccer field she was a force, a boiling tyrant who kicked, scored, and defended her team's way to many wins. And when she walked down the halls with her awkward smile and her haphazard pile of books, even the boys who smoked cigarettes and pierced their ears began to make way.

Amanda frowned at the thought of what she had once looked like. The ghost of that image was always there, looking back at her from the mirror no matter what she did. Sometimes she allowed herself a small consolation when other men's eyes wandered toward her the way children will gravitate toward a puppy. She would of course frown them off. She didn't want the attention of other men. Still, the attention gave her hope, hope that she had distanced herself forever from the homely little girl with carrot hair and glasses.

She looked at her watch and wondered where Parker and Glenda had gotten to. Glenda's softball games were scheduled at the same time as Teddy's baseball games, but usually she finished first. Maybe Parker had taken her for ice cream. Amanda thought about Parker's enthusiasm when she told him she'd been offered Marco's position at the Bureau. There were only a dozen assistant special agents in charge in the National Center for the Analysis of Violent Crime. NCAVC had absorbed the former child abduction unit, the serial killer unit, and the profiling unit into one entity, but each former unit had four ASAICs—and now Amanda was being offered one of those laudable positions.

Of course, there was no way she could take it. She appreciated the honor of being chosen, but Marco's death still bothered her immensely. She had seen a therapist about what happened. She knew she shouldn't blame herself. Still . . .

She was at the end of her allowed sabbatical, but she wondered if she could delay going back to her old position even longer. Even dealing with the guilt and the mourning over Marco, there had been a pleasant element to the summer that she couldn't explain. She felt like she had been the best mother she'd ever been. They'd taken a trip to the Outer Banks and spent another week at her brother-in-law's cabin near the Shenandoah National Forest. It wasn't far, but a turbulent waterfall nearby cooled the woods around the cabin and provided them with rock pools and slides to swim in. She worked with Glenda for hours on end, trying to get her ready to swim without a life jacket.

Every night before bed, vacation or otherwise, Amanda read to them from the Harry Potter series. Besides taking care of the house, she was always ready to throw the baseball with Teddy and kick the soccer ball back and forth with Glenda. More important, it seemed that lately a day didn't go by without Teddy giving her an unsolicited hug. Maybe she could keep that going, even if she did return to the Bureau. Maybe she could only take assignments that were close to home. Amanda took a deep breath.

As the game played on, the tree line on the edge of the park finally extinguished the sun's sweltering orange rays and brought the first relief all day from the early-summer heat. Amanda reached down and picked up a bottle of water lying in the dry grass beneath her chair. She took a long cool drink, then rested the sweaty plastic against her cheek and then her bare thigh. Teddy scored and his team took the lead going into the final inning. As her son's team took the field, a loud low rumble prompted her and the rest of the parents to turn their attention to the parking lot behind them.

A shiny black vehicle, its armor glistening like a beetle, rumbled right up behind the backstop and shut down. The monstrous machine had the heartless countenance of a big truck combined with the awkwardness of a tank. It was a Humvee, a troop carrier for the army that had been converted into a road vehicle. They were rare sights in suburbia, freakish machines that cost as much as a Mercedes sedan. Like everyone else, Amanda peered intently to see who on earth would be driving such a thing in a quiet middle-class town like Manassas. Amanda was shocked to see her own grinning husband and just the top of what must be Glenda's green softball cap in the passenger seat.

"Come on! Let's play ball!" the umpire shouted.

Amanda felt her cheeks flush when she realized that the entire game had stopped to view the spectacle of Parker climbing down from the gleaming paramilitary vehicle. As he strode her way across the grass, his giant smile was betrayed by the shifty eyes of a little boy who had been caught stealing. He knew buying a machine like that was irresponsible, but Amanda had serious doubts as to whether he would ever admit it.

"Hi, honey," she said, giving Glenda a kiss and a smile as if nothing was wrong.

Then, hissing under her breath to Parker, she said, "What is that thing?"

Without waiting for his response, she turned back toward the action on the field.

The game was under way again and the evening came to life with the shrill cries of "No batter, no batter, no batter!"

"What?" Parker said in a low tone. She knew he'd taken offense. "What the hell is that supposed to mean? You know what it is. It's a Humvee. It's what I've been talking about getting for, like, forever. Only now with our extra income, I figured, Hey, this is the safest vehicle on the road. Do you know driving our kids around town is statistically the most dangerous thing we do? Because it is, you know."

"You bought that thing?"

His silence answered her question.

"Parker," she said, shooting a glare his way and holding up her hand to try and cut him off, "don't even try that with me. This isn't a Volvo, Parker. You bought a troop carrier, a troop carrier that we can't afford."

"Not so goddamn loud, Amanda," Parker said.

"Damnit," he said, kicking the dusty grass beneath them. People turned to look. Parker's round red face and twinkling eyes had gone sour. "Can you come over here so we can talk?"

"Honey, you sit right here and watch your brother," Amanda said to Glenda. "We'll be right back."

She got up and followed Parker into the parking lot, out of earshot from the rest of the parents.

"You're getting a big raise, Amanda," Parker said. "And I got promoted. We can afford it, and you know I've been wanting this. You're the one who gave me the idea."

"*I* gave you the idea?"

"Yes, you," he said. "You were the one who started

going on about how the money would let us do some things we'd always wanted to do. Damn, I thought that's what you were getting at. This is perfect for us. It fits us all, and I can take it off road for hunting, and look at it. No one's got a truck like this, Amanda."

"Parker," she said, "we talked about setting up college funds. That's what we talked about. Besides, I'm not taking the new job."

"What?"

"I said I'm not taking the job, Parker."

"Well, you got to go back to work," he said.

"Not as the ASAIC, I don't."

"Why not?" he said in bewilderment.

"Don't you ever listen? I've been in therapy for months to get over watching my partner die and now I'll take his job? Does that do anything for you?

"And I'm not staying away from the kids anymore," she said, "just so you can parade around town like some suburban Arnold Schwarzenegger. If I took that job, I'd be gone way too much."

Parker wore a frown that didn't suit him at all. He was a cheerful man who liked to hunt and fish and play with his kids. Everyone liked Parker because he was always that way. To see him otherwise made Amanda feel like she'd run a traffic light with the kids in the backseat.

"Amanda," Parker said, "I didn't honestly think there was a job on this earth that could take you away more than you already are . . ."

He spoke without rancor. Instead his words were heavy with unhappy acceptance. He looked like an old dog that knew it was going to be put down, sad, but all the same full of that faithful love. A thousand bitter retorts sprang to life in Amanda's mind, but her heart sank, failing her and leaving her with nothing but a helpless shrug and a small stream of silent tears.

Something in her life had to change.

CHAPTER 19

Sergeant Emerson Tidwell was used to his subjects skipping town. Two out of ten usually did. And when they either never showed up from the beginning of their release from jail or simply got tired of reporting in to him on a regular basis as time went on, the resulting warrant was flat-out useless. Nevertheless, Tidwell always filled out the appropriate paperwork. Diligence was something his grandmother had taught him at an early age.

So when Gilbert Drake failed to appear on July 17 at his eleven A.M. appointment, Tidwell left a message on Drake's answering machine as a reminder. After hearing nothing for a week Tidwell began to fill out the warrant at promptly eleven A.M. As always, it was neat and precise, despite the fact that it was a meaningless exercise. The system had created Tidwell's job when Pennsylvania adopted its own version of Meghan's Law, named for a girl abducted and killed by a prior sex offender who had moved into her New Jersey neighborhood next to Meghan's parents. After Meghan's murder, her parents lobbied successfully to help protect other families from the dangerous molesters turned loose in their midst.

Sex offenders were divided into three levels and monitored accordingly when they were released from jail. If they came to Pittsburgh, they had to report to Tidwell. He put them in his file and explained the process to them—appearances every three months for level threes and immediate notification upon any change of address for all offenders.

Tidwell pursed his lips as he looked at Drake's record. The sag in his big drooping eyes seemed even more pronounced. His cheeks puffed out and a long thin hissing sound escaped him. Drake had a history of abducting and violating young women. He had been living in a tough area over near the V.A. hospital, rife with cheap apartments and dilapidated crack houses. It was one of the neighborhoods typical to Tidwell's charges. Of the 207 level-three offenders floating around his city, two-thirds of them could be found in three or four neighborhoods.

In truth, Tidwell didn't put much stock in the subdirectory. Because most of the offenders were living in a few small geographic areas, the chief of police had restricted notification to the public at large. Tidwell was all for giving out the information in his files to the media, neighborhood groups, and schools. The chief, however, in conjunction with the mayor's office, didn't want to incite panic or riots. Despite the law making the information public knowledge, most times what people didn't know wouldn't hurt them. Tidwell knew differently, but still his request had been denied.

With his work complete, he placed his pen in its spot on the desk, went downstairs, and crossed the street to the courthouse, where he processed his warrant. Not one of the hundred or more warrants he had filed over the last seven years had ever been served. On the rare occasions one of his subjects was picked up on some other charge, the penalty for failing to appear before Tidwell was treated as a joke. Never had he seen or even heard of a judge who would mete out anything more serious than a conditional discharge. There was a fear from above that if someone was arrested for failing to comply with the reporting laws, the charges very well might fail a constitutional challenge. Sometimes Tidwell wanted to put a copy of the Constitution in the outhouse behind his hunting camp.

He jogged down the stone steps of the courthouse, his massive belly jiggling beneath his sweat-stained uniform, and out onto the sidewalk. Heat waffled up off the pavement, giving everything up and down the street a liquid quality. Around the corner was a deli whose specialty sandwich was called a Hog Hoagie. Tidwell was good for two of them, washing down any remains with a pint of AriZona tea, and always leaving one small heel from one bun on his plate as an homage to the low-carbohydrate diet he knew he should be on. But he was a man who enjoyed his food, and he cheerfully reminded himself of that as he dug in. A dusty fan blew warm air down on the patrons from the corner of the deli. After his meal Tidwell dabbed the thick folds of his dark brow with a handful of napkins before rising to go. It was so hot it made him think about the cool stream that he used to splash in as a kid.

It was late in the afternoon before he received a call from homicide.

"Tidwell."

The voice on the other end was sharp and nasal.

"This is Zuckerman. You just filed a warrant on a body I got over near the V.A. hospital. One of your pervs got shot up pretty good. You know anything about it?"

Zuckerman was a homicide detective—not a sergeant or a lieutenant, but a beat detective. Granted, he was in homicide, and that was a prestigious thing. But at the age of fifty-four, he wasn't unlike the eleventh man on a basketball team. He got in the game when it was junk time. Maybe that was why he had a bad attitude.

"Gilbert Drake?" Tidwell heard himself say. The black-and-white mug shot of the forty-year-old man was still fresh in his mind—the nappy head, the creamy brown skin, the broad flat nose, and those small dark empty eyes.

"That's him," Zuckerman shot back. "I bet you got an encyclopedia on who'd want to take this shit bird out."

Tidwell felt a jumble of words escape from his mouth, an unintelligible stammering. There were plenty of people he imagined would want to kill Gilbert Drake. How about the families of the victims whose lives he'd destroyed? How about some father or husband who discovered that he was up to his old tricks near the V.A. hospital? And then this was the second such call he'd received in the last two months.

"What's that?" Zuckerman asked.

"Nothing," Tidwell said, fixed now on his answer. "I don't know anything about anyone who'd want to kill him."

It was a stupid response, but one that Zuckerman accepted without any qualms. He was a man who went through the motions of his job as if they were nothing more than sweeping the same patch of floor he'd gone over every day for twenty years. "Well," he said, "just send me over his family information and his prison record. I guess I'll have to try and get a hold of them . . ."

Tidwell didn't know how he was supposed to respond to that. It was almost as if Zuckerman wanted his opinion, but Tidwell's experience with homicide detectives told him that they didn't want advice from anyone. That was part of the reason why he didn't say anything to Zuckerman about Gilbert Drake being the second sex offender on his list in the last two months to get whacked.

"How was he killed?" he asked, his words dropping from his thoughts like ripe fruit.

"What?" Zuckerman sounded slightly confused as well as mildly offended.

Tidwell wasn't surprised. That wasn't his business, but he felt Zuckerman had somehow left the door open with his loose banter.

"How was he killed?" he said again.

"Swiss cheese," Zuckerman said.

"Swiss cheese?"

"Filled him full of holes," Zuckerman replied with delight. "Someone shot him about twelve times. Made a hell of a mess out of his apartment. No one heard anything, either, or they say they didn't. He's been dead about a week, so we're not sure exactly when. Come to think about it, he smelled like old cheese, too."

Tidwell was silent for a time.

Finally Zuckerman said, "So, you'll send that stuff over, right?"

"Yes."

Tidwell hung up and gathered the information the detective had asked for. Then he looked at his watch and cleaned up his desk. It was early to leave, but he was leaving anyway. He needed to think.

CHAPTER 20

At home Tidwell found his wife and two kids out back at the pool. He watched them through the window of the house, their shrieks of delight muted by the glass. They lived in a cramped middle-class neighborhood and had stuffed their little backyard with an inexpensive above-ground pool. His wife, as small as Tidwell was big, was sitting in a plastic chair reading a magazine while his son and daughter splashed around, whacking each other with brightly colored foam noodles.

Tidwell felt a smile curling the corners of his mouth as he removed his shirt and tie and pulled on an enormous pair of flowery blue trunks. Downstairs, he took a can of Budweiser from the fridge and slid open the screen door. The grass was dry and brown and tickled his bare feet. Tidwell noted with satisfaction that because of the heat, he hadn't had the lawn mower out of the shed in two weeks. As he mounted the pressure-treated steps to the pool, his kids erupted in cries of joy.

"Daddy! Daddy! Daddy's home!"

Tidwell burst into a grin and bent down like a giant over his wife for a kiss.

"You're early," she said, slapping his hand away from her thigh, but still obviously pleased with the surprise. At her feet a dozen freshly stained Popsicle sticks were stacked up like bones.

"I needed to think," he told her over the cries of their children.

"Think?" she said as if that were the strangest thing she'd ever heard of.

"Yeah," he said, "after a swim."

With that, he set his beer can down on the deck and lightly spun around, launching himself into the middle of the small round pool. The ensuing splash bowed the aluminum sidewalls, swamping gallons of water over the edge and bringing more squeals from his children, who were now clutching their noodles like life preservers. Up and down Tidwell heaved himself at the pool's center, creating a personal tidal wave amid a gale of laughter. Up and down he pumped the water until his breath became short and wheezy. He stopped to watch the children pitch about on the crests of the waves and laughed out loud.

Wearily, he waded to the edge and hoisted himself up onto the deck that was now stained dark from the water.

"That looks so fun," his wife said.

In one corner of the rectangular deck a bright blue tarp covered an old recliner. Tidwell dried himself and whipped the tarp off the chair. The imitation leather was faded and patched with black electrical tape. He picked up his beer, draped a towel over his back, then sat down with a heavy gasp.

"Damn," he said, sipping his beer.

"What?" his wife asked.

"My sunglasses," he said.

"I'll get them."

"No, that's okay," he said, but she was already up and

halfway down the stairs. When she came back, and he had his beer and his sunglasses and his chair and the sun and his children were playing between themselves again, Tidwell began to think. His wife left him alone, as did his children after a stern warning from their mother to give him a minute to unwind. In the peace of the hot sun he turned over in his mind exactly what he should do.

No, that wasn't it at all, he thought. He knew what he should do. The question was: What was he going to do?

He snorted again. Who wouldn't want either of them dead? He remembered being offered a position on the sex crimes unit years ago. It would have been a promotion for Tidwell at the time, and something that was hard to pass up. But those were the investigators who got called to the scene when a person was sexually victimized in any way. Often the perpetrators were family members, still present at the scene.

"I wouldn't be any good at it, Lieutenant," he'd said to the supervisor who interviewed him. "If I showed up and saw one of those women or kids after one of them sons-of-bitches did what they do and they were around, you'd have a murder on your hands on top of everything else."

That was what he'd said, that he'd kill someone who did a thing like that if he had to see it. He meant it, too. He couldn't even think of coming face-to-face with those victims, to see the tears, the horror, and not react. Cor-ralling these perverts the way he did, like animals, that was okay. He could do that with a certain detachment. And he was proud of his job, even if it didn't go far enough.

Now someone had seen it through a little farther than he did, and Tidwell was pretty sure he knew who that someone was. Mark Kane. Probably not the man's real name, but Tidwell could see Kane's face clearly in his mind, his straight blond hair, his small round glasses. It struck him as peculiar when Kane had come back to examine the subdirectory for a second time. That was just two weeks after the first time and only a few days before Roland Lincoln had been found dead.

At the time, even though Tidwell thought it was strange, he hadn't connected the death of Lincoln with the blond-headed man called Mark Kane. Now, though, with two of his sex offenders killed in the exact same bullet-ridden fashion, Tidwell couldn't help piecing the whole thing together. His mind came to the conclusion the way a child will automatically finish a rhyme.

If he did pass on his information to the detectives, there were no guarantees that they would find Mark Kane. But if he did nothing, he knew Kane would never be caught. Neither Zuckerman nor Nelson was going to bust his hump on this one.

"Honey," Tidwell said suddenly to his wife. He was watching the kids from behind his dark glasses. During his reverie his wife had replenished him with a fresh can of beer, and he sipped at it gently.

"Yes love?" she replied, reaching across the space that divided them and taking his hand into hers.

"Don't do that, Bill!" he barked out abruptly. His ten-year-old boy, big like Tidwell, was dunking his twelve-year-old sister under the water. The boy immediately stopped and his sister began to defend his actions.

"Those are the rules," he said flatly, hiding his inner pleasure at the girl's loyalty, "and I don't want to hear no more."

He glowered at the kids for a few moments, making his point, before saying to his wife, "You know the kind of people I have to keep track of."

"I do," she said, uncertain. Tidwell rarely talked about work.

"There's someone out there killing them," he said.

"Emerson?"

"A guy came in about two months ago," he explained, "a sharp-dressed guy in a suit with blond hair—good-looking guy. Blue eyes. Quiet. A lawyer, so he said. He wanted to see the directory."

"There's nothing wrong with that, right?" his wife said.

"No," he replied, "not at all. Anyone has the right to look at it. It's just that most people don't, that's all. Don't have the stomach for it. Talk themselves out of it. Pretend things like that can't happen to them. Pretend that it's always someone else, somewhere else. But if they knew . . . If they knew . . ."

Tidwell shook his head, then realized he had wandered off the subject. "So a couple of pretty bad ones have been murdered and I'm pretty sure it has something to do with the blond guy, the lawyer," he said.

"How can you think that?" she asked.

"I just do," he said simply, "that's all. Asking to see the directory once, that's one thing. Twice, that's strange. Throw two murders on top and you have to connect them all. You just have to."

"But people get killed all the time," she said.

"They do," he said, "but not the same type of person in the same exact way. Both of them were kidnappers, rapists. And both were shot to pieces right in their homes.

Both crime scenes were clean, crazy clean, like a professional job . . . Whenever you think you have just a coincidence, you probably don't."

"So what are you going to do about it?"

"Technically," he said, "it's not my job. I'm not a homicide detective and the guys who are, I promise you, wouldn't be happy to hear my opinions."

"But you could tell them at least," his wife said.

"I could," Tidwell said, staring at his kids, "and that's the problem. I could, and I probably should, and they might find this guy. But the problem is, honey, I don't want them to find this guy . . . That's just the truth and that's the problem. I'm a cop, and I don't want them to find this guy who's a killer."

Tidwell looked at his wife. She returned his gaze with a placid expression of understanding.

"Can you imagine?" Tidwell said, raising his beer can in the direction of their children.

"No," she said sharply. "Don't. Don't even say it."

CHAPTER 21

Jack found a garbage bag under the sink. It smelled under there, so he ran the disposal. It still smelled. He went into the refrigerator for a lemon and opened one of the plastic drawers at the bottom. Blue and white mold had taken over three peaches. Jack's face crinkled in disgust. He picked them up with one finger and his thumb and dumped them into the garbage bag. Below them was the lemon, brown and soft but remarkably free from most of the mold.

The lemon went into the disposal. Jack ran the water and ground it up, then sniffed the sink. Better. He went back to the refrigerator and began to throw things in, half-empty red-and-white boxes of Chinese food, a carton of spoiled milk, other things he didn't even know he had. He filled the bag, then went back under the sink for another.

Beth was coming. They were going to a show in the city: *Blue Man Group: Tubes*. Jack had seen it years ago on a trip to Chicago with Angela. She didn't get it. Jack couldn't forget. They were mimes who did an incredible production of percussion, acrobatics, and comedy. He knew Beth would like it. They liked the same things. Art-house movies and books. Vivaldi's *Four Seasons*. Bruce

Springsteen and the Red Hot Chili Peppers. Carole King. She even liked the smell of chestnuts roasting in the summertime on the corner by Central Park. They'd taken a walk there the last time they'd gone into the city.

This time, instead of Jack driving out to get her on the eastern end of the island, then going to the city, then driving her back, then coming home, Beth suggested they leave from his house. She would be the first person aside from him to walk through the door since Angela had walked out. He thought they might have a drink before they left. That meant he had to at least clean the kitchen, the living room, the front hall, and the bathroom. For everything else, he'd just shut the doors.

In the living room he began to pick up cans. He went back to the kitchen to clear the counters and the floor. Three bags later he started to mop and vacuum. Then he found an old towel and wiped all the countertops and tabletops before cleaning out the bathroom with lemon-scented ammonia. There was filth everywhere, but nothing that he couldn't get rid of with some effort. When the whole downstairs smelled like lemons, he washed out his rag and toted it upstairs along with the vacuum. His bedroom was next.

There was no need to clean it for Beth. They weren't that far along, but the sound of squeaking wood on his coffee table and the smell of lemon everywhere had inspired him. On his way down the upstairs hall, he glanced into Janet's room. Dust lay like a white film of snow on top of her desk. Her computer screen was gray with it. There was a book on geometry no one had bothered to take back to the school. Cobwebs hung from the recessed light fixtures. Stuffed animals sat in a fading pile on her bed. Jack felt his breath leave him.

He should clean this room. She might come home. Not today or tomorrow, but one day she might. Her room shouldn't be this way. He pushed open the door and stepped tentatively inside. He sneezed and his eyes began to water.

He plugged in the vacuum and began to run it over the carpet, leaving broad clean blue tracks in its wake. It felt good. When the visible part of the rug was done, he switched off the vacuum and moved the bed. Underneath it was even worse, but he could clean that, too. There was a small suitcase jammed under there, and a soccer ball. Jack picked up the ball and turned it over in his hands. On the wall were posters. The Dave Matthews Band. Britney Spears. There was a bookcase across from the bed. Trophies rested, heavy and dull in their coats of dust.

A flicker of the nightmare flashed in Jack's mind. His breathing came now in short staggered gulps. He grew dizzy again. He threw the soccer ball into the bookcase and heard himself scream. The trophies toppled from their shelves. Jack attacked them, throwing them across the room two or three at a time, punching holes in the sheetrock.

When they were gone he pulled the bookcase down with a crash. He turned to the desk and swept the book and the computer off onto the floor. The computer exploded in a rain of sparks. Jack grabbed the screen to smash it again and the shock knocked him flat. There was ringing in his ears. There was ringing in the air mingled with the smell of burning plastic.

He lay for a long time before the ringing stopped.

After it did, he heard someone calling his name. He shut his eyes and felt the tears roll down his dirty cheeks. He shut them even tighter and tried to stifle his sobs.

He felt a hand touching his. It was that same hand. That warm hand, full of life.

"Jack," Beth said, "what happened? Are you all right?"

Jack nodded and sat up slowly. He pulled her to him and held her.

"Jack?" she said.

"I'm okay," he said. "I was just . . . cleaning and I . . . I just don't know if she'll ever be better."

"Oh, Jack," she said, clutching him tight, gently rubbing the back of his head. "I'm so sorry."

She helped him to his feet and together they looked at the mess.

"Come on. Let's go," Jack said. He felt his cheeks flush with embarrassment.

"I want to help you," she said. She put her hand on the back of his neck and gave it a gentle squeeze

"I know, but let's go. I've got the tickets."

"We don't have to." She glanced down at the computer, which had begun to smoke again.

"No, I want to. You'll love these guys. It's weird, but you'll like it," he said. "Forget about this. Just forget it. I was cleaning up and I kind of lost it. It just happens to me. I'm sorry."

"I could help you pick up," she said. She left him to unplug the broken computer from the wall.

"Not now," he said. "I don't want to be here."

"Let's go downstairs, okay?" Beth took his hand and led him out of the room and down the stairs.

"Can I get you something?" she asked. "A glass of water?"

"Maybe a beer," he said. "But I can get it."

"No, you sit down. I'll get it. We can talk."

She led him to the couch, and he watched her march across the room and into the kitchen as if she'd been there a thousand times. Jack heard the bottles inside the door of his refrigerator rattle.

"Do you want a glass?" she asked from in there.

"No, that's okay."

Beth returned with a can of Foster's and a small green bottle of Perrier. He'd bought a six-pack of the stuff just for her.

"With lemon," she said, looking at the bottle and handing him the beer. "That was nice."

Jack cracked the can of beer open with a hiss and took a long drink. The frosty metal chilled the tips of his fingers and he set the can down on the coffee table. Beth looked around and found an old *Newsweek* magazine in a rack beside the couch. She slid it under his beer can.

"Thanks," he said.

"It's a nice table," she said. "What is that? Cherry?"

"Mahogany I think."

"You have to take care of it if you want it to stay nice." She was smiling at him and he knew she didn't mean it in a bad way.

"You should have seen it an hour ago," he said, looking around. "This place was a mess."

"I smell a lot of lemon cleaner," she said.

"It didn't really bother me," he said. "I didn't even notice to tell you the truth and then you said you'd come over and I was like, wow, what a pigsty. I got on a roll and I started to do the upstairs and I realized that I never . . . That was the first time I even went in her room since . . . Isn't it weird how you can go past something every day and never really see it?"

Jack drank some more of his beer and looked at the floor.

"You did good," she said. "I like that smell. My mom used to polish the woodwork with lemon Pledge. It's kind of like that."

"Thank you."

She smiled at him again.

"No, not for that," he said. "Thanks for not turning around and never coming back."

"I wouldn't do that. Do you think I'd do that?"

"No," he said. "I know you feel too sorry for me to do that, I guess."

Beth put her hand up to his face and ran her fingers through his hair. "Do you think that's why I'm here? Because I feel sorry for you?"

"Partly, I guess."

Her smile grew sad. She tilted her head and her eyes bore into his. She shook her head slowly and spoke in a quiet voice.

"That's not why I'm here," she said. "I'm here because you're nice and you're smart, and maybe even a little because you look like Robert Redford."

"Robert Redford?"

"When he was young. In a way. Not exactly.

"You're a good man, Jack," she said after a while.

"No," he said. "I'm not. I'm really not."

CHAPTER 22

Three weeks later Beth wanted to see an art-house movie about a kid in England who wanted to dance in the ballet. Jack wanted to make her happy in just about any way he could, so he agreed without comment. For the first thirty minutes he thought of nothing but his daughter and escape plans and hidden guns and vengeance. But soon the movie screen overtook what was inside his head. Instead of a lot of dancing, the movie was really about realizing your dreams and becoming whole. When the credits rolled his face was wet with tears. His cheeks grew warm when Beth noticed. She grabbed his hand.

It was hope, not despair, that left him wiping the tear tracks from his face as the two of them walked out of the theater and into the balmy night. Jack drew a deep breath before letting it out slowly.

"I liked that," Beth said. "Did you?"

"Would you like a drink?" He didn't want to talk about the movie.

"Sure," she said, looking up at him with her easy smile and the small space between her teeth.

"Jack?" She reached up and touched his cheek. "Are you all right?"

"Yeah," he said, smiling back. "Just a little shaky. I'm sorry."

"Don't say that."

He tilted his head to kiss her, oblivious to the other moviegoers surging past them in the dull glow of the parking lot. When their lips met, it was Beth who pulled him close, pressing her body against his and turning the kiss into something more than what he had meant it to be, reminding him of high school. She wore a long burgundy blazer over a snug white halter top. He wrapped his arm under the blazer and felt her hot, bare skin.

Without speaking, she gently pulled away.

"I liked that," she said in a whisper that he'd never heard before.

"I liked that, too . . . ," he said, his voice cracking. "How 'bout that drink?"

Jack took her to a restaurant in a nearby shopping center. A quiet place with soft music and small leather booths. A place where the flicker of candles heightened the dreamy intimacy between two people who had yet to know all there was to know about each other.

When they arrived, a teenage valet took the car from them to a lot out back. When Beth saw a woman in an evening dress on the arm of a man in a suit emerge from the place, she was reluctant to go in dressed in jeans, but Jack insisted that they were fine. The host who greeted them at the door felt otherwise. He was in his midtwenties with a tan face and a strong broad chin. He had greased his shoulder-length hair over his head and wore a large diamond earring. His clothes were completely black.

"We don't allow jeans at La Maison," he said.

Jack turned on him and his face dropped from a complacent smile into a forbidding frown. His eyes narrowed slightly, the life suddenly draining from them.

"I think you should make an exception for us," he said.

The man snorted and combed through his greasy locks with his fingers. The stereo above played some horrible jazz fusion. "Sorry," he said. "There's an Applebee's next door."

Jack took another step toward the man with his body tense and coiled as if ready to spring. "I'm sure you'll be heading there after work for some potato skins and a couple of margaritas, jackass, but I think I'm fine right here," he said. He moved in close, smelling the man's tangy, overripe cologne. "I'll be at the bar if you'd like to help yourself to a good old-fashioned ass kicking. Better yet, maybe you want to call the police and have them charge her with wearing denim?"

The man pressed his lips tightly together, boiling. He continued to sneer, but bowed his head and waved them in with sarcastic assent.

"Good," Jack said. He turned and took Beth by the arm. The bartender winked at them and nodded appreciatively. Jack smiled back thankfully and ordered their drinks, his voice back to normal.

Jack took two healthy swallows of his vodka tonic while Beth sipped tentatively at a glass of red wine.

"You got quiet," he said gently.

She had pulled her hair back with a mother-of-pearl-inlaid comb; it fell in two perfect curtains of silk just behind either ear. She was looking down, her eyes hidden by their own long lashes.

After clearing her throat, she said, "Just when I think I'm getting to know you, I realize that I don't.

"It's funny," she said with the whisper of a laugh. "Most people, the more time you spend with them, the better you know them. But it's the opposite with you. It seems like the more I know you, the more I don't know you."

"I'm sorry," he said. His hands quivering around the wet rim of the glass. "I just get angry sometimes."

"No," she said, waving her hand in a dismissive manner. "I don't care about that. I'm glad you didn't just let him run us out of here. I would have. No, it's just that I was surprised you did it.

"I think I'm glad you did," she added hastily.

Jack considered her for a moment before asking, "Why did that surprise you so much?"

"You're so . . . quiet, I guess," she said. "You're quiet and smart. It's like you're shy, but not shy in a bad way. And then you just, like, turned vicious. I don't think it was so much what you said that made him back down. It was how you said it. All of a sudden, I felt my heart pounding because I knew you meant it. I thought, you know, that you'd really hit him or something."

"I used to just let things happen to me," Jack said. He spoke softly, gazing down at his glass as he swirled the melted shapes of ice in his drink. "But lately, I guess since Janet . . .

"Lately I don't care as much what people think in situations like that. I guess I got pushed around by people, not in an overt way, but subtly—subtly pushed around my whole life. I think I got pushed around at my law firm and probably by my ex-wife. I think maybe I'm just not going to let that happen anymore. That's all it is . . ."

She reached over and touched his cheek, drawing his lips to hers.

"I don't want to push you around, Jack," she whispered. "But I want to know you."

Jack swallowed and looked into her eyes. He considered her carefully and for some time before he worked up the courage to speak.

"Do you want to . . . I don't know, do you want to stay at my place tonight?" he asked.

Beth shut her eyes and nodded. "Yes," she said, "that's what I want. I want that very much."

Jack paid the bartender. Outside, there was no sign of the valet. They waited for a few minutes in silence. Impatient, Jack rounded the corner of the building to where he'd seen his car disappear. Still there was no sign of the valet. The Saab sat right there in front of them and on a hunch, Jack slid inside and found the keys stashed above the visor.

"Come on," he said to Beth as he started the engine.

On the way back to his house they held hands in the front seat and said nothing. Jack felt himself coming back to her, to them, then and there. They had never spent the night together. Even though their age difference wasn't unusual, he still felt a slight pang of discomfort. He was nearly ten years older than she was.

They drove with the top down and the warm summer air whipped through their hair, cooling them. Beth's hand, however, was warm so Jack didn't even bother asking if she wanted the top up. As he pulled into the driveway of what had so recently been his family's home,

Jack's blood was running too high for him to even think about how strange it was to have this woman by his side.

He led her by the hand into the house and they kissed again just inside the door before he took her up the stairs. Together they stood in the middle of his bedroom. Jack put the radio on next to the bed and he heard a song he knew from his law school days, Bruce Springsteen tenderly on fire. Light fell in from the hallway, and Jack tried to subdue the frantic desire he had to tear the clothes from her body. He ran his trembling hands up under her white top until she stopped him.

She let her jacket slide off her arms to the floor and with both hands pulled the top off up over her head. Half naked, she began to undress him, brushing his warm bare skin with her dampened lips as she worked. When Jack's clothes were in a pile on the floor, Beth slipped out of her pants and clung to him. Jack kissed her hard. He ran his hands gently over the firm contours beneath her warm skin. Finally he pushed her gently back toward the bed. She stopped to remove the comb and then lay back. Her long silky hair spilled down around her pale shoulders and onto the plush down comforter, black as ink in the dim yellow light from the hall.

CHAPTER 23

Jack awoke with a start. Beth groaned softly, momentarily tightening her grip on his ribs. At the same time she softly pressed her lips into the muscles of his chest. Her hair had somehow fallen across the ridges of his stomach, warming him with its silky touch. Jack breathed deeply, enjoying the naked warmth of her skin. After a while, though, his mind began to tumble upward and he slipped out from underneath her gentle grasp and the warm nest of bedclothes. He pulled on a pair of shorts and walked barefoot into the bathroom.

As he washed his hands he noticed for the first time the toothpaste smeared about the vanity, the tube lying open amid the mess. He hadn't expected her to spend the night. Dried spatters of soapy water and foam blemished the mirror. He found a relatively clean washcloth in the closet, dampened it, and began to wipe up the worst of it. Then he straightened up, putting his deodorant, his shaving cream, and a bottle of mint Listerine beneath the sink. An armful of towels from the floor went into the bottom of the closet along with a mental note to do some laundry.

He padded back across the cold granite floor and into the bedroom. Beth lay sprawled out amid a wild tangle of covers. He gazed at her with a mixture of pleasure and pain. He slipped out of the bedroom and into the wide hall. Everything was the same, the wallpaper, the slightly crooked oil painting of an Atlantic seascape in winter, and the occasional muffled thump of the furnace vent as the air-conditioning kicked on. It seemed impossible to him that everything could be the same when nothing really was.

Hatred suddenly boiled up inside of Jack. His wife, Angela, had twisted and stretched him throughout their marriage. That was bad luck or a bad decision by him. But when she blamed him for what happened? Inside, he had already blamed himself.

Jack's hands clamped instinctively into fists. When he felt this way, his only consolation was the thought of cleansing the world of more human poison. It gave meaning to his life and alleviated at least some of the horrible guilt.

He knew he would never get back to sleep, and lying awake in bed in the state he was in now would only tarnish the brief moments of happiness that he'd experienced with Beth. Instead he went downstairs to the library, where his computer sat atop his massive tiger maple desk. Books lined the shelves, many of them leather collectibles. Jack had read them all, mostly sitting in the overstuffed chair by the big window overlooking the back lawn. Some of them he'd read aloud to Janet when she was young: *A Tale of Two Cities, Black Beauty, Treasure Island.*

He sat down in the large leather chair at the desk and turned on his machine. Things had changed since Hans Strauss in Oswego. He was getting good. It didn't make the act of killing any less distasteful, but it certainly made him less apprehensive. It wasn't unlike the expertise he had acquired in a power-plant acquisition, where once confusing details now read with the simplicity of a road sign.

He had discovered a Web site compiled by volunteers from the families of other victims. It posted the sex offender registry information of nearly every jurisdiction over the Internet. Jack could quickly locate the worst of the scum from different cities or counties. After reflecting, he knew that what he'd done in Pittsburgh had been a mistake. Two similar murders in the same place could arouse suspicion.

Since then he had targeted only one sex offender in any police jurisdiction so that no pattern would emerge for investigators to lock onto. During his last power-plant transaction in Dayton, Ohio, he had chosen second and third victims in nearby Springfield and the outskirts of Cincinnati. Jack knew that police forces rarely communicated among themselves, even regarding the worst crimes. It wasn't impossible to cross-reference crimes either by e-mails or Teletype, but Jack knew that there were investigations and there were investigations. No cop he ever knew would bust his tail to find the killer of a level-three sex offender.

One thing he had not done was strike within his own geographic area. He wanted to. He wanted to stop at least one predatory criminal from victimizing another teenage girl like his daughter. He had buried six serial rapists so far, none of them from Long Island. Before now, he'd been too cautious. But with his newfound confidence, he presumed that if he did it just once, his own proximity to the crime wouldn't matter.

In the glow of the computer screen Jack's face would have looked to anyone who could have seen him like the visage of a dark angel, so grim and full of vengeful determination that he looked like something either more or less than human. He scanned through the files of people who had done unthinkable things. There were so many to choose from that it sickened him. By his means of assessment, all of them deserved to die, but he was only one man and he had to make a choice. He selected Lawrence Brice.

Like Eugene Tupp, Brice had a long list of prior incidents that began at an early age. He was eighteen when he kidnapped, beat, and raped a high school classmate. He served less than two years. Within eight months of his release he dragged a pregnant woman bound and gagged into some woods. She was miraculously rescued by a passing off-duty police officer. Brice was found guilty not of assault, or kidnapping, but for something called unlawful retention, a relatively minor infraction. Despite his previous record, he served just six months. Two years later he was charged with the rape and assault of a coed from Hofstra University. But like Eugene Tupp, Brice had escaped conviction. At trial, the pipe Brice had used to beat the girl was excluded from evidence, also because of an unlawful-search-and-seizure ruling. Given the chance, he was the kind of man who would do something similar to what Eugene Tupp had done to Janet. Probably he already had.

Brice lived on Longcut Road, out where Long Island actually became somewhat rural. It was near the Brookhaven National Laboratory and not far from where Beth had her apartment in Medford. It would be convenient for him to scope out Brice, either before or after picking up Beth for a date. While he recognized the efficiency of the location on the surface, deep down it made him uneasy, dropping off Beth and then reconnoitering a victim just a few minutes away.

A noise by the door yanked him back from his dark reverie. Beth stood there, the tails of one of his dress shirts hanging to her knees. The shirt's white cuffs had fallen down over her hands, but as she reached up to sweep her hair back from her face one of them fell free, revealing her long elegant fingers.

"Beth," he said, standing up and coming out from behind his desk. Instead of crossing the room to embrace her, he stood awkwardly on the rug in the center of the library and shifted uneasily in his shorts from one foot to the other.

"What are you doing?" she asked sleepily, peering at the computer.

"Nothing," he said. The word snapped in the space between them.

"Oh come on," she said. With a playful expression she moved toward his desk, craning her neck. "I gotta see whatever it is that could get you out of bed in the middle of the night. I gotta know what my competition is. Not some weakness in the intellectual armor like a video game . . ."

"No!" Jack yelled, cutting her off.

CHAPTER 24

Beth stopped and looked at him with disbelief.

"That's my work," he said.

"Whatever," she said.

"I'm sorry," he said. He crossed the room and tried to touch her shoulder. Beth shook free and stepped back.

"Will you please take me home?" she asked, looking away.

"Beth, I . . ."

"Now," she said, looking at the floor. She had her arms folded tightly in front of her, and her mouth was closed tight.

"Yes," he said. He looked up at the antique clock on one of the bookshelves. It was just past five. "Yes, of course."

Dawn was beginning to seep in through the tall mullioned windows. While Beth changed upstairs, Jack scribbled down Brice's address and turned off the computer. Upstairs, he pulled on a pair of jeans and a T-shirt. With a grim frown he removed the locked silver metal briefcase from his closet and put it in the trunk of the car. Beth climbed into the front seat without comment.

They rode in a painful silence. When he got off the expressway exit for Medford, Jack said he was sorry again.

"Don't worry about it," she said. Her tone and her distant gaze said much more than her words.

Jack noticed that he was clenching the steering wheel. He sighed, and then let go. He knew there was something powerful he should say, something clever and romantic. He was forty-two years old and all he could think of was the same old losing strategy that he had seen his own father employ: to say that he was sorry and wait.

He pulled up in front of her apartment, a gray New England-style three-story complex with white railings and shutters. The sun was nearly up by now and the nearby expressway had already come to life with the steady hum of traffic, although there was no other sign of life in the parking lot itself.

Jack hesitated, then he leaned over to kiss Beth's cheek. It was too late. She was already out of the car.

"Beth," he said, but she shut the door in his face.

Jack put down the window.

"I'm . . ." he said, and then stopped, his mouth half open. It was there, just beyond his reach like a forgotten name on the tip of his tongue.

"I'm sorry," he said. "Beth, I'm sorry."

She kept walking. He watched her back as she disappeared into her apartment.

Jack held his breath for a minute, waiting to see if she'd come back out. She didn't. He looked at his watch and slammed the Saab into gear, driving out through the parking lot and onto the open highway.

Fifteen minutes later he was driving slowly down a rural road with sandy brown shoulders and thick-needled pine trees. After passing by a couple of ranch houses, Jack came to an opening where an old gray house sat alone with its naked wood decaying among a tangle of weeds, tall grass, and brambles. The only sign of life was an old brown utility van that had been run up the two sandy ruts and rested next to the weather-beaten house. Paint on the clapboard siding hadn't been a concern for decades; the few patches that remained were so grimy that they served only to enhance the overall sense of blight.

The windows were intact except for one, which was miraculous considering the pile of corroded junk that was stacked up on the porch beside a broken refrigerator. The rusted bodies of three cars lurked in the weeds. The blood in Jack's temples began to thump. His mind reached a clarity that seemed almost drug-induced. The trees and the freshly laid blacktop on the road, even his car bathed in the brightening sky, were like the shiny silver images seen in a mirror.

Jack drove a little farther down the road, discovering nothing but the dirt access road for a gas distribution pumphouse. He pulled off the pavement and tucked his car under the eaves of some trees. With his shirt untucked and his gun stuck into the waist of his jeans, Jack walked back down the road toward the sagging gray house. At the mailbox he looked either way before pulling on his leather driving gloves and starting up the sandy ruts toward the house. He climbed onto the porch, stepping up on an upside-down bucket. Two cats leapt from their resting places in the junk and disappeared from sight. A fetid odor seeped up from underneath the porch. Jack felt his stomach tighten.

The cheap brass handle on the door had faded long ago to a dull brown. Heart surging, Jack tried it. It was locked. He knocked twice and waited. The sun cast a single beam up over the treetops, stabbing at the earth with the day's first barb of August heat. Jack knocked again, harder this time, insistent. This time he heard the creak of floorboards and a sleepy aggravated groan. He removed the gun from his waist and held it snug to his pant leg.

Brice opened the door bleary-eyed without asking who or what it was. He was unshaven and rough looking with long dark hair and deep blue eyes. His mouth was small and puckered, his nose long and bent, and his chin melded right into his gangly neck almost without a point of demarcation. He was naked to the waist, and his pale sunken chest was split by a black streak of long thin hair that ran straight through his navel and into his dirty yellow sweatpants.

Jack pulled up his gun and fired a round into the center of Brice's chest. Brice staggered back with a confused look on his face, looking quickly from the scarlet hole in his torso to Jack before throwing his hands up in front of his face with a high-pitched scream. Jack stepped through the door and began firing more rounds. Splinters of wood flew through the air. Blood sprang from Brice's arm, his shoulder, and his chest in three different places now. Jack kept firing, aiming more carefully now that his victim was on the floor. A bullet struck Brice under one eye and he stopped moving except for a tremor that seemed to run through the length of his body.

Jack snorted as he mechanically emptied what was left of the magazine into Brice's bloody chest with a steady *clank-clank-clank* from the action of the gun. When he was finished, he fought back the wave of vomit surging up into his throat. The taste of bile filled the back of his mouth.

The gore of so many bullet holes was a logical necessity. He couldn't leave a victim who could live to tell about it. Jack knew the human body was miraculously resilient. He once prosecuted a case with the Brooklyn D.A.'s office using an eyewitness account of a victim who'd been shot seven times, five of them in the chest, and lived. His attacker did twenty years for assault and attempted murder.

Even through his gloves, the silencer on the end of the Glock felt hot. Jack kept it at his side, thinking back to the time in Pittsburgh when he'd burned his skin with the hot gun by stuffing it back into his pants too quickly. He crouched to the floor and began picking up the spent shells, his mind swimming with the horror of the act he had again committed.

There were no other details for him to consider as he locked the door and closed it behind him. His method was as flawless as it could be. Six times prior to this he had successfully gone into his victims' homes, killed them, and disappeared without a trace. His gloves prevented any fingerprints. His flat-soled shoes left no discernible marks and they, like the rest of the clothes he was wearing, would soon be disposed of. None of his victims had ever been able to scratch him or cut him so he never left behind any visible source of DNA. The only things that remained were the slugs he fired, and they were inconsequential. Because of the Glock's unique polygonal barrel, they were unidentifiable.

Outside, the full force of the steamy sun had hit the porch and cooked up the smell of spent motor oil mixing with the sour stench that was already there. One of the stray cats scurried back under a broken baby carriage; a half-dead mouse skittered between Jack's feet, dragging its hindquarters and causing him to leap almost two feet into the air. The mouse disappeared down a hole in the corner, leaving a thin trail of blood across the dusty wood. Jack caught his breath and jumped down off the porch without bothering to step on the pail.

Without looking back, he hurried down the rutted driveway to the road with the empty shell casings clinking in his pocket. As he walked along on the sandy shoulder toward his car, a sense of relief at having survived began to wash away his overwhelming sense of revulsion. He hadn't reconnoitered the area. He hadn't even known for certain if Brice was alone.

But as quickly as they had risen, Jack's soaring spirits plunged when a dilapidated pickup truck chugged up over the rise in the road. It was coming his way trailing a blue plume of exhaust, and it was beginning to slow down.

CHAPTER 25

The stench was like a punch in the face. The smell of spoiling human blood and entrails cooked by the late-summer heat in an old wooden home was enough to make most men ill. David McGrew stepped across the threshold and drew in a deep breath to make a statement. The statement was this: I'm a homicide cop to the bone, one-third tough, another third cunning, and one-half crazy.

He wasn't supposed to be there in the first place. The crime scene technicians weren't quite finished, and they didn't like the detectives swarming through the scene contaminating things. But McGrew took advantage of everyone's attention being drawn to the TV truck that had raced up outside. The lieutenant had started fluffing up his hair in the reflection of his car window, and everyone else gaped at the brunette reporter who got out and began doing the same. McGrew wasn't the one being interviewed, so he wanted to get inside and check things out before anyone else.

McGrew was just twenty-eight, and he imagined himself as one of the cops he saw in the movies. He was the star. Other people were either minor supporting characters or extras. If he thought the scene called for a certain amount of macho indifference, then he had the stuff to do it. With Lawrence Brice's bloated body offending the noses of passing traffic all the way out on Longcut Road, McGrew knew inhaling deeply was exactly what Clint Eastwood would have done in the original *Dirty Harry*.

McGrew's sentiments weren't limited to daydreaming. He possessed an extraordinary sense of confidence that was very real, even if at times it was unfounded. He was blessed with an innate sense that he was born to succeed. Everything in life to McGrew boiled down to winning and losing. He was an investigator and a damn good one, a winner. If he was on a case, he got his man. The fact that Lawrence Brice was a psycho pervert who deserved every slug that the M.E. would fish out of his rotten corpse made no difference to McGrew. It was a case. It was his case.

One of the laboratory technicians, a bleached blonde with long lashes and big brown eyes, stopped what she was doing to stare at McGrew from behind her filtration mask. She also knew he shouldn't be there. McGrew stroked the small wisp of beard that grew from beneath his lower lip and winked at her. He liked the look of her shape and the slightly trashy air about her. McGrew knew his own shortcomings. His hair was going. His eyes were on the small side and his teeth weren't the straightest in the world, but his personality more than made up for it with the ladies. Besides, it was his self-confidence that got them. He knew for a fact—a lesson direct from his Dale Carnegie course—that some women found it even more attractive than a strong chin and big blue eyes.

He looked intelligently at the dried patches of blood as though he could read the signs of the struggle. In fact, it was simple logic and not the smears of gore that told him

Brice had been whacked by one of three things. A family member was not unusual in almost any murder. A drug buyer or dealer was also typical. Or, and this was a titillating notion, the killer in this case could be intimately connected to one of Brice's victims. McGrew already knew that Brice was a perv. The officer responding to the complaint of the bad smell that had reached the road had already run a check on the man. Everyone now knew that he was a psychotic rapist out on parole.

McGrew didn't let that bother him, though. When the call came in to the station, he was one of the first ones into his car, racing to the scene. Some of the old-timers actually sat disinterestedly, looking up from their desks and then back to their work when they heard the stiff was a level-three sex offender. But not McGrew. A dead body was a dead body. McGrew was out to make a name.

He had a good start already. He had an influential uncle—the congressman representing eastern Suffolk County and a member of the powerful appropriations committee—whose name he wasn't afraid to drop in the right places. More important, he was seventeen out of seventeen on cases he had participated in and an impressive three for three on cases gone cold that he had been assigned to work. That was his record as a homicide cop, and he didn't intend to ruin his perfect string of wins. McGrew could see his future. He might burn through partners, he might not get asked over to other cops' homes for cheesy weekend cookouts, but his day would come. One day the young cops coming up through would punch one another's lights out for a chance to work with McGrew. It might be tough, it might be lonely, but the ones who wanted to get the bad guys more than anything would look to him.

"Are you all set for us to let the rest of them in, Detective?" asked a short fat crime scene tech. He was being sarcastic. They both knew McGrew wasn't supposed to be there.

But McGrew wasn't mad. He looked solemnly at the plastic bag and gave one more audacious sniff, searching his mind for the right line.

After a moment of consideration he lowered his voice and said, "Yeah, let 'em in."

He glanced at the blonde, who was pulling a slug out of the floor with a pair of heavy tweezers. She heard it. McGrew knew he should get his ass out of there. The lieutenant would finish his TV gig and come walking in any minute. The tech people were beginning to migrate toward their van. They were loaded down with plastic bags full of evidence. He lingered in the entryway, eyeing things up like a golfer getting ready for a long putt. The blonde kept her back to him, and that allowed McGrew to carefully study her curves. She had a lot going on.

She turned and faced him, and he could tell from the wrinkles around her eyes that she was smiling from behind her mask. McGrew sensed something vaguely erotic about the mask and the cheap blonde and the stench, but he couldn't put his finger on it. Maybe it was just the sense of danger from being where he knew he shouldn't. Whatever it was, he quickly wiped the look of confusion from his face and asked her name.

"Lindsey," she said. "I'm from Tampa. I just started."

"I'm McGrew. Detective McGrew. David McGrew. Homicide."

McGrew held out his small hand. Lindsey removed her mask and one of her rubber gloves. The rest of her face was a little disappointing for McGrew. Her nose was off kilter and her lips didn't have much color to them. They looked chapped. Her chin was too small for her to be called pretty, but still, there was something sexy about her. And that backside. He liked those curves. Her fingers were long and cool and rough. McGrew held them longer than was necessary or proper in a greeting between two coworkers.

"Maybe I could buy you a drink sometime, kinda like the welcome wagon or something," he said with an expert wink.

"That's nice," she said. "I really don't know anyone yet. My mom had to move up here. Her doctor wanted her here, so I came, too."

"What's your number?" he said. "I'll give you a call."

Lindsey looked at him and waited.

"Don't you want to write it down?" she asked.

McGrew tapped his head. "It all goes right here. In the computer. McGrew doesn't need paper and pencil for a pretty woman's phone number."

She smiled and recited her number for him. "Well," she said. "I better be going. We're finished and they'll be waiting for me."

"Hey," he said as she made her way past him, "you forgot your slugs."

"What?"

"Your slugs," he said, nodding toward the plastic bags lying on the floor, "your bullets. The evidence."

"Oh," she said. And then as if to change the subject she asked, "What do you think happened?"

McGrew shrugged and said, "I got a couple ideas banging around, yeah. I'll find him."

"How do you know it was a 'him'?" she asked. "You said 'him.'"

"Women don't kill like that," he told her, narrowing his eyes. That was the cheapest bit of knowledge in the book, something you could learn from any one of a thousand B movies. He checked to make sure she wasn't playing with him before saying, "They might pop a guy, but they don't unload the whole magazine into someone, blood everywhere, the guy flopping around, screaming like a stuck pig."

He looked out of the corner of his eye to gauge her reaction.

"No?" she said. Her eyes widened. "How do you know that?"

"Because," he said, dramatically lowering his voice and stepping closer to her, "I know women. I know women very well . . . But whoever did it, though, they made one big mistake."

"What's that?" she said, eagerly searching the bloody scene for some obvious clue she herself had overlooked.

McGrew glanced warily around to make sure that none of his counterparts had arrived.

"You know how they say you don't shit where you eat?" he asked. It was a cagey line that he'd heard somewhere. He spoke in a low conspiratorial tone. "Well, this guy? He took a shit where *I* eat . . . And let me tell you, this guy? Whoever he is? I'll get him. I haven't come across a case yet that I haven't solved."

CHAPTER 26

McGrew watched the morning news over a bowl of Lucky Charms, fervently hoping to hear his own sound bite coming back at him. Because of the brutal nature of the slaying, there was a lot of media play on the Lawrence Brice murder. A local plumber had seen all the hoopla and finally come forth with a story of his own, their first real lead.

McGrew personally leaked the plumber lead to the press and did several interviews, but somehow they got hold of the plumber himself. McGrew scowled as he watched the plumber on TV describing a blond-headed man with glasses whom he'd seen walking down Long-cut Road one morning around the date that the murder was thought to have taken place. The damn toilet plunger was taking up his spotlight. This was a scene for the star of the show, not some old fart missing a front tooth.

McGrew tossed his spoon into the bowl. Milk splashed onto the table.

"Fucking guy," he said.

The plumber wasn't even that much of a help. His description was too vague. The old guy wasn't able to give them a straight answer on how the killer looked besides the glasses and blond hair. A monkey could have done that. They didn't even have a credible composite from this dope. No way did he deserve to upstage McGrew in the quote department. The old man had no media appeal whatsoever. McGrew shut off the TV and refilled his juice glass.

Already two weeks had gone by. The investigation had started out fifteen strong, three shifts, around the clock. Now it was just McGrew. Another big case came along after only a week—a rich woman stabbed to death and found floating in Noyack Bay—and everyone else's attention got diverted. McGrew asked to have the Brice job for himself and he got his wish. No one else seemed to really care about going undefeated. No one seemed to care about becoming a legend.

It was now the second Saturday of September. The summer season had ended in the Hamptons and McGrew, thanks to his uncle the congressman, had moved in to house-sit a beachfront mansion in Quogue. He was still keeping his apartment in Riverside so he didn't have to store his black lacquered furniture set and his leopard couch. And even though he wouldn't have easy access to his gym, the mansion had its own weight room full of Nautilus equipment, so McGrew could keep his cuts. Looking good was a big part of his game.

The best thing about the temporary move to Quogue was that it put him close to the scene of the crime. McGrew went back to the run-down house where Brice lived, sometimes first thing in the morning, sometimes late at night when he couldn't sleep. He was going to go over everything two, three, even four times a day, whatever it took. Today he was going to pay a second visit to Brice's mom. That's how you made something out of nothing. That's how you won where others failed. You kept digging.

The crazy old bitch lived in a trailer wedged into a wooded lot that some farmer had used as a dump for all his old equipment for about fifty years. Mrs. Brice had a nest of ratty gray hair and about three teeth to her name. She mumbled when she talked and McGrew knew by the way she stuttered and shuffled that he made her uncomfortable, but that was just too bad. He was on a case.

He drank the milk from his bowl and slurped down his last few Charms, then went to the billionaire's master bedroom suite and strapped on his gun. McGrew smiled at himself in the big mirror in front of the bed. He'd been told to use the guest quarters, but the Jacuzzi tub, the pink granite fireplace, and the extraordinary view out over the dunes was too much for him to resist. He'd jimmied the lock on the master bedroom within the first hour of his arrival. So far he'd slept in the big sleigh bed by himself, but someday the ladies would recognize his talent. He was expecting Lindsey to fall into the win column any day now.

McGrew's car was parked outside on the circular drive beneath a massive roof that extended off the front of the house and was supported by two giant white columns. As he circled the sand-swept driveway, he stole a glance at the mansion. It was more a castle than a home.

He pulled out of the big place and onto Dune Road. The drive to Mrs. Brice's trailer took him less than ten minutes. A small patchy dog on a chain barked at him as he got out of his car, and McGrew fantasized putting a bullet in the little mutt's head.

"Here poochy," he said, glanced at the trailer, and then kicked the dirty little beggar in the ribs.

He picked his way through the junk.

"Acorn don't fall far from the tree," he said, thinking of the son's dilapidated hovel.

He knocked hard on the door about ten times.

"I'm coming. I'm coming," the old hag said with a shriek.

"What do you want?" she asked through a crack in the door. Immediately she began to gnaw on the lower part of her mouth. She was mumbling something about police.

McGrew wedged his foot in the door and then opened it, slowly pushing her back. There was a hoard of empty Campbell's soup cans on the little kitchen counter; lying in the middle of the floor amid the other refuse was a tidy little mess that the dog had left behind as a memento. In the old woman's hand was a filthy dishrag.

"Thanks for asking me in, Mrs. Brice," he said. "I hate to interrupt your Saturday cleaning, but I need to ask you a few questions. Sit right down there."

He helped her into the small booth in the kitchen and, after brushing some toast crumbs off the seat, sat down opposite her and smiled. He was going to twist her until she sang.

CHAPTER 27

Isn't this nice, just you and me?" McGrew asked. "No other police investigators around to make you nervous?"

Mrs. Brice muttered something and began to finger a ragged hole in the front of her old dress. He could see the blue-green flesh of her breast and his stomach turned a little somersault.

"I want to know if you ever saw your son with a blond-haired man with glasses, Mrs. Brice," he said. "Come on now, a sick fuck like Lawrence didn't have too many friends now, did he? Think hard, Mrs. Brice. You can just nod if you remember. I need to know, Mrs. Brice. Then I can help you. He might want to do the same thing to you that he did to Lawrence . . ."

That got her attention. The old woman's eyes darted at McGrew. Their whites had gone yellow long ago, and they had a creamy buildup on them that he found fascinating. He stared.

"Yeah, that blond-haired man, about five foot ten, maybe six feet. My height, straight blond hair, and little round glasses. You remember him?"

"He ain't coming for me?" she said.

"He might be," McGrew said, leaning close enough to smell the rancid tomato soup on her breath.

"I never saw no man like that," she said, alarmed. "I never did. Lawrence, he never came by with no friends, not since he growed up."

McGrew nodded. More of the same crap, but he wasn't going to be deterred.

"I think you better start thinking harder, Mrs. Brice," he said. "I can help you, but not if you don't help me."

"I don't need no help, do I?"

"You might," McGrew said. He shrugged, then looked around the trailer. His eyes came back to rest on her with an accusatory glare.

"You sure you don't want to tell me who that blond guy is?" he asked.

That really set her to mumbling and twisting. McGrew watched her for a time before he got up and went to the door with a sigh.

"You call me if you do," he said.

"I ain't got no phone," she said.

"Where do you do your shopping?" he asked. "For food?"

"Seven-Eleven up the road."

"Well, they got a pay phone there. I suggest you think about all this and use it."

McGrew fished a quarter out of his pocket and flipped it across the trailer onto the little table.

"Then maybe I can help you," he said. "Maybe I can keep him from coming after you." Then he left.

Something about going back to the root of it all stimulated McGrew. The crappy trailer where Brice grew up, the haggard old woman who was his mom, it got him inside their world and that's where he believed he needed to be to find the answer. He had ruled out the obvious: a drug deal gone bad or a revenge killing. There were no drugs and all the top suspects—the family members of prior victims—all had bulletproof alibis. With all the bullet holes in Brice, some had speculated a crime of passion.

But everything told McGrew that Brice was a loner. He stocked shelves at a grocery store in town, but spoke to no one. His human interaction was limited to his mom and whatever stimulation he could get over the Internet. McGrew believed the mother didn't know the blond man. Maybe Brice didn't know him, either? Maybe, for whatever reason, Brice had been killed by a professional. After all, the scene had been strangely devoid of evidence . . .

McGrew felt his heart pumping fast. He spun his wheel and headed back for the mansion and his computer. He took his machine out on the covered terrace off the kitchen and placed it atop a glass-topped rattan table. He fired up his machine, plugged in a phone line, lit a cigarette, and got to work. He logged onto his own department's internal system, and from there into the national Teletype. He was searching for other crimes in the last three years that might create a link to the killing on Long-cut Road.

They had been wrong all along. It wasn't anyone connected with Brice. It couldn't be. The scene was too clean, the killing too smooth. Besides the messiness of it, it was exactly how McGrew would have killed someone if he were a bad guy. He should have thought of it before: The absence of shell casings or any other physical evidence had to mean a professional.

He didn't know why. Maybe it had some connection to

the smut Brice was into on the Internet. Whatever the reason, if it was a professional, then there would be other killings. A professional by definition never killed just once. So while this particular murderer didn't leave any physical evidence, he would likely have left the same general footprint somewhere else.

Somewhere, McGrew suspected, this person, this hit man, had killed other people by riddling their bodies with a 9mm Glock, also leaving no other trace. But that might be enough, at least to find a pattern. From there, other possibilities might show themselves. Who knew? Maybe he'd find a batch of other dead pervs somewhere.

After two hours McGrew blinked his eyes then stood up rubbing them. He had plowed through six weeks of Teletypes poring over descriptions of murders from all over the country and come up with nothing. There were two other homicides, one in L.A. and one in New Orleans, that came close. Both had been committed with the same type of weapon, but neither was as clean a crime scene as Brice's. In both instances there was plenty of other evidence to go along with the 9mm Glock. And the pattern didn't fit. One victim had been shot only once in the head in a barroom fight, the other one took three slugs in the body, all in the back. Neither sounded like a professional job at all.

McGrew lit up another cigarette, brewing up a cloud of smoke. He squinted at his watch. He decided to get the blood flowing back in his legs with a stroll on the beach. At the end of the teak boardwalk he stopped to survey the long stretch of white sand. It was empty except for a family having a picnic about a hundred yards up. The father had one of the kids on his back and the other two were racing around him like puppies. The mother was unloading a basket of food onto a blanket spread across the sand. McGrew took a long drag and blew the smoke out his nose. That's one role he didn't see himself playing: the family man.

McGrew coughed and hacked up a bit of phlegm, then spit into the sea grass before turning back toward the house. He was going to work right up until Lindsey, the crime scene tech, returned his call about going out for dinner tonight. He'd put in twelve calls to her already, and he just had the feeling she would be ringing him up this afternoon.

What if she wasn't calling because she was going to just show up? He'd left a lengthy message all about this place. With her in mind, he stripped off his shirt. A big soaring eagle covered the smooth surface of his chest. Its wing tip dipped down below the waist of his Levi's; its yellow beak tweaked his armpit. Lindsey would like it. He could imagine what the scene would look like. Bogart and Bacall, her walking in on him. He composed a few lines.

"Where've you been?"

"Working."

"All day? It's Saturday, you know."

"I've got a killer to catch. I haven't lost on a case yet and I'm not going to start now. Sit down and I'll be with you when I'm done. By the way, I hope you're wearing that lace underwear I like."

McGrew lit a cigarette and let it dangle from the corner of his mouth. Those lines would sound great coming from him out of a wreath of smoke. He sighed, then hunched down over his computer and got back to work.

McGrew remained motionless except for his eyes. They darted back and forth across the screen like frantic roaches for nearly an hour. He stopped only to light up again and once to see if his cell phone ringer was on. Still no call.

Then it happened.

"I got it," he said, his voice breaking with the excitement. He pumped his fist in the air. "Cincinnati, Ohio. A dead perv shot to shit with twelve nine-millimeter slugs. I got a bead on the son-of-a-bitch now."

CHAPTER 28

If Amanda had been able to know just who would become her new boss at the Bureau, she would probably never have passed up the promotion. She'd never intended to make a mortal enemy of Benjamin Hanover, but it had happened.

Hanover was in his late fifties. Most of his peers in the Bureau had either moved upward into better positions or to the private sector to make their fortunes. Hanover wasn't an unintelligent man, but his career was blemished with bungled investigations and embarrassing complaints from inside and outside the agency. Hanover had been in the wrong place at the wrong time more than once.

Never had that been more pronounced than his first encounter with Amanda. After a series of remarkable successes early on, the agency began to use her as a kind of troubleshooter. Hanover had been working with a young agent by the name of Melinda Gross on a case where the killer was using a meat cleaver on his victims. Hanover and Gross were apparently closing in when they discovered what they believed to be the killer's name on a car rental receipt in some motel trash. But the name turned up nothing. The media began to stir over the butchery. Inside the agency, pressure mounted from above.

Amanda didn't consider her assistance as the high point of her career. She had simply asked to see the original car rental receipt. After all, the man staying in the hotel room where it came from matched the description of an unknown man spotted near one of the crime scenes. The name of the man registered in the hotel didn't match the car rental receipt, and that gave Amanda the unshakable feeling that something was amiss. She double-checked the lead.

As it turned out, the name on the receipt was Douglas F. Emmons. The name Hanover had searched for in the database was Douglas *S*. Emmons. Hanover was on a two-day leave to attend his mother's funeral when Amanda made her discovery. By the time he returned, she and Melinda Gross had arrested Emmons. Amanda said nothing about the error, but Hanover's partner wasn't as discreet and before she knew it, everyone knew.

He became the running joke in the office. E-mails even started going around to other FBI offices around the country.

Amanda remembered one in particular.

Hanover goes into an appliance store and asks to buy a TV. The slick-looking salesman says he doesn't sell TVs to washed-out FBI agents. Hanover goes out and gets himself a dark wig, sunglasses, and some bell-bottoms. When he comes back he points to the TV and says he wants it. The salesman refuses and says he still won't sell to washed-out FBI agents. Hanover whips off his disguise and says, "What gave away my disguise?" "Nothing," says the salesman, "but that's a microwave."

Amanda, on the other hand, was celebrated. That case proved she had common sense, too. Because she came out looking so good and he so bad, Hanover blamed her for all of it. When she tried to explain that it wasn't her doing, he had glared maliciously at her.

"You're a liar and a bitch, but you'll get yours one day," he'd said, spitting his words at her before he walked away. They hadn't spoken a word to each other since.

Amanda parked her car in the garage and took the elevator up to the third floor. She marched down the hallway, nodding and smiling to the familiar faces that she hadn't seen all summer without stopping to chat. Hanover now had his own secretary and a large office lined with windows. He made Amanda wait outside for twenty minutes in the hall before the secretary finally showed her in. Hanover didn't bother to get up or even shake hands. Amanda sat down.

"Are you lost?" Hanover asked.

Hanover had silver hair, tan skin, and a wiry athletic frame in spite of his years. Only the lines of worry around his pale green eyes and the downturned creases in the corners of his mouth hinted at his bitterness. That was, until he spoke. His tone of voice was split evenly between blatant condescension and scathing impatience.

"I'd like an extension of my sabbatical," Amanda said.

"Oh?" Hanover said, raising his eyebrows. He made a temple of his fingertips and placed them beneath his nose.

"Yes," she said. "I'd like to extend it for a year."

Hanover snorted in amusement.

"We don't have sabbaticals that last that long," he said.

"You've already used up your sabbatical. I'll be happy to give you a leave of absence, though . . ."

A leave of absence meant that Amanda would lose all her seniority. That would cost her in salary, pension, and vacation when she came back. And she definitely wanted to come back. She just wasn't sure when, and that's why she was hoping to continue the sabbatical they had given her after Marco's death. That was before Hanover had become the ASAIC over her.

"If I come back," Amanda said, "I'd like to be with Mike Collins."

Mike Collins had been the agent assigned to follow up on the Oswald case. Amanda hadn't completely lost touch with the office during her recovery. The investigation had continued. She really had seen a second man. A witness apparently saw him escape out the kitchen window and down a fire escape after Amanda shot Oswald. If Hanover was going to force her to come back, then that was where she should be, working on that case.

But Hanover was smiling.

"I'm sorry," he said. "I know someone of your incredible talent probably didn't realize it, but the FBI just kept going. Even when you had a breakdown.

"Let's see," he said, picking a folder up off his desk. "I have a homicide detective from Long Island, New York, and I've been told to begin a joint investigation. He has a very important uncle. That would be good for you. You could curry some more favor . . . or given your fragile condition, maybe you'll take that leave of absence."

"I appreciate your concern," Amanda said. "Maybe I will."

"Should I start the paperwork?" Hanover said with mock concern.

"No," Amanda said, rising from her seat. "I'll let you know when I'm sure. I'll decide, not you."

Without a good-bye he picked up the phone and began dialing as if Amanda were already gone.

She stomped down the hall and into the elevator. Those who knew her busied themselves as she stormed past.

She looked at her watch. She had to hurry. Teddy had forgotten his lunch and she had to drop it off at baseball camp, then pick Glenda up from her horse riding camp the next town over. How important was that really? She was a taxi service.

Oh, it hurt when she missed certain things. There was the time her flight from Minneapolis was late and the school play had ended, Glenda teary-eyed in her Pumba costume when Amanda finally met them at Dairy Queen, Parker going on and on about how she could see it all when they got home. He kept tapping his stupid VHS camera, which was sitting on the tabletop next to a leaky banana boat sundae.

But what about the three girls she found tied up in a cabin in the backwoods of Minnesota? Wasn't that more important? Couldn't everyone see that? Hers wasn't just that same old middle-American dilemma: the financial need for two incomes. Her job was important. She was out there, finding killers and stopping the worst kind of monsters, protecting families like her own so they could have their little costume plays and ice cream sundae celebrations.

Parker had played that tape over and over for a week

and it did something to Amanda. Their life in the bedroom went to hell. They were partners the way two former friends might share a vacation home between their
families. They worked things out. They got along for the
good of everyone. But she knew her prowess ate his heart
out. Without saying so, both of them knew he wasn't half
the man that she was.

When she arrived at home, Parker was in the driveway
washing his Humvee. The sale was final, and as it turned
out, Parker had paid too much. For him to try to sell it to
someone else now would cost them even more money.
The shiny black paint showed through beneath the swirls
of white suds. A green chamois cloth hung from his back
pocket. She rolled down her window.

"Hi," she said.

Parker looked pointedly at his watch.

"I've got a big poker game tonight, remember?" he
said.

"And?"

"Well, when the hell are we going to eat?" he asked.

This wasn't the first time something like this had happened. Little incidents from the past month popped into
the forefront of Amanda's mind. By themselves they
were just dots. A complaint about the bathtub ring. A
charred hamburger. Running out of tissues. Coupons for
laundry detergent. Teddy blaming her for a frog that got
away. Glenda saying *shut up*. All together, they painted a
portrait of a highly educated and very talented woman
who was squandering both. A wifelike character out of
some television program about the 1950s.

Parker's words to her just now and his attitude had just
put her over the edge. This was not going to be her life.

She slammed her car door without another word and went into the kitchen, where she proceeded to fill a mixing bowl with cornflakes. She caught herself wondering what the case with the homicide cop from Long Island was all about. She wondered how many other school plays she would miss. How many games? How many Brownie meetings? Tears welled up in her eyes and spilled freely down her cheeks and still, she called Parker in to his dinner with a smile. In her mind, she was already back in the game.

CHAPTER 29

The vista of mountains and sky was suddenly lost as the Saab descended a twisting curve in the empty two-lane highway, but another unfolded, equally stunning: a dark lake bordered by an army of cedars. Reflected in the still water was the perfect mirror image of the cedars and the sky.

"Looks like a Wyeth painting," Beth said, almost to herself. The wind was beating her hair through the open window.

The top was down and her head was covered with a black-and-gold silk scarf. Both of them had on jackets for the trip. Although it was a sunny day, the air in the mountains was cooler than the balmy late-summer air so close to New York City.

"I knew you'd love it," he said. "I used to come up here . . . a while ago."

Beth nodded. She said nothing, but reached over and scratched the back of his neck, then kneaded the muscles there.

"I'm glad you came," he said.

He slowed down a little so they could talk better.

"I thought after that night in the library that my art-house movie days were over," he said. It had been nearly a month ago, and although he'd come up with a brilliant explanation for acting like an ass, they had never really gotten into it.

"I'm sorry about that," she said.

"You're sorry? I'm the one who's sorry."

"Jack," she said. "I thought you were . . . e-mailing your ex-wife or some other woman or something. The first night we're together and you're off to the races . . . But after you told me what you were really doing . . . well, I wasn't going to bring it up again, but I'm glad we're talking about it, Jack. I want us to talk."

"I know," he said. It wasn't a complete lie that he'd told her, and that was some comfort. It was a cathartic process he was going through. And even though he wasn't really writing a private memoir about his broken life like he said he was, his work on the computer did help him. It helped him survive. He couldn't have told her the truth. He had done what was best for them both.

"I haven't had a day away since . . . I can't even remember," he said. "God, look at the way the wind has made the top of that pine tree grow."

Beth gave him a pained expression. He knew she wanted to talk more, but he couldn't help the way he felt. He slowly sped up.

"When can you visit Janet again?" Beth asked.

Jack glanced at her, startled, as if she'd slapped him. Her fingers continued to work without pause. He tried to focus on that, tried to let his neck relax.

"I don't know," he said. "Dr. Steinberg said she needs more therapy—and more time.

"I just want to see her," he said after a pause. "Sometimes I think I'd rather see her, even if she . . . hates me, than not see her at all . . . but that's stupid."

"It's not stupid," she said. "You love her."

Jack squinted into the sun despite his sunglasses. From the car floor beneath his seat, he fished around for his bottle of Maalox and took a swig.

Beth watched him but said nothing.

She gripped his leg above the knee and held it. He could feel the warmth of her hand and her strength.

He began to concentrate on the road. A sign told him to turn off the main highway. The town of Racquet Lake was just a mile away. They rambled through a grassy fen and over an old wooden bridge that clacked noisily as if to warn them away. The town consisted of an abandoned mill, a hotel, a bar, a gas station, and a general store. Except for the mill, each of the other establishments was part of a large green three-story building built in the early 1900s at the southern edge of the lake. It had once been the last train stop for the millionaires as they made their seasonal trek from the sweltering heat and filth of New York City to the cool beauty of the Adirondack Mountains.

Now the only people in sight were a family of four with a black Lab puppy. They were unloading a bright yellow canoe and an equally colorful cluster of camping gear off the top of their dusty minivan. A towering spruce filtered the sun's rays, allowing only patches of light to reach the ground where pavement and gravel and smooth oily sand somehow coexisted in harmony beneath a single gas pump. Jack got out and stretched his legs as he ambled toward the store. Beth twined her fingers with his and walked along beside him, deeply inhaling the fresh air. They stopped momentarily to look north, across the lake, over the treetops at Blue Mountain, dominant among the other peaks.

The grocery store seemed almost empty. Several feet of mint-green wooden shelf space separated one group of items from the next. On Long Island goods were stacked to the ceiling. One whole portion of this store, about a third of its total space, was completely empty. In the back corner was a scant butcher's case, but no one stood behind the stainless-steel and glass counter. The only person in the store was an older woman with long kinky hair dyed so black it was nearly blue. She was smoking a cigarette and staring at them with a disinterested sneer.

"We're looking for a cabin to spend the night," Jack said to her. "Do you know of any places that are still open?"

"People don't usually come this far this late in the season. 'Course, you wouldn't know the season was over by the looks of the sun," she said, turning her attention outside to the sparkling surface of the dark lake.

Jack waited for a moment before asking again. "Is there anyplace you know of that's still open? We're looking for a cabin . . . on the water. Someplace quiet."

"Ha," she said. "Everyplace around here is quiet.

"Hotel's open," she said, indicating with her sagging chin the rooms that apparently waited for them just above. "It's dirty, but it's open."

Jack decided to try again. If this crone with her grimy nails and ketchup-stained blouse was calling it dirty, he didn't want to even look.

"No," he said, "I think a cabin is what we want to try to find. I guess I'll try up at Blue Mountain."

"You might want to try Steffenhausers," she said. "You go north on twenty-eight for about four miles and you'll see a sign. It's got a big purple teddy bear on it. You can't miss it. I guess that's why they do it."

Jack thanked the woman, then bought a six-pack of Bud Light and a damp box of pretzels as a recompense for the information.

They soon came to the purple bear, and Jack turned off the highway once again. Halfway down the long arcing drive, which led to a cluster of cabins on the lakeshore, they came upon the owner of the place busy in the midst of several great woodpiles. Steffenhauser was a large burly man with a big gray beard, thick black plastic glasses, and a faded green fisherman's hat. He was splitting wood. He noticed them and stopped to wipe his eyes and clean his glasses with a red bandanna that he'd removed from his back pocket.

Jack got out and walked over, asking if he had a place for them to stay.

"Give you my best cabin on the point for a hundred dollars," he said, speaking so fast his words were hard to digest. "I got twice that two weeks ago."

"Before the season ended," Jack said.

"Wouldn't know the season was over by the looks of the day," he said. "Nice car. Almost got me a convertible once, a Mustang. Wife wouldn't allow it though. Would simply not allow it. How'd you hear about us anyway?"

"The woman at the general store told us," Jack said.

"She did?" he said, his round face falling. "Well, she'll be here for her ten percent I imagine and it'll be in the bartender's drawer at the Dirty Spoon by sundown. Not that I blame the old girl. Tough life that one, Claire Conner. Got a son, Tom. Tom Conner. Went to jail.

"You watch yourself, miss"—he directed his rapid flow of words at Beth—"you don't ever want to stay down on Seventh Lake. Some people think it's me trying to hurt the competition, but it's not."

He dropped his voice and spoke to just Jack.

"I just think people like knowin'," he said. "I'd want to know if I wasn't from around here. He lives by himself right there, on the hill overlooking the inn. He killed a bunch of girls a while back. Raped 'em and killed 'em and now he's out and livin' right there."

CHAPTER 30

I just think people ought to know," Steffenhauser said. "People with young ladies in their party ought to, but you folks are wanting to get into that cabin. Birch Bow, we call it. There is a birch tree right there, you'll see it, planted by my granddad. Squatter, he was. No land deeds back then, but well—"

"If you just give me the key," Jack said, "I'll find it."

"The key. Oh, yes, the key," he said, considering the problem with a knitted brow. "Well, you best talk to my wife about the key, she's in the office and if you don't mind, don't tell her about the ten percent coming to Claire. I'll just handle that on the back side.

"If she knew that, she'd sure as hellfire charge you a hundred and ten, just to pay Claire," he said. "But I'll take care of that on the back side." He winked broadly. "Well, back to work!"

With that, Steffenhauser went after a massive chunk of wood with surprising intensity. Jack looked at Beth, who smiled from the front seat of the car.

"I couldn't hear what he was saying," Beth said with a laugh as they continued up the drive, "but he sure was saying it fast."

Inside the office Jack rang the shiny little dome-shaped

bell on the counter. Moments later he was confronted with the sour visage of a tiny white-haired woman with piercing brown eyes.

"That old fool," she said in a mutter after listening to Jack. "I just cleaned Birch Bow for the winter yesterday. He knows that. No, maybe he doesn't. If the old fool would ever stop talking and listen," she said under her breath. Then to Jack she said, "You can have Red Squirrel. It's next door to Birch Bow and it's got a phone. Only cabin that does. Phone and a fridge. I'll let you have it for one fifty. I got one seventy-five two weeks ago, but it's out of season now. Not that you'd know."

Jack paid in cash and took the key without a word.

They spent the afternoon simply lounging in a comfortable hammock slung between two cedars at the water's edge. At one point a broad beam of the afternoon sun fell directly onto them from between the trees and Jack stripped down to his shorts. After a time, he took a swim. They were in the lee of the small south breeze, and it was almost as if the summer had truly returned for an encore. Bright green ferns waved gently in the golden light that found its way to the forest floor. Nestled together, the two of them read their books, swinging gently and breathing in the rich warm scent of balsam.

Jack was absorbed in *Shogun*, a novel he'd read before, and one he remembered as powerful enough to distract his active mind. But instead the book and its revealing perspective on the Asian psyche—where death was no more significant than the petal of a blossom falling to the earth—brought him inexorably back to Tom Conner. And as engaging as Jack found the book, he hadn't read through very many pages before his mind came to rest again on the old man's words about the ex-con who lived only one lake to the south. The ominous warning about young women haunted him.

"Are you hungry?" he asked, forcing himself to break the train of thought.

"If you are," Beth said.

"I am," he said. "Let's go back to that place we saw back in Inlet. It looked halfway decent."

"I'm getting cold anyway," she said, shivering slightly and burying her icy nose into his neck.

"You are cold," he said drawing her lips toward his own.

"And you're warm," she said, breaking away just long enough to add in a husky voice, "you're always warm. Hey, how about sharing some of that heat?"

"I could do that," he said. He stroked a long strand of hair away from her face.

When they emerged from the cabin forty-five minutes later, both were freshly showered and in clean clothes. As they drove toward Inlet—a town of two gas stations, a hardware store, and a small movie theater along with a handful of restaurants—the sun set and the air began to cool fast. The top of the Saab was already up, but now Jack closed up the crack in his window and Beth did the same.

When they passed by the Seventh Lake Inn, Jack couldn't keep his eyes off the peeling blue Victorian on the hilltop across the street. A single light shone from a corner window. Something vicious stirred in his veins.

He'd had his afternoon in the sun. Too much time had gone by since he'd done something to pay for his past sins. He didn't deserve to leisurely lounge around in a hammock when his daughter was inside a mental hospital.

At dinner, Beth said, "You're quiet."

"I'm always quiet, remember?" he said. He looked at the bubbles rising up one by one in his beer glass against the backdrop of the red linen tablecloth. The place was half empty, and the smell of stale beer along with someone's cigarette smoke drifted into the dining room from the bar.

"Look at me, Jack," she said. "Look at me. I thought we were making a breakthrough here today . . ."

"I like that space between your front teeth," he said.

She nodded. "Now we're getting somewhere. What about my eyes?"

"They're like . . . they're so blue, and every guy in the place almost fell off his seat when we walked through the bar."

"That's it? You're supposed to be a wordsmith?"

"I'm a lawyer," Jack said. He was beginning to smile.

"What do you call a hundred lawyers at the bottom of the ocean?" she asked.

"A start."

"You heard."

"I like your nose, too," he said. He took a drink of beer. "The way it kind of turns up at the end, just a little. And your hair."

"I like your eyes, too," she said. "They're blue like the intense color in Renoir's flowers."

"Wow."

"I know," she said. "I have it all."

He stared.

"You know I love you," he said. He reached across the

table and grabbed her hand. Beth gazed back at him. It was the first time he'd ever said that. He had thought it before now, but something kept him from saying it. Her eyes were moist.

"And I love you, Jack Ruskin," she said. "I love you so very much . . ."

"Sometimes I worry that a lot of this is you just feeling sorry for me."

"You need to get past that," she said. "The first time I really talked to you it was because I felt bad, but that has nothing to do with anything now.

"When I'm not with you, I'm thinking about the next time I will be. When it's cold and you offer me your jacket or hold my hand across the table and sit there looking at me the way you do listening to every word I say, I'm like . . . I feel special.

"I never had that before. I had guys who looked around the room when I was talking. I never met a man as handsome as you who wasn't totally self-absorbed. You're special. That's why I love you."

For quite a while the two of them simply stared at one another, their hands intertwined atop the table. Their waitress brought them coffee.

When she was gone, Beth said, "I'm not a counselor or a psychologist or anything like that, but I have to say that I know something is bothering you, something more than normal. I know it hurts you for me to even say that, or for me to even mention things like Janet's name, but you brought it up. I mean . . .

"I guess I kind of feel like I did when I was a little girl and my family went camping on Sandy Pond up on Lake Ontario. I had this new kite and I was trying to get it to fly. The wind was blowing good, but it just kept dragging along in the sand no matter how hard I ran.

"I needed help, Jack," she said. "I just needed someone to help me the littlest bit. My brother Caleb finally came along and he gave it just the slightest lift, just to get it started, and it took off and I let all the string out and it kept going . . .

"And then I let the string go and I imagined that it just went forever. That's what I asked my mom, if it would go forever, and she told me that yes, as far as she knew, it would. And when I went to sleep every night for about a week, I'd think of that kite just going on and on. But at the beginning, I needed help to get it started. And now . . . I feel like I need you to help here and it could be really good. I guess that's a silly story . . ."

"Well," Jack said, clearing his throat after a moment of silence between them. "I think that's something that I can do and I want to do . . . And it's something I will do. There are some things that . . . I just need you to be patient with me. I'll get there. I just don't know when."

Beth pressed her lips together and nodded slowly, signaling that she had pushed as far as she was going to.

Jack paid the check and led her out into the night. The cold air slapped his face. The stars burned across the darkness above them like a million diamonds. Beth clasped his hand as they crossed the gravel parking lot to his car. They rode in silence back up the winding road toward Racquet Lake with the radio playing softly.

As they passed the Seventh Lake Inn, Jack tried not to slow down. He tried not to look at the old house on the hill. He failed. The nightmare flickered vaguely, unwanted, in the back of his mind.

In the murky shadows of the starlit night, the peak of Tom Conner's roof seemed sharper and the sockets of the windows deeper and darker. The window that glowed on their way to dinner was now a black void and Jack wondered if the monster named Tom Conner was sleeping or out, stalking someone in the inky night.

"What are you looking at?" Beth asked.

"Nothing," he said. He calmly redirected his attention to the road, but his heart was racing. In his mind's eye he could see himself mounting the steps to the porch and knocking on the front door. Jack felt suddenly constricted, almost short of breath. His mind was flooded with a thought that was as wildly dangerous as it was exhilarating. He felt drawn to it in the way a person might feel the urge to jump from a staggering height.

He hadn't done the proper setup, but he hadn't done it with Brice either. That was dicey for a while, after the plumber in the van had seen him. But that was over now. This was different. The setting was so isolated and the target so certain that he couldn't go wrong. He had no right to be holding hands and carrying on like a teenager. He had to think about others.

Thinking about himself was what had gotten him here in the first place. He should have been thinking about Janet. He should have been there. And now he should be thinking about Tom Conner. He should be thinking about wiping that human excrement from the face of the earth. He didn't need much, just his nerve and his Glock, and that was nestled in its metallic case . . . in the safest place a person could hide something—in the trunk of one's car.

CHAPTER 31

Jack stepped on the gas and leaned forward, feeling for the knob that would make the music louder.

Beth seemed to sense his discomfort. She reached over and ran her fingers along the back of his neck. He took a few moments and concentrated on his breathing, regaining his composure.

When he looked at her, he couldn't ignore the hint of youthful hunger in her expression. He forced his mind back into the here and now. If he was going to pull this off, he had to appear normal.

Inside the cabin they undressed each other and slipped beneath the clean white sheets worn soft from years of use.

The chill of the mountain air had crept into the cabin, but Jack didn't notice until Beth was asleep in the crook of his arm. By the light that spilled into the room through a crack in the bathroom door, Jack thought he even detected the wisps of his own breath.

He tried to ignore it and pulled Beth's firm naked body tightly to his own. She was nearly flawless.

". . . heat," he murmured.

It was too cold to ignore. If he didn't do something, they'd wake up with frost on their eyebrows. He slipped out of the bed and danced lightly across the icy floor. When she awoke to a toasty cabin he could tell her what he'd done. A real gentleman. Beth groaned sleepily and snuggled down deeper into the blankets and the warm spot he'd left behind.

Jack rotated the thermostat dial upward. The luxury of heat from a dial seemed almost out of place in a cabin built from rough-cut cedar planks. It stared back at Jack like a rheumy eye, unblinking and unaffected. There was no sound, no click from the mercury switch, and no aching groan from the metal registers near the floor. He bent down and touched one of the long narrow metal boxes. It was stone cold.

"Damn," Jack said. He listened to the silence. He twisted the dial back and forth several times and flicked the switch on the side up and down. Nothing worked.

His hands were now stiffening in the cold. He puffed them full of warm air and cursed again. The warmth of the bed was beckoning like a siren, but he had to do something. He pulled on his jeans, stiff and chilled from their abandonment on the floor, and stepped into his shoes. There was a heavy jacket in his travel bag. He took it out along with a change of clothes and shoes and buttoned it up, covering his bare chest. Quietly he opened the door, but instead of following the gravel drive he jogged down the sandy path that went through the trees and back to the office. He could see more clearly now, coming from this angle, that the office was nothing more than a room attached to the side of the Steffenhausers' house.

There was a light on downstairs in the house. Jack walked into the office, circled the desk, and rapped on the

door that led to the Steffenhausers' kitchen. Old man
Steffenhauser appeared with his finger straight up in the
air and jammed tightly against his constricted lips.

"Shhhhhh!" he said.

Then, after rolling his eyes warily at the ceiling and a
moment of silence, he said in a quiet voice, "Mrs. Steffenhauser's asleep and she'll kill us both, by damn. Quiet.
Just be quiet."

The old man's emphatic expression would have been
comical if Jack didn't suspect that he was actually afraid.
Instead Jack felt mildly annoyed.

"We need some heat, Mr. Steffenhauser," he said in a
quiet voice, but refusing to whisper. "The heat's not
working."

"Shhhhh!" the man hissed again, his eyes rolling in
panic at the ceiling. "I'm coming. I'm coming."

Without bothering to put on a coat or even a pair of
shoes, the old man took a flashlight from the shelf, then
grasped Jack by the arm and led him out into the night.
Barefoot and wearing a pair of red-and-white striped pajamas, Steffenhauser led Jack back up the path, speaking
in a panicked whisper as he went.

"You don't want to wake Mrs. Steffenhauser," he said.
"She's as mad as a wet hornet when woken. She'd kill the
cat. She'd cut out my liver. She'd burn the house down.
She'd . . . she'd be God-awful mad, my friend," he said,
apparently having run out of horrible things he could
think of. "I know just what you need and I can do it in the
blink of an eye better'n telling you."

Jack followed in silence, shivering and marveling at
the cabin owner's obvious disregard of the frigid night.
When they got to the cabin Steffenhauser swung the

beam of his light side to side and rounded the corner to the back. Tucked behind the gleaming hundred-gallon tank of propane gas that fed the stove was a breaker box. The old man popped it open and flipped a switch.

"That'll do it," he said. "I'll wait on the porch, just to make sure. You go in and give her a try, son."

Jack did. He heard the rapid click of expanding metal as the coils inside the registers—crammed with current—began to glow. Outside on the porch Steffenhauser waited patiently, staring out over the rippling water at the hulking mountains and the brilliant star-studded sky beyond. Jack, relieved and confident that he and Beth wouldn't freeze to death during the night, noticed the view that had mesmerized his host.

"You still like to look at it?" Jack said stepping lightly out onto the porch.

"Oh yes, son," Mr. Steffenhauser said without turning his head. "Oh yes."

"Would you like to borrow my jacket, Mr. Steffenhauser?" Jack asked, glancing down at the old man's wide flat feet, which were splayed out on the plank floor like raw pancakes.

Steffenhauser wiggled his toes.

"No son, but that's mighty kind of you. I'll just move on back to the house warmed to my core by the fact that Mrs. Steffenhauser is still asleep. I don't want to alarm you but I do believe it was a near run thing back there when you failed to whisper. Not that I blame you, son. You haven't lived with the missus these forty-seven years and more, so you can't know the hellfire of her wrath. Hellfire it is, pure and simple. Best avoided at all times but absolutely essential after dark."

The old man chuckled wisely, then with a slap on his leg he said, "Well, I best be getting back. You got your heat now and I got . . . I got the missus."

"Mr. Steffenhauser," Jack said. "Can I ask you a question?"

"Sure."

"You spoke earlier about Tom Conner," Jack said.

The old man's merry countenance melted.

"And I wondered what it was exactly that he did . . ."

Steffenhauser turned toward him and flipped on his flashlight, shining it on the floor, illuminating them both in an eerie glow.

"You're serious," he said, peering at him gravely. It wasn't a question. It was an affirmation.

"Yes," Jack said, his blood suddenly racing.

Steffenhauser stared for a moment, then shut out his light. Everything went black.

CHAPTER 32

While their eyes adjusted to the night Steffenhauser said, "For several years there'd be a girl or two every summer who would disappear. Most people thought they was lost, wandered off into the woods, that kind of thing. Then they found one of them way out in the woods. She'd been hurt and beaten, beaten bad and left to die. It was Tom Conner that did it."

In the blackness, the old man's voice was rich with hatred and disgust. He paused for a minute, and then continued.

"He was working for Governor's at the time, a boat rental place on Fourth Lake. He'd see a family or a group of teenagers come in and he'd get their vacation address from the paperwork. Then he'd get them at night. Every one of the girls who disappeared had gone to Governor's within a week of having disappeared. But no one ever put the whole thing together until that one girl identified him. They were mostly girls who belonged to city people on vacation, but a few were high school kids from right around these parts.

"They never did prove it was Tom Conner that did it to the others. No one ever found those other girls, but folks knew pretty damn well that it was him. There was some talk about some of the boys taking him out in the woods and shooting him between the eyes like a rabid coon, but it was just talk. That was back in July of 'eighty-eight. I'll never forget that summer. He got out maybe four years ago. Didn't seem like he spent enough time in jail for what he did . . .

"But," the old man said with a heavy sigh, "they couldn't prove he shot no one, and it was the first time he'd been caught doing anything bad. That's the law. I tell you true, though, if it'd been one of my daughters or one of my grandkids he did that to, I'd a taken my deer rifle out and killed him myself."

The old man flashed the light back on and Jack saw the wild look in his eyes.

"I mean it, son," he said, his bushy white eyebrows knit into a fearsome scowl. "I would have."

Then it was black again. The two of them stood there for a long while, neither moving, both staring out at the bejeweled sky. A star suddenly tumbled headlong like a wayward rocket and disappeared behind the sleeping mountains. Jack felt a ridiculous urge to take this half-crazy old man into his confidence: to tell him that he, Jack Ruskin, had done what the old man yearned to have done himself.

The moment seemed frozen in time and in it Jack felt the frame of his carefully constructed plan bow under the full weight of the terrible secret. What a relief it would be if someone else could just know and tell him it was good. He felt a pressure building inside him. He was risking his life for people he didn't even know, but it was more than that. He had to do it.

Jack opened his mouth to talk.

"I—" he said. Then he stopped. His mouth began to move and the words began to spill out, words he couldn't explain.

"I think it's important for people to forgive, Mr. Steffenhauser," he said, lying with all his heart, sounding self-righteous, placing himself outside the realm of suspicion for the act he knew he was about to commit.

"That's what the Bible tells us," he said. "That's what God wants . . ."

The old man shifted uncomfortably and Jack felt the tension on the little porch expand until it seemed there was barely room enough for the two of them to stand side by side.

Finally Steffenhauser sighed heavily and spoke. "That's what the minister said, son. But it weren't his kids that it happened to. Seems to me that would change things a piece, but I ain't going to argue with the Bible any more than I'd argue with the missus. That I won't do, so instead, I'll just say good night."

Jack watched the old man shuffle down the trail, his striped pajamas glowing faintly in the starlight. When he was gone, Jack slipped back into the cabin. Beth was sound asleep in the bedroom, and part of Jack envied her peaceful slumber.

Then a wonderful idea came to him.

From his briefcase, he removed his notebook computer. In the small living room off the bedroom was a desk that looked out through a picture window, across the porch and out on the lake. He set the computer down and accessed his law office over the phone line. He logged onto LexisNexis, a legal and news archive of colossal proportions. What did the old man say? The summer, July

1988. Jack searched that month joined with the name *Tom Conner* and the key words *kidnap* or *sex crime* or *rape* or *sodomy*. There were seven matches. One was an AP wire story, four pieces in the *Utica Statesman,* and two in the *Adirondack News*.

Jack searched through them and the full horror of Tom Conner's crimes came to life. His stomach tightened into a knot of rage. In one of the Utica paper's stories was the thing Jack wanted: a quote from the father of a girl who had disappeared. As Steffenhauser said, her family had also rented a boat at Governor's. It was presumed that Tom Conner had taken her and tortured her in the same way as the girl he had chained up, only this girl never made it home. Her father's name was Arthur Campion. He was a doctor from Albany, and the emptiness of his words in print recalled for Jack his own shock after what had happened to Janet.

"We just hope she's all right. We have to hope."

Jack logged off of LexisNexis and brought up a new document within his personal files. Then he began to write. When he was finished, he went back through and edited, cutting and changing some things so as not to incriminate himself.

He accessed the Albany phone directory and found an address for Dr. Arthur Campion. With that he was able to find an e-mail address on-line. When the time was right, Jack would attach a new wire story about Tom Conner that had yet to be written—gunned down in his Seventh Lake home and left to rot—to this letter and then send them both from a special Web site that guaranteed anonymity. Jack could send his e-mail to the doctor without leaving an electronic trail that the police could trace back to him. Not that Dr. Campion would want to lead them to Jack even if he could.

Before Jack closed out the file, he reread the letter one last time. It was an explicit description of what he was going to do to Tom Conner and why. It said that he hoped that Dr. Campion would find some solace in the vengeance he was about to visit on the monster responsible for taking his daughter from him. It was unsigned, of course, and for some reason that bothered Jack. He wanted a moniker at least, something that connected the letter to him.

He thought of his biblical words to Steffenhauser and on a whim he got up and went into the bedroom. Beth had turned over but was still sleeping quietly. In the drawer beside the bed was a green Bible. Jack took it into the next room and opened it to Revelation.

He had a vague idea about an avenging angel. That's what he was. For fifteen minutes he searched, and then he found it: the fifth angel of the apocalypse. The fifth angel would bring a vial of death and pain to the throne of Satan. There, he would pour out its contents, mercilessly avenging the evil done by Satan and all his followers. That was Jack. He was the fifth angel and that was how he signed his letter.

CHAPTER 33

After closing the document and storing it in a secure file, Jack shut down his computer and searched through his duffel bag for a different set of clothes and a windbreaker. Hyped up by the existence of his letter and the sense of justice it would bring to the parent of another victim, Jack hurried outside. There was a slight incline down to the main loop and Jack put the Saab in neutral, letting it roll away from the cabin. When it stopped, he started up the car and rolled down the windows to listen. The engine purred quietly, making less noise than the sound of crunching gravel beneath the tires.

The driveway—he knew from a small map given to him when he checked in—was a broad semicircle whose other end would take Jack to the highway without having to pass the main house. Nevertheless he crawled along with his headlights off until he came to the road. His hands trembled and he gripped the wheel tightly, forcing himself not to speed and breathing deeply in order to better concentrate on his impromptu plan. The sickening fear had crept up inside him, trickling into his core like a cesspool. He was going to kill someone and he couldn't stop it. Even more, he felt compelled to do it. He found the bottle of Maalox but put it down untouched. The grinding in his gut would keep him alert.

When he passed the inn and Tom Conner's house he began to search for an appropriate place to pull off the road. Less than a quarter mile away he came to a gas station. There were several cars lined up outside awaiting repair, and Jack pulled in next to them. For several minutes he sat in the darkness, looking and listening. The engine ticked; otherwise all was quiet.

He got out of the car and circled the building, searching for signs of people within. Satisfied that the place was just a garage, he went to the trunk of the Saab and removed a pair of leather driving gloves and then his gun and holster from its metal case. The road was empty and Jack reached the driveway to Tom Conner's house in just a few minutes.

He looked up the winding path at the old house that rose like a canker from the hilltop, gaping down upon the road and the inn across the way. Jack felt his face tighten into a grim mask. He looked around and then climbed the hill, quiet except for his own heavy breathing. As he reached the top, he could see a dilapidated green panel van parked next to the side of the house. Fresh tire marks in the sand told him the van was in use and suggested that Tom Conner was at home. He moved closer to the house, removing the pistol with its weighty silencer from the holster beneath his arm.

The stillness of the run-down old house surrounded him like a heavy mist, pressing him from all sides. The weight of his foot on the first step caused its rusty nails to shriek in protest. Jack froze with his heart pummeling the inside of his chest like a fighter working the heavy bag.

But the noise shouldn't matter. He would have to knock anyway. The noise of his footsteps was a natural precursor to that. He took a deep breath and climbed to the porch amid a tempest of groaning planks and squeaking nails. The front door, battered from years of weather against its naked face, was nevertheless solid as rock slag. Jack rapped his knuckles against it, the sound barely resonating. In the door's center was the snarling face of a corroded cast-iron lion. Jack lifted its massive lower jaw and slammed it down three times. Not a sound came from within.

He waited several more minutes, then went to the nearest window and began rapping on its ancient panes. That's when he noticed that one piece of glass was missing. He reached his hand through the opening and pushed aside the moldy-smelling curtain, peering into the darkness of the house where he could make out the faint outline of a doorway. His rush instantly returned. It appeared to be a door beneath the staircase. Was there a basement? If there was a basement in an old house like this, it was apt not to have windows.

That would be the place someone like Tom Conner would be. It would also explain why no one had answered the door. Maybe that's where he was, down there, planning, scheming, or secretly watching the kind of porn that stirred a really sick mind. Jack felt for the window's latch. He found it and forced it open. Letting the curtain fall back into place, he grasped the frame of the window and tried to force it open. It was hopelessly jammed.

With a frustrated huff he left it alone and began to circle the house, moved by an unseen hand. It was possible that there was a door in the back that wasn't locked. If so, he could enter there. If not, he'd come back and try to open the ancient window again. It wouldn't do to come this far and simply give up. Past the van, in the back of the house there was another entrance. It was a newer door, locked, but with the kind of latch that Jack knew could be opened by sliding a durable card between the door and the frame. He removed the wallet from the back of his pants pocket and extracted his driver's license. Carefully he began to work the card into the door frame below the lock with the Glock still gripped tightly in his other hand.

The sense of someone else's presence drew his attention away from the door. The unexpected sight of Tom Conner's bearded face and dark menacing form rounding the far corner of the house made Jack jump and cry out in shock at the same instant. An orange burst of flame lit the night, an explosion ripped through the silence, and Jack felt the impact of a shotgun blast tearing into his flesh, spinning him up into the air and throwing him backward like a lifeless puppet down onto the sandy blood-speckled ground.

CHAPTER 34

Jack lay still.

The dark heavy figure of Tom Conner approached him. He moved through the gloom, silent except for the sound of his raspy breathing because he was so fat. The shotgun was still leveled at Jack's chest. Finally Conner stopped. He was six feet away and peering anxiously for confirmation of his kill the way a jackal will nervously sniff at a carcass.

Jack held his breath. The shotgun slowly drifted off its mark. Conner edged closer, shuffling his feet in halting tentative steps. Jack's fingers felt the smooth handle of the Glock in his hand. Suddenly Conner's shotgun swung back on target. Jack winced. When no shot came, he eased his eyes back open again—two slits. Even in the dark he could see that Conner was just two feet away now, and again the gun had drifted.

With snakelike quickness Jack jerked his own gun up and into play, firing fast and furiously with a raging cry. The shotgun exploded again. Jack felt the sting of hot powder, but the slug sang past his head and smacked into the earth with a resounding thud. It was Conner's last shot. Bullets struck the fat man like punches, jolting him backward, doubling him over with pain and finally dropping him in his tracks amid the thwack of the hushed 9mm slugs as they buried themselves into flesh, organ, and bone.

Jack sprang to his feet and emptied everything he had left into Conner's quivering frame. He staggered. The weight of the heavy ache in his shoulder and the hot wet blood soaking his shirt made him light-headed. The world seemed to spin. Even when he closed his eyes, the gruesome image of the dead man filled his mind. He stumbled to the ground and began to vomit uncontrollably, heaving painfully even after his stomach was empty.

He stood huffing over Conner and carefully assessed the situation. He'd been shot. There would be blood on the ground, his blood, and vomit. They would have his DNA.

A cold sobering thought suddenly splashed against his face. Was he trying to get caught?

Maybe that was the only way out. Jack seemed unable to stop the vicious acts of vengeance on his own. He looked at the motionless body of Tom Conner. Stains of blood riddled his corpulent frame. A dark pool had begun to form beneath him. Out of habit Jack got down in the sandy grass and began to grope around for his own 9mm shell casings. With the help of a small penlight he kept in his pocket, he found twelve without a problem, but soon grew frantic in his search for the remaining five.

Then he stopped. On his hands and knees in the dark, he realized it was probably irrelevant. The casings could tie the act to his gun, but a sample of DNA was more telling than a shell casing or a cloth fiber or even a fingerprint.

An abrupt flash of light made Jack start to his feet. He realized almost right away that it was only a lightning flash. The rumble of thunder came soon afterward, and small breeze rustled the dry leaves of the trees. Jack looked up and waited. After a minute came another flash, and in its light he could make out the heavy billowing clouds approaching from the southwest. His mouth hung open, awed by the relief he suddenly felt. There would be rain.

He dropped back down on all fours with the small light in his mouth and renewed his search for the shell casings. They had to be there, not more than six or eight feet away. He just had to be patient.

As his fingers sifted through the grass he considered the implications of the rain. It was divine. The next flash of lightning revealed the shiny rectangle of his driver's license. It was the license he had been using to open the door, the license he had forgotten all about. Accidentally leaving it there in the grass would have provided the police with exactly what they needed to connect him to the crime. Yet there it was, revealed to him as if by magic.

Why had he doubted himself? This was meant to be. He scooped the license up out of the grass. He had erred in his approach tonight, that was certain. But even his blood would be washed away. There was another biblical analogy there, but he shunned it. History was littered with lunatics thinking they were God Himself or somehow in possession of His divine powers. Jack needed to ground his thought in reality.

He found two more shell casings. His search was calmer now, confident beyond reason that he would find the remaining three. The lightning began to flicker now with increased frequency. The wind picked up. Sandy grit stung his cheeks. His shoulder ached, but it was no longer a concern. His mind was clear. He fished open the rip in his shirt and looked objectively at the three-inch trench of deep purple flesh beneath the penlight's beam. Blood oozed out, but slowly now, sticky from the clotting.

In his mind he quickly constructed a plausible story for Beth: He had gone to the main office to find Mr. Steffenhauser about the heat. The old man came and turned it on. The two of them admired the vista from the porch. And when the old man had left Jack decided to go to the water's edge for a more complete view. As he made his way through the trees, he had taken a nasty spill and gored open his shoulder on the sharp stub of a broken branch on a pine tree.

Walking through the woods earlier in the day, he had noticed the random spikes of wood, and they would suit his purpose.

Jack found the remaining shells just as the first drops of rain began to fall. The single heavy beads seemed to pop on contact with the earth. The sky grew angrier still, and that gladdened him. The storm would be big enough to wipe everything clean.

By the time he reached his car, the sky was black and teeming. Jack shed his wet clothes and put them into a garbage bag with the shell casings and tossed the whole thing into a half-full Dumpster behind the garage. With fresh clothes on his body, he set out for the cabin.

When he got there Beth dashed outside through the pouring rain and into the headlights of the Saab. Steffenhauser was soon beside her. Jack turned off the car and got out.

"Are you all right?" she asked.

"I'm fine," he said. He glanced uncomfortably at the old man. Steffenhauser's face was partially protected from the rain by a broad-brimmed green felt hat. The three of them now stood in the wet orange glow of the cabin lights, the lightning giving them sporadic glimpses of one another and the woods around them in a brilliant blue hue.

"Come inside," Jack said. His tone gave away none of the anxiety he felt. "I'll tell you what happened, but everything is fine. I'm sorry for the fuss. I just didn't want to wake you."

"I'm sorry, too," Steffenhauser said. He was cheerful despite his dripping wet hat. "I didn't mean to cause a ruckus with all this, but when the lady here came to the house with you gone and the car, too, well, just to be safe . . . I called the police."

CHAPTER 35

Amanda was up at six. She ran her six miles hard in a light gray rain. As she finished, the early-morning sun broke through the clouds. Drops of water glistened and dripped from the trees. Wet brown leaves blanketed the yard and gave off the musty smell of early fall.

After a shower she got out the box of oatmeal and poured some into a saucepan. She measured out her water and lit the stove then dashed back up the stairs to pack her things. She unfolded a narrow garment bag with wheels. Two changes of clothes. Some pictures the kids drew. Her FBI jacket, in case it got cool or rained. A small leather pouch of toiletries. Sneakers. Workout clothes.

The zip of her zipper woke up Parker.

"Sorry," she said. She went to the drawer where she kept her gun. It was coated in a thin film of dust.

"What time is it?" Parker asked.

"Almost seven-thirty."

Parker sat up and rubbed his puffy eyes.

"Where are you . . ." he said. "Oh, I forgot. Back to crime fighting."

"Why did you say it like that?" she asked, strapping on her gun.

He shrugged. "You didn't think I was going to sing a song, did you?"

"I thought you'd appreciate what I'm doing."

"You do enough of that for both of us."

"Do you know what I do?" she asked.

"Do you know what I do?" he said. "Did you ever think about that? Me, running around with the kids. Me and all the moms."

"That's not fair," she said.

"I'm sorry," he said. "You're right. I'm being selfish. We just miss you when you go. Lots."

"Breakfast is ready when you are," she said. She scooped up her bag and jogged down the stairs. The smell hit her before she reached the bottom.

"Damn," she said and hurried into the kitchen.

Burned oatmeal bubbled up out of the pan, hissing and sputtering in the flames. A small shriek escaped her. The kids tumbled in after her.

"Awesome," Teddy said.

Amanda took the pan off the fire and flipped off the gas. She quickly scooped the cereal out into the bowls she'd lined up on the counter.

"Sit down, kids," she said.

They were chattering a mile a minute, excited by the flames.

"Sit down."

Amanda got out brown sugar and milk and put some bread in the toaster. She threw together a pot of coffee and poured the juice. The round clock on the wall above the table was working against her.

Glenda started in.

"Mommy, this isn't—"

"Just eat it, Glenda," she said, scraping some butter onto the toast.

"It's bad, Mom," Teddy said.

Parker arrived. "Coffee ready?" he asked.

"Sit," she said to him.

She poured some coffee from the pot even though it hadn't finished percolating. It looked thin, but the toaster dinged again. She set the coffee down in front of Parker along with a bowl of the oatmeal.

"Honey," Parker said. "This is burned. Honey?"

"Why is Mommy crying?" Glenda asked.

"I'm not crying," Amanda said. She sniffed and wiped her eyes on the back of her hand. "I'm sweating. It's warm in here."

"She's crying," Teddy said. "Definitely."

"Mommy's got a lot on her mind," Parker said. He got up from the table and tried to take the butter knife from her.

"I've got it, Parker," she said. "Sit down. Please."

"It's eight," he said.

"Damn."

The kids were wide-eyed.

"I didn't mean that," she said. She put the toast down on the table and went to the refrigerator. She took out two brown bags and set them in front of the kids.

"Lunch," she said. "Look inside."

"Aw, Mom, Gushers," Teddy said, peeking into the bag, "this is totally awesome."

"You said Gushers make cavities," Glenda said. She held her bag of the sticky little synthetic fruit pieces between her finger and her thumb.

"Only when you have them all the time," Amanda said.

"Oh," Glenda said. "That's good."

"I just thought you'd like something special," Amanda said.

"For what?"

Amanda shrugged and picked up Parker's coffee cup to take a sip. It was pitifully thin.

"I don't know," she said. "To celebrate my going back to work I guess."

They sat there, all three of them, saying nothing. The smell of burned oatmeal drifted up from the table. No one was eating it anyway. Parker cleared his throat.

"Mom and I are going to start working on setting up a college fund," he said. "She's going back to work so you guys can go to college one day."

"I don't want to go to college," Teddy said.

"Yes you do," Amanda said. She kissed him on the lips, then Glenda.

"I love you both," she said. "I've got to go."

CHAPTER 36

Amanda glanced at the shiny wet Humvee as she backed out of the driveway. She wanted to smash into it. Instead she backed out into the road and tried to think about her job. That's what she should be doing.

This was no great assignment she was undertaking, but it was work. Although it happened from time to time, no FBI agent wanted to be paired with a local cop. It was just short of an insult. The fact that the detective's uncle was a powerful congressman on Capitol Hill did nothing to change that.

But that's what it was. The uncle was on the appropriations committee. He had called the director himself. The director called Hanover's boss, and so it went. At least the case wasn't a total loser. Also, while McGrew sounded young and brash over the phone, it was also clear that he was extremely committed to the case.

He had uncovered a series of murders whose M.O.'s were similar enough to be considered at least in theory as the work of a single serial killer. McGrew had already fed his information to the people at VCAP, the FBI's Violent Crime Apprehension Program. Working off that they had already uncovered three more possible matches: sex offenders murdered at close range with a 9mm Glock. Each crime scene was unusually bereft of evidence. It was an interesting file to say the least.

Amanda picked up her cell phone and started to dial home. No, she'd said good-bye. Now she was gone. She had to learn to let it be. It was like her running. She had to build herself up again, get strong.

At Washington National Airport she parked her car and dashed inside. She checked her gun at security and found her gate for the flight to Pittsburgh. It was a short flight, up and down, but it gave her enough time to ponder the uniqueness of the case. McGrew's theory about a professional killer made some sense. It was possible that some underground pornography ring linked all the victims. After all, each had been a level-three sex offender.

But Amanda thought there was another possibility as well. The killer might have been the victim of a sex crime himself. He might have suppressed the event, a horror from years ago that had secretly festered in the back of his mind. Such a thing could grow until it was strong enough to commandeer his psyche, steering it from the bounds of normality into the murky world of a psychopathic killer.

After a while Amanda decided to clear her mind, mentally walk away from the problem to better consider it later with a fresh perspective. There was a shopping catalog in the seat pocket in front of her. She opened it. There were some neat toys. She could just see Teddy on the miniature four-wheel-drive Jeep. There was also one of those new swing sets with the big yellow tube for a slide. She shook her head and let out a short quick breath.

She had to stop doing this to herself. It was like a dual

major. Mother. FBI agent. She had to remember that and keep her focus.

She put the catalog back and took out the USAir magazine. There was a story in there about a young author named Ace Atkins. He lived on a hundred-year-old-farm in Mississippi, teaching at the University in Oxford by day and following the paths of Faulkner and James Lee Burke by night. She made a mental note to look for his book in the airport. Now that she was on the road again, she needed something to read. She had actually read less during her time off than she did when she was working. That was another thing to look forward to.

When she landed in Pittsburgh, McGrew was waiting for her outside security. He was easy to pick out. There were only a handful of other people staring up the escalator waiting for passengers, and none of them but McGrew looked like a cop. His white dress shirt, open at the collar, worn with cowboy boots, blue jeans, and a wool herringbone blazer with outdated elbow patches was just less than respectable looking. He had a wild shock of gelled hair that protruded ridiculously straight up from the forefront of his receding hairline. His small dark deep-set eyes glowed with the same enthusiasm Amanda had sensed over the phone. McGrew wasn't a handsome man by any means, but he certainly wasn't acting as if he knew it.

As she approached, McGrew didn't bother to hide his careful top-to-bottom assessment of her, allowing his eyes to linger at the curves in evidence even beneath her olive business suit.

Amanda marched off the escalator and held out her

hand. "I'm Special Agent Lee. You must be Detective McGrew."

McGrew was obviously caught off guard.

"I didn't . . . you look . . . different," he said.

"We've never met before," Amanda said.

"Different than I expected," he said, unable to keep his eyes from conducting another quick frisk.

Amanda backed him right down with an intense look that said it all. McGrew seemed to take notice. He cleared his throat and in a tone that was nearly apologetic asked if she had any other luggage.

"This is it," she said.

"Well," McGrew said, clapping his hands together with a single energetic smack, "let's go then. I caught an earlier flight than I was supposed to. I've been here since this morning, and I've already got something that you're gonna like. My uncle told me you're a real hotshot at the Bureau. Anyway, I got this guy, a big black sergeant by the name of Emerson Tidwell. Now, get this: He knows I know something about who killed these pervs. Now, he doesn't know I know *he* knows it, but he does. He's got some big-time information that he's holding out on. I don't know why, but when he knows I know he knows . . ."

McGrew shared with Amanda a heartfelt, if ridiculously wicked grin.

"When he does . . ." McGrew said, "he's gonna talk, and we're gonna have ourselves a killer."

CHAPTER 37

Tidwell stared at the young cop and then looked at Amanda with raised eyebrows.

"What'd he say?" Tidwell asked.

The three of them were sitting by themselves in the same interview room on the third floor.

"Sergeant," Amanda said, "if you're not willing to talk to us, just say it. You know what he said."

"That's a pretty funky accent," Tidwell said.

"Right," Amanda said.

"I said," McGrew said, speaking slowly as though he were addressing a three-year-old, "despite what you're telling us, we already know from someone right here in this office that there was a man here during the time we're talking about who asked to see the subdirectory. Twice."

"Then why don't you talk to whoever that was?" Tidwell said. "Because I don't know what you're talking about."

"We already talked to her," McGrew said. He was smiling falsely now. "That's how we know you're the one in charge of letting people into this little fucking room to thumb through the perv files.

"And we know that the guy we're looking for was in

here," McGrew said. "A blond guy with glasses. But you were the one who talked to him. You were the one who probably wrote down his name . . .

"And we know," he said, "we know, Tidwell, that you don't have more than a handful of people come in here every month. If that. So what in the fuck is your problem?"

McGrew stood up and looked at Amanda.

"Let's go talk to the chief," he said. "I'm ready to take some action here."

Amanda hung back and watched Tidwell's face. He didn't sweat or blink. He just formed a thick fake smile on his lips and looked at McGrew like you would a shoe after stepping in dog crap.

"You want to take action?" Tidwell said. He stood, too, now looking down at the shorter man. "Come on, brother. I been waitin' for this since you walked in the door at about ten o'clock this morning."

McGrew lunged at Tidwell and grabbed him by the front of his shirt. "Don't fuck with me," he yelled. "This is a major case, you idiot."

"McGrew!" Amanda shouted, grabbing him by the shoulders and pulling him back. "McGrew. Let go, you jackass."

Tidwell swatted McGrew's hands off of him with ease and stood breathing hard and blinking slowly at the two of them.

"I'm sorry," she said to Tidwell. "Give us a second."

McGrew huffed and stared at Tidwell. Then he snarled gamely and said, "Yeah, you better look at me, big man. Get a good look, 'cause I'm not through. I know you're hiding something and I ain't gonna rest until you tell us who the fuck that guy is."

"McGrew!" Amanda said.

Tidwell rounded the table and let himself out, closing the door softly behind him.

"Shit," McGrew said, shrugging Amanda off of him and slumping down in his chair. "Shit."

"What the hell was that?" Amanda demanded.

"What?" McGrew asked. "That? That was nothing. That was me letting him know that we mean business, that we ain't going away."

Amanda shook her head, her face distorted with incredulity. "You can't act that way. And don't say *we*. That's not we, McGrew. I'm an FBI agent. We don't do that."

"Yeah," McGrew said. He muttered something Amanda didn't catch.

"What was that?" she asked.

He didn't answer.

She was about ready to throw a chop right to this jerk's throat and leave him flopping around on the floor like a dying fish. "They had to send you to me," she said, reaching for the door. "Of all the things . . ."

"Hey," McGrew said. "Where the hell are you going? This is a fucking investigation. There's a serial killer out there. If I'm off base, then I'm off base. I'm sorry. I care about this shit, you know. I've never lost on a case."

"I'm not here to baby-sit you," Amanda said. "I don't care who your uncle is—I'm not going to be a part of this nonsense, this . . ."

"Tell me I'm not right," McGrew said. "Tell me he's not hiding something."

Amanda stopped.

"I can't tell you that," she said.

"Ha. I'm right and you know it."

"Whether you're right or not isn't the issue," she said, closing the door and turning back to face him. "This isn't good cop, bad cop. I graduated from that in fifth grade. Get your shit together."

"We're onto something," he said.

"I know that," she said.

"You do?"

"McGrew," she said, "a child could see he was lying to us, but you also have to see the big picture. He's not going to help us, at least not now, not after that stunt you just pulled."

McGrew shrugged and said, "Okay. I'm done with that. I'll follow your lead. Can you get anything more out of him?"

Amanda frowned to herself and thought. After a moment of consideration she said, "No, not after that."

"What about threatening his boss?" McGrew said. "Don't you have some kind of federal habeas corpus or something like that that you can threaten everybody with?"

"Habeas corpus?" Amanda said raising an eyebrow in puzzlement. "No, that's wh— Haven't you ever just tried to ask for help? You have to build relationships, McGrew. That's how cops work together. After what you did with Tidwell, that's now out of the question."

"So you say we just leave it alone?" McGrew asked.

Amanda looked at the door through which Tidwell had disappeared. "I think I'll go talk to him. I'll give him my card and tell him if he changes his mind to call me. I'll apologize for you."

"Good," McGrew said cheerily. "But you know it's the blond guy, right? We can go and check out the murder scene. The place by the university got cleaned up and rented out already, but the scene by the hospital is still pretty much the same as it was the day that Drake pervert got whacked. A guy named Zuckerman is in charge of the case. I lined it up for him to take us out there. He sounded like a stiff on the phone, but you never know, do you?"

"No," Amanda said. "You don't. And if you go at it right, you might even build a relationship or something. I'll meet you downstairs at the front desk."

"Better than that," he said, "I'll pull the car out front to pick you up and I'll call Zuckerman so he's ready.

"I feel good about this now," McGrew said. "Do you?"

Amanda looked at him for a moment.

"I don't know if I feel 'good,'" she said. "But I know we've just confirmed that the man your plumber saw on Long Island is the same guy who came in here looking for sex offenders to kill. We've got a long way to go, Mc-Grew. Don't forget that. And we may never get there. But I also know this: We're onto something big."

CHAPTER 38

Amanda found Sergeant Tidwell in his cubicle, going over some paperwork as if nothing had happened. He looked up at her from beneath his heavy eyelids and actually smiled.

"I'm sorry," she said. "That was totally uncalled for. I don't want to sound condescending, but that's not how we do things at the Bureau, and Detective McGrew is not from the FBI. We've been teamed up on this case temporarily. He's from New York. You know? Enough said."

Tidwell waved his hand in the air. "That's nothing . . . like a gnat. I'm fine. Look, I understand where your partner's coming from, too. I'm a cop, but some folks just don't have as good recollection powers as others; that's all. Mine fails me on this one. I just don't recall anything about it."

Amanda looked at him for a minute. She liked him.

"We've got a man out there who's killing people," she said. "He's dangerous. He's going to do it again."

Tidwell returned her stare without expression and nodded. "Yes, we do."

Amanda sighed and took a card from her shoulder bag. "Would you call me if anything jogs your memory?" she asked. "That happens sometimes . . ."

Tidwell shrugged and took her card in his enormous hand, slipping it into the top drawer of his desk after running his thumb over the raised golden Bureau seal.

"You never know," he said.

"Thank you," Amanda replied.

Outside, McGrew sat waiting patiently in the car.

"That's Zuckerman right there," he said, pointing to the unmarked cruiser at the curb ahead. They followed the car through the streets of Pittsburgh to a crumbling neighborhood sprawled beneath the shadow of an ancient V.A. hospital. When they stopped in front of a three-story brick tenement, Amanda and McGrew got out of their rental car and approached the Pittsburgh detective.

Zuckerman rolled down his window and pointed to the building with his thumb. "It's on the second floor, number twenty-one twenty-one. You can't miss it. Here's the key."

"You want to go in with us?" McGrew asked.

Zuckerman looked at him blandly and shifted in the cruiser's well-worn cloth seat before saying, "No. I got some calls I need to make. I'll be right here."

As proof, the graying detective held up his cell phone.

McGrew was off and Amanda followed him up to the building. A handful of young men in oversize pants and an array of colorful jerseys glared at them from their roost on the steps as they entered. McGrew glared right back. The elevator was broken and by the smell of it, Amanda thought she'd be just as happy to take the stairs, until she got a whiff of the stairwell.

McGrew jogged up the metal steps like he was seeing his college dorm room for the first time. Breathing through her mouth to avoid the stench, Amanda placed her hand on the railing, only to yank it back after touching something foul and jellylike. Choosing her steps amid the refuse that littered the stairs, she picked her way carefully to the second floor. McGrew was waiting for her impatiently in the hall. A man rolled up in newspaper and reeking of alcohol and the pungent body odor of the unwashed was lying against the wall.

McGrew, impervious to the wretched sights and smells, turned and strode down the hallway until he came to a door marked by a web of plastic yellow crime scene tape. After tearing aside the tape the young detective unlocked the door and swung it open.

"He would have knocked," McGrew said out loud without looking at Amanda. "Then, when Drake comes to the door and opens it: Pow. Pow. Pow. He just starts banging away."

"From what I've seen in the reports," Amanda said, "no one heard anything, here or anywhere. What about a silencer?"

McGrew nodded. "Definitely. This guy is a pro."

He walked into the room and began to examine the bullet holes still remaining in the floor next to the chalked-off shape of Gilbert Drake's body.

"I still think he's not," Amanda said, watching him from the doorway. "Too many shots for a professional, way too messy."

"You said that on the phone," McGrew muttered, sticking his finger into one of the holes and wiggling it around.

Suddenly he popped up and said, "Let's talk to the neighbors."

Amanda nodded. Next door, an older woman with

glasses answered their knock. After carefully examining their badges she removed the chain from the door and swung it open enough for them to see her red terry-cloth bathrobe and the powder-blue shower cap atop her graying head. She stood barring the way in, however, and Amanda spoke for them both from the hall. The woman listened carefully before her brow grew dark and her mouth turned down beneath her scowling eyes.

"That's why you're coming here?" she asked. "You think we aren't glad he's gone? That was the Lord's will.

"You," she said, pointing her finger at Amanda, "you coming all the way up here from Washington, D.C., to find out who killed that Gilbert Drake? You know what he did? Well, no one told us what he did. They just moved him right in here next door to me.

"But I read about it in the paper after he was dead. He got what he deserved if you're asking me. The Lord punished that man, I say. And didn't no one try to find the people that killed my boy when he was shot dead right out on the street!" she said. "No one came up here from Washington, D.C., then. You ought to be ashamed of yourselves, coming all this way for a man like that. If I knew who did it, I'd shake his hand, praise God. Now go away and leave an old woman in peace."

With that, she slammed the door in their faces.

"That relationship was doomed from the start," McGrew said. "You can't blame me for that one."

They fared little better with the rest of the neighbors.

"At least no one else slammed the door," Amanda pointed out.

After returning the key to Zuckerman, the two of them got into their rented car and headed back to their hotel.

They had an appointment with Zuckerman's counterpart, the investigator on the Lincoln case, in the morning.

"You want to get a drink?" McGrew asked, pulling up in front of the lobby.

"No thanks," she said, "I want to think. I'm going to get a run in."

"A run?" McGrew looked puzzled.

"You know," she said, getting out of the car, "with sneakers, like the thing they do in Boston every spring."

"That's a marathon," McGrew said, throwing the car in park and getting out after her.

"Well," she said, heading for the door, "I'm not running a marathon, but I'm going to clear my head."

"Great," he said. "I'm with you. When?"

Amanda stopped and looked back at him doubtfully.

"I'm going as soon as I get checked in and changed," she said. "If you want to, you can try and keep up, but I'm not slowing down."

"I wouldn't want you to," he said.

She was already gone.

CHAPTER 39

Amanda unpacked her bag, hanging her suit for the next day and carefully removing two watercolor pictures from the bottom of her things. They were the children's paintings, one by Teddy, one by Glenda. She slipped their edges beneath the frames of the hotel artwork hanging on the wall opposite her bed. Teddy's painting was a tree with bright red apples hanging from its thick branches. A sun blazed in the corner and green grass covered the ground where a squirrel sat. Glenda's was of a girl with a horse. Amanda inserted a wallet-size school photo of each child in the bottom corner of each picture and stood back to look.

She smiled to herself, kissed her fingertips, pressed them to the photos, and then got changed. McGrew was waiting for her in sneakers and a pair of black dress socks. He looked down at them and shrugged apologetically.

"It doesn't bother me," she said. "Here we go."

She set out at a fast pace, trying to burn him off right away, but after a time, she realized he wasn't going down so she settled into her usual pace.

They arrived back at the hotel in a sweat. McGrew was buried, but to his credit, he'd hung on the whole way. Still, he didn't have enough left to do anything but nod and watch and she was able to bid him good night amid the confusion of valets, bellcaps, and a throng of Japanese tourists disembarking from a tour bus.

The sun was nearly down. Amanda went to her room, ordered some food from room service, and made her calls to home. The Gushers were a hit and Parker had taken them out for Dairy Queen after homework. Things seemed settled and Amanda was able to breathe a little easier. But her call was disrupted by someone knocking insistently on her door. It was just after nine. She hung up and went to answer it.

She had presumed that she'd seen the last of McGrew until the next morning, but she had no idea who else it could be. She heard his voice. Definitely McGrew.

"What, McGrew?" she asked through the bolted door. "What do you want?"

Amanda looked out through the peephole. She could see him fidgeting in the hallway as if he'd been stung by a bee. Suddenly, he put his eye right up to the hole.

"Open up," he said. "We've got to go."

Amanda thought for a moment then opened the door.

"What?" she asked.

"I just got a call," he said. "I know an investigator in the New York State troopers' office. We could wait for a flight tomorrow, but it'll waste time and I can't sleep anyway. You can sleep. I'll drive. We can be there first thing in the morning."

"Drive where?" Amanda asked. "What are you talking about?"

McGrew stopped and tilted his head dubiously. "I'm sure you never heard of it. It's a place in the Adirondack Mountains up in New York State. It's called Racquet Lake."

CHAPTER 40

"Hey Ben."

Benjamin Hanover started from his reverie. He whipped his feet down off his desk and scowled.

"Mike," he said. "Damn, no one even calls me Ben anymore. You kind of startled me."

"Lots to think about?" Collins asked. He was a tall man, tall and thick with curly brown hair and a serious face.

"Oh, yeah," Hanover said. "You don't even know. ASAIC, man, it isn't easy. Sit down."

"No thanks," Collins said; he was just inside the doorway. "I just wanted to run something by you. I've got a guy—his name is Charles Wheeler. I don't have anything to prove it, but I'll bet dollars to doughnuts that he's the other guy who was in that apartment in Jackson. He and Oswald shared a cell together in Angola."

"Oswald?"

"You know, the Hubble Sanderson guy . . . Marco."

It came to Hanover. Hubble Sanderson was the real name of the man Amanda had killed, the man who'd murdered Marco. Collins, and every other agent who worked on the case, never stopped referring to him as Oswald, the alias he had sometimes used. Hanover just forgot. He had a lot on his mind.

"So this Charles Wheeler guy was in Angola for assault, but if you read into the arrest report, it sounds like he's a pervert, same as Oswald," Collins said. "I guess things got pretty rough for the two of them at The Farm, you know how that goes. Even the bad guys hate a pervert. From what I know, Wheeler and Oswald kept to themselves. They got pretty tight."

Hanover smirked at that.

"Wheeler's been on the move since Amanda Lee shot Oswald," Collins said. "We didn't even know who we were looking for until I did a background on Hubble Sanderson. About five years ago, when these two beauties got out of Angola, Wheeler came into some money. A lot. His grandmother died and left him almost a million dollars and these two fruits started running around Key West."

"Fit right in there, huh?" Hanover said.

"No, not really," Collins said. "The word I got was they were into some pretty bad shit. Kid stuff and snuff films. They got tossed out on their ass just everywhere they went and then they just disappeared. It wasn't hard with all that money."

"I guess not," Hanover said.

"The point is," Collins said, "he disappeared again. After I found out who he was, and what these two were into, I put my foot on the gas. I figured Wheeler had to be Oswald's partner.

"In a way I'm surprised we haven't had another body yet. Maybe they're out there and we just don't know it. Maybe Wheeler's just being a lot more careful now that he's alone. I think Wheeler is just as bad as Oswald, maybe worse. He put a screwdriver through some guy's hand to land in Angola and that's just what he got caught for. He had a bunch of arrests that never got prosecuted. Perv stuff."

"And you can't find him?" Hanover asked.

"Not until today," Collins said. "I guess Amanda's out on the road, so I thought I'd give it to you so you can track her down and let her know. I mean, I'm all over this guy, but she should know anyway."

"Amanda? What's this got to do with her?"

"This guy's now living in a nice little apartment complex outside Alexandria," Collins said. "It's about a ten-minute drive from Manassas."

Hanover was puzzled.

Collins said, "That's where Amanda lives. It's no coincidence, Ben. She killed his partner. I think he's out to get her."

CHAPTER 41

Can I help you?"

He turned around. She was a dumpy little bitch and he didn't like her. She had no style with her drab pigtails and her bottle-thick glasses.

"I like these kittens," he said.

"They are nice."

No shit, dumpy bitch. Do you want to know why I need them? I bet you do. People always like to know my business, but I won't tell.

"I want two, and I can't make up my mind," he said, thoughtfully stroking his goatee. "One is for my little niece and one is for my nephew."

"That's a nice present."

"Their mother is kind of a bitch," he said, offhand. "But they're very nice little children."

He forced a smile and saw her looking. He ran his hand across the tight black synthetic material. Cycling pants. His fingertips swept across his waist and then danced lightly all the way up to where his nipple rings made little bumps in his suit. The rings were from Hubble. He always liked them.

"The orange-and-white one is nice," she said, stepping back a little.

"I like black, black and white," he said, turning his attention back to the kittens frolicking in their bed of wood chips. "I like the little black one there and the little white one there. You know, I'll take them both."

"Okay."

She took a quick breath and went back down the aisle, taking the long way to get to the back of the display. She took the kittens out and put them in a box.

He put on his wraparound sunglasses and snaked his way through the mall with his box of kittens. Outside was a big white Tahoe with tinted windows. At the rear, a shiny black bicycle waited on its rack.

The drive to the bitch's neighborhood was short. There was a park at the entrance to the development and that's where he parked his truck. The children liked the swing set there. The little girl spent most of her time on the swings. The boy liked to throw rocks at the metal slide. And there they were.

He got out and took down his bike, then walked with it and the box of kittens to a place in the grass. It was later in the day. People were everywhere. There were other bikers and runners, too. He wasn't the only one in tight clothes.

He sat down and crossed his legs, opening the box like a picnic basket, plucking out the kittens and setting them down on the grass where they immediately began to wrestle.

The girl came over first, then the boy.

"Would you like to pet them?" he asked. His voice trembled with excitement. His fingers danced across his chest.

"You look scary," said the boy.

"I do?" he said, pointing at his own chest.

"Yeah," the boy said, reaching down to pet the black one.

"We don't talk to strangers," the girl said.

"You're very good children," he said.

"I'm the good one," the girl said, "Teddy always gets in trouble. Dad says he's a $martass."

"Glenda," the boy said with a scowl, "you said my name."

"So what?" she said, picking the white one up and sticking her little finger into his mouth so he could bite it. She gave a little shriek but hung on.

He just looked at them. He didn't have to say anything. He knew that. Children loved kittens.

CHAPTER 42

The Indian summer was now gone. Cool air was dropping down on the Northeast from Canada. The sun hadn't shown its face in the last four days, and from the thickness of the gray morning clouds Jack supposed that today would make it five. The sound of wet tires kissing the street outside the Holiday Inn was muffled by the drizzle drifting down from the overburdened sky. Jack pulled his raincoat tight around his shoulders. The ache from the gunshot wound was nothing more now than a reminder of what he'd done to Tom Conner. The bleeding had stopped several days ago, alleviating the need for a bandage or a dressing.

He hurried across the street dodging irritable morning commuters with coffee cups in one hand and steering wheels in the other. One horn blared but Jack never looked back. He crossed the parking lot of an old diner with a stainless-steel shell and a red neon sign that proclaimed its name: TROY DINER.

Inside, Jack was greeted not only by the warmth, but the friendly sound of clinking plates and glasses and the rich smell of fresh coffee riding a wave of seared breakfast meat and steaming eggs. He took a paper off the rack and dropped two quarters on the counter. A plump middle-aged woman in a pink-and-white-striped outfit smiled and led him to a small booth along the window in the back. Jack ordered his breakfast and began turning through the pages of the *Albany Times-Union*. On page three his heart leapt into his throat. The headline read: ADIRONDACKS SLAYING: NO SUSPECTS. He reached into the pocket of his coat that he'd hung on a hook at the end of the booth, removed the ubiquitous blue bottle, and took several big gulps.

It had been a little more than a week since Racquet Lake. In the background of his mind, he recalled the events that occurred when he arrived back at Steffenhausers' that crazy night. He wasn't proud of lying to Beth again, but the bottom line was that it worked. After his arrival he had quickly convinced her and the old man that he had taken a spill in the woods and gashed open his shoulder. Instead of disturbing the Steffenhausers for a second time that night, he told them he'd gone to look for a twenty-four-hour pharmacy.

"You'd have to go all the way to Utica to find that," the old man had said.

"I know," Jack said. "I just kept going and going, you know, thinking the next town would have something."

Jack then insisted that Steffenhauser call the sheriff's department to say that it was a false alarm. Steffenhauser had. Luck was with him. The deputy in the area was still in the midst of sorting out a bloody bar fight outside of Inlet. He hadn't been able to respond immediately anyway. When Jack heard that news, it only furthered the growing sense that he was merely a player in some divine plan. He knew what he'd done was dangerous, maybe even stupid, but he couldn't help the sense that some pre-ordained fate was at work.

That was why now he was taking such care with his next victim.

Dante Pollard was a fifty-three-year-old three-time loser. Jack knew firsthand that human filth like Pollard never stopped. If they were caught and convicted of assault, or kidnapping, or rape, they did a few years at most. That was if they were convicted of everything they'd done. Unfortunately, this was all too rare.

In Jack's daughter's case Tupp had been convicted only of second-degree rape. After excluding the abduction van from evidence, Tupp's attorney was able to knock out almost everything that proved Tupp not only had raped his daughter, but was also the man who'd abducted and tortured her. Without the van there was almost no way to prove those other elements of the crime. It appeared to Jack that Dante Pollard had committed a very similar crime and like Tupp, he had been sentenced to less than four years for a crime that Jack thought deserved death.

Eugene Tupp. He would be out of jail in less than a year. Jack had to be careful. If he kept taking wild chances, he'd be caught. He'd seen it as a prosecutor—criminals becoming emboldened by their success, growing sloppy. If there was something at work in his subconscious, some part of him that secretly wanted all this to stop, Jack had to keep it at bay at least until Tupp got out.

His breakfast arrived.

"Here's your omelet, honey," the waitress said. "Broccoli and cheese."

Jack began to eat. He chewed mechanically and counted each mouthful. He would be certain to take at least ten. He had to stay strong. Between tallying the mouthfuls with a pen, he sketched out Pollard's home on the same napkin. He drew the trailer, the driveway, and the thick hedge along the road. He put an X where he'd be hiding. He added Pollard's car in the driveway, the moment he'd come home. Jack drew an arrow from the X to the car, then swallowed down number ten.

He spilled some coffee on the plan and then crumpled it up into an indecipherable wad. He left with most of the omelet uneaten, paid the bill, and crossed the street back to the hotel parking lot and his rental car. The rest of the day he spent working out of a conference room in the law offices of Hiscock & Barclay, finalizing the last few steps for the purchase of a nearby steam station by a power company from Baltimore. One of their lawyers politely asked him to dinner.

"No, but thank you," he said. He told the lawyer he wasn't hungry. That was the truth.

The trailer where Dante Pollard lived was in the country, a few miles outside the small town of Bennington, Vermont. Jack slowed down and rolled past. A single streetlight illuminated a battered black mailbox and a deep culvert beneath its harsh glow. It was the only light for miles and it marked the beginning of the long straight gravel drive that cut through the tall hedge Jack had drawn on the napkin. If you went slow enough, you could catch a glimpse of Pollard's seedy white trailer. It lay like a decaying cocoon in the midst of an overgrown field.

Jack stopped and closed his eyes for a moment. He imagined the sound of his own knocking on Pollard's door. He could see the startled expression on Pollard's face as the serial rapist saw the gun and began to feel the hot lead ripping through his body.

Jack opened his eyes. Soft yellow light came from a broken light fixture hanging by its bare wires just above the tattered screen door. A dirty silver tank of propane was attached to the trailer's side like a swollen tick, but the big gold Chevy Impala that normally presided over the scene from its patch of dirt was gone. Something was wrong.

CHAPTER 43

Jack felt his stomach heave. He quelled it and kept on going.

A quarter mile from Pollard's trailer he pulled off the rural highway and into a small abandoned gravel pit. In total silence he changed his clothes. There was a bottle of Maalox in his bag. He removed it and stuffed it into the pocket of his black jacket before tucking the Glock into its holster and walking furtively down the road. Except for the broken porch light, the trailer was dark. Pollard should be there, but he wasn't. Something told Jack to leave.

He had watched Pollard on and off for over a week. He knew the man worked during the day at a tree nursery in Bennington and would typically return to his trailer after a fast-food meal and a couple of hours in the video arcade at a nearby shopping mall. Not once had Jack seen him vary from that routine, so he was unsettled by Pollard's absence.

But Jack had prepared for this night in detail, so he decided to wait. He walked back down the rural road, cut up into Pollard's driveway and into the cover of the overgrown hedge. He was impervious to the cold drizzle and the wet leaves that soaked him as he pushed his way into the thick darkness of the foliage. Despite the weather, Jack felt warm and alive with anticipation. After a time his stomach began to hurt. Jack took a couple of swallows from the bottle in his jacket, then removed Janet's school photo from his wallet, the antidote that he could always count on to keep him going when he got nervous. He hunched over to protect the photo from the rain.

The sound of the gold Impala with its cracked muffler could be heard from a great way off. Jack jumped up, flexing his fingers. They had begun to chill beneath the damp leather of the gloves. He had plenty of time. He needed to relax. He put the school photo back in its place and took out his pistol. Maybe he could use Pollard's late arrival to his advantage. He remembered Tom Conner, skulking around the back of his house, getting the jump on Jack. Wouldn't it be best to kill Pollard before he could get back inside the trailer? It would.

When the car's headlights swung past the hedgerow, Jack slipped out of the thick cover and, crouching low in the high grass, made his way quickly toward the trailer. When the car came to its usual resting place, Jack was just twenty feet away, the Glock in his hand, ready to spring forward from beyond the glow of the porch light and the cover of the waist-high grass. But instead of going toward the trailer, when he got out of the car, Pollard looked nervously around and made for the Impala's enormous trunk. Pollard was dressed nicer than usual in dark slacks and a white button-down oxford shirt beneath a black leather bomber jacket. His large round eyes, long straight nose, and the gentle wisps of thinning brown hair gave him the look of a kindly if nervous schoolteacher.

Jack stayed where he was but kept his eyes just above

the tops of the overgrown grass, his gun directed at Pollard. If the man should see him, Jack would simply open fire. He preferred, however, to close the considerable gap, knowing that he was no marksman when it came to shooting the pistol. When Pollard reached the trunk, he turned his back to the night once again and Jack, his heart pounding, used the opportunity to sneak closer still. Pollard fidgeted with the lock and the trunk swung up, opening wide like the mouth of a cave, a small light winking from within. Jack was close enough now to strike. He half stood, raising the Glock above the level of the grass as the man bent down into the trunk.

Jack froze, unable to fire. His entire being was upended by the sight of Pollard as he removed from the trunk the frail, struggling form of a young teenage girl, bound and gagged with thick silvery bands of duct tape.

Jack was so stunned that he felt an enormous breath of air rush into his chest; he was momentarily helpless. The wide-eyed horror of the girl as she fought against her bonds and the look of wicked delight that lit Pollard's face registered in Jack's brain simultaneously, overloading his capacity to think or react.

Pollard turned and made his way toward the trailer, too consumed with the object of his perversions to notice Jack's dark form beyond the halo of light. Shaking, gasping for breath, Jack stood helpless, his limbs still frozen and useless as if he were in some terrible dream.

CHAPTER 44

Pollard was at the door now, and still Jack was unable to move. Horror and agony had overrun Jack's mind and incapacitated his body. He felt the terror of his own little girl, and now the girl before him, and every human being ever abused by a fiend like Pollard. The nightmare came back. The nightmare was real. The weight of guilt and despair—his own, this child's parents, and every other parent helpless in the struggle to keep their own safe from these monsters—was crushing him.

A cry of total madness escaped Jack, giving him away. Pollard spun in a panic, dropping the young girl into the mud. Pollard fumbled for his key, already in the lock, and struggled with it, cringing at the same time. Jack raced toward him. The door finally sprang open and Pollard fell into the blackness of the trailer. Jack leapt over the thin girl, landing on the top step.

Pollard had disappeared. The inside of the trailer was as dark as a pit. The light from the yellow bulb outside the door did nothing more than nick the edge of the blackness. Jack looked right, and then left. It was silent. He stood still, listening. His own breath came and went in noisy buckets. He tried to calm himself, but his heart was a rabid machine. He groped the wall for a switch, but found none.

Was there a noise? He thought he'd detected just the hint of a sound to his left, the scratching of paper or the wheels of a drawer. Jack crouched and aimed his gun, waiting. Not wanting to be a target himself, he eased into the darkness.

Something whistled past his head and he turned involuntarily as something shattered behind him. Jack spun back and fired wildly into the dark. He was promptly bowled over, knocked to the floor of the trailer by the frantic Pollard, scrambling for his life. Jack sensed him dash out of the trailer. He jumped to his feet, the gun still in his hands, and charged for the door. Pollard was sprinting across the gravel, past his car for the road. His left arm dangled uselessly. Jack aimed and fired. He missed.

He fired again and again. Flame flickered from the barrel of the Glock. Time began to crawl. He kept missing! And with each moment, Pollard got farther and farther away. Jack was acutely aware that he was running out of bullets.

Panic crept in, and then on his next shot Pollard spilled to the ground. Jack jumped down the steps and ran toward him. Pollard was in the grass now, its waving tips betraying him in the faint yellow light. He was crawling faster than most men could walk. Jack caught him and fired his gun into the middle of Pollard's back. Pollard stopped and then started again, then turned on Jack like a wild animal.

Jack fired again, this time striking Pollard squarely in the face. He aimed and pulled the trigger one more time. Nothing happened. Jack backed away and dropped to his knees, fighting back the urge to retch. After a time, he rose and took a few steps back toward Pollard. He had more bullets, but they were in the car. He took out his penlight and saw there was no need to worry. The last shot had exited through the back of Pollard's skull, leaving a massive jagged crater in its wake.

Jack tucked away his light and the gun and scoured the trampled grass looking for the shell casings. His limbs were filled with lead. He forced himself to walk back to the trailer. The girl. She lay bound, looking up at him glassy-eyed and whimpering pitifully from her place in the mud.

"Oh, no," Jack said, a new surge of emotion bursting forth from his core. "Oh, no. No, no, no. I won't hurt you."

He crouched over the girl and pulled her light trembling form tightly to his chest. She was sobbing uncontrollably beneath the tape. Jack shook his head and stroked her muddy hair. Tears began to course down his cheeks.

"No," he said, "don't. It's okay. You're all right. I won't hurt you. You're all right now."

Jack held her for a time that seemed eternal, gulping down his own bile and whispering softly to her. He rocked her until he realized she had either fallen asleep or more likely relapsed into some drug-induced state. Jack lifted himself and the girl off the step. His paternal instincts told him she was better off sleeping in her bonds than enduring the trauma of their removal. He stepped inside the trailer, his flat-soled shoes smearing the blood from Pollard's arm across the floor as he searched for the light switch. He found it and then lay the girl down on a couch. It was worn but clean looking, and over its back lay an afghan fastidiously folded in the manner of a grandmother. Jack pulled the blanket free and covered the girl.

He then set to work scouring the area for the rest of his shell casings. The mindless task gave him the opportunity to consider what should be done. The safest thing would be to leave the girl and call the police from a pay phone, but Jack wasn't going to do that. When she awoke, it would be someplace safe and warm, not alone the way his own daughter must have been in the prison of a filthy fishing shack, not bound and gagged and wondering if the dark angel who had delivered her was nothing more than a dream. So where could he take her?

The answer came to Jack as he extracted the seventeenth and final shell casing from the mud beneath the steps. He stuffed the bag of brass casings into his pocket and went back into the trailer to retrieve the unconscious girl. She was an easy burden at first, but by the time he reached his rental car Jack's back was aching from the strain. He denied himself the relief of setting her down until he could put her in the backseat of the black Town Car.

Free from her extra weight, Jack nimbly stripped off his outer layer of clothes on the spot and stuffed them along with the casings into a garbage bag he'd taken from the trunk. Finally he returned the pistol and holster to their metal case, shut the trunk, and got behind the wheel. He stopped briefly to dispose of the garbage bag in a Dumpster behind a darkened pharmacy, then made his way through town, driving cautiously and heading for the Bennington Emergency Medical Center.

Jack pulled up outside the sandy colored single-story building and watched. He felt his agitation double. There was nothing to see. The glass double doors leading to the inside were frosted white. Outside, there was no sign of life. The girl stirred in the backseat and Jack felt a bolt of panic. His plan was predicated on her unconscious state. But after a gentle groan she turned over and dropped off again with only her head visible beneath the soft covering.

Jack decided to move quickly. He hurried out of the car and removed the girl as gently as he could from the backseat. As he marched across the parking lot in through the emergency doors, Jack hoisted the girl's form up in front of his face. The doors swung open with a loud rattle, revealing a young nurse sitting behind a desk chatting with a middle-aged doctor who was leaning against the wall with his hands in his pockets. There were no other patients to be seen.

Jack rushed toward them, screaming.

"Help me! She's not breathing!"

The nurse froze, but the doctor stood abruptly and Jack pushed the girl into his arms, spinning instantly and running back through the open doors.

He raced to the car, jumped in, and squealed out of the lot. As he swerved around the corner, Jack stole a quick glance back. He cursed and stamped on the accelerator. The nurse had run out of the medical center. He had seen the pale glow of her face. She had seen his car.

There was a reckless voice inside him that didn't even care. He'd killed another monster. He only wished he could get them all.

CHAPTER 45

He backed the plunger away from his vein, filling the syringe with his own blood. The amber liquid swirled with angry red clouds until it all turned to Mars. He shut his eyes and he pumped the liquid joy back into his body, letting it sweep over him. Time passed. Pleasant floating, naked on an undulating wave. Everything was fine.

Then he heard the little brat's words. They rang like a bell.

"You look *scary*."

Scary. He went to the mirror and looked. His limbs were thin and white like a Grecian statue, shaved clean of the disgusting black forest of hair. The way Hubble liked it.

He toyed with his nipple rings, then lifted his arms. Only the faintest hint of stubble. Very clean. Nothing scary.

He leaned toward the mirror. His face was sharp, but Hubble said he was beautiful. He traced a pointed fingernail across the high cheekbone, out, and down along the hatchet edge of his jaw. Eyes like tar pits. His nose, surgically reduced to the thinnest, the straightest line. The way Hubble liked.

Hubble was gone now. The bitch. She shot him. Now it was her turn to feel pain.

Hubble. The pointed goatee was his idea, too.

"Moloch," Hubble told him. "That's you."

Moloch. The first angel Satan called to arms.

He grinned at himself, still floating, hearing Hubble. Then a frown. His teeth. They were dull. The stumps of hewn trees.

"You look scary."

He would give them scary. He staggered into the kitchen, his feet slapping the linoleum. A toolbox rested beside the water heater in a dusty utility closet. Hammers. Nails. A hacksaw. He grinned. Tools he could use for fun.

A small file.

He took it and returned to the mirror. Still naked and white and smooth, still beautiful. He pulled his top lip up and away, his red gums grinning back, angry. The white teeth sitting like harmless lumps. Like little children.

Sharp. Sharp and *scary.* They didn't even know. He'd give them scary.

The file rasped fragments of tooth onto his tongue and dusted his lip. White flakes nestled in his black beard. A distant sensation of pain. That made him mad. He worked harder, faster, the smell of burning bone.

He'd burn their bones. He'd make them pay for this pain. He'd give them scary. He leaned back and curled his top lip up and away. A single stalactite, wicked and dangerous. Scary.

He went back to work. Bone dust everywhere. The

pain excruciating, but somehow delicious in its distance. Time blinking with pain.

Done.

He smiled. Look at him now. A pumpkin smile. Two sharp points where his canines had been. Empty blackness on either side. He stretched his mouth open wide, then let it ease back into a grin.

"Scary," he said.

He would show them.

CHAPTER 46

Amanda stared frowning at the damp sandy gravel. Tom Conner's body had already been taken away. A crisp breeze blew through the pine trees overhead. They swayed in the blue sky, hushing the staccato cry of a red squirrel claiming its territory. Thick white puffs of cloud drifted past, casting dark shadows on the green mountains in the distance.

Amanda took the pictures that were handed to her and held them up in the morning sunlight, sifting through them and imagining the scene as it was first found. McGrew watched her, and so did Lieutenant Briggs. After a few moments Amanda turned to the state trooper and handed him back the photos.

"The slugs were from a Glock?" she said. Despite the sun, there she could see a hint of her breath in the chilly mountain air.

"Right," Briggs said. "No markings."

"And you found no traces of anything in this entire area?" She shivered and pulled her jacket close. On the back were the yellow letters: FBI. "No shell casings, no footprints, no blood, no fibers?"

Briggs shook his head. "Our lab people are pretty good, Agent Lee," he said. His voice was thick like his eyebrows. Amanda would have liked him but for the obvious deference he paid to McGrew.

Briggs was relatively young, but he already had the air of a seasoned cop. He also had the air of a climber, a political animal looking to gain favor. If Briggs hadn't mentioned McGrew's uncle a dozen times then he hadn't mentioned him once. Amanda didn't go for that. Still, his size and deportment commanded a certain degree of respect.

"I'm sure they are," she said.

"They had a heavy rain the night we think he was killed," Briggs said. "That was more than two weeks ago. We didn't get called but just two days ago. And then, like I said, I heard about Detective McGrew's investigation from a buddy of mine who works in the governor's office. His uncle, the congressman, just happened to be telling the governor about Detective McGrew's working with you folks down in Washington and . . ."

"Is your uncle a congressman?" Amanda asked McGrew.

Briggs's face turned red and he looked at her uncertainly.

"I'm kidding," she said. "I didn't mean anything. We're lucky you called. With something like this, every day counts. Every hour."

Amanda knelt down again, fingering the spot where the shotgun slug had been removed.

"Two shots were fired," she said, almost to herself, then she looked up at Briggs. "But the other slug is definitely missing?"

Briggs looked around at the endless swaying trees.

"That slug could have gone anywhere. It could be

down there in the lake if he shot in the air. If it was any-where close," he said, "I'd have it. Believe me."

"How many hospitals are . . . within a hundred miles?" she asked.

Briggs looked from Amanda to McGrew and said, "The nearest medical center is in Old Forge. We checked that out already."

"Okay," Amanda said, "that's a good start. Maybe that slug is in the lake, but maybe it ended up in our man. Can you have your people find everything within a hundred miles and start checking? I could get my own agents to do it, but it would take time and I'm sure your people know the area better."

"I'll get my people on it," Briggs said. "I got the word right from the governor's office to help any way I can."

"Great," she said. "We're looking for a blond man, medium build, straight hair and glasses. Right, Mc-Grew?"

"Yes," McGrew said. He seemed foggy from driving all night. Amanda liked him that way.

"We'll be at that place across the street, the Seventh Lake Inn," she said to Briggs. "I want to poke around town, talk to some of the locals. I'll give you my cell phone number."

"Won't work up here," Briggs said.

"Anywhere?" she asked.

"Up on that ridge," Briggs said. "That's about it."

"All right," she said, "I'll check back there every two hours. If you find anything, leave me a message, please."

Briggs nodded and started around the side of the house for his cruiser, issuing orders as he went.

Amanda turned to McGrew and said, "You better get some rest."

"Oh no," he said. "I just need some coffee. I'm coming with you."

"Okay, I want to change," she said. She was wearing a pair of jeans and a sweatshirt beneath her FBI windbreaker. "Let's go get checked into the inn. You can get some coffee and we can get started. I want to talk to Mrs. Conner."

CHAPTER 47

There were no framed pictures hanging on the knotty-pine wall, so Amanda laid her children's pictures out on the small desk by the window then unpacked her things. She took a quick shower in the soft lake water and changed into a dark pantsuit, strapping on her USP 40 underneath the blazer.

Downstairs, there was a small gift shop just off the lobby. McGrew wasn't there yet, so she wandered in and began to poke around. There was an imitation flintlock pistol that she knew Teddy would love. She picked it up and also a small box of red caps that he could load one at a time to make the gun pop. For Glenda she found a necklace made out of small wooden beads. In the middle hung a little hand-carved black bear. Amanda tried to roust up a feeling of satisfaction. She forced her lips up into a smile. No use.

When she came out of the gift shop, McGrew was waiting for her. He stood, smiling his crooked smile at the young woman behind the desk.

Amanda paid for her souvenirs.

"What's that?" McGrew asked.

Amanda felt her face grow warm. She was supposed to

be a professional on assignment. "Just some things," she said. "I was waiting for you."

McGrew just took out his keys, shrugged, and said, "Okay, let's go."

Mrs. Conner lived down a long oiled dirt road that ran along a power line. It was a rickety two-story place with rough-cut pine siding that had faded itself nearly white. The red tin roof had faded, too. It looked a hundred years old. The front yard was mostly sand, although a few tall sprigs of grass struggled up. Two big Dobermans were chained to a massive pine tree whose trunk had been wrapped in sheet metal to keep from being girdled by the crazed animals.

"Fucking mutts," McGrew said over the din and the dust.

Amanda's attention was drawn to movement in one of the two second-floor windows above. The old woman stood behind the glass clutching a blanket up to her with one hand and holding a bottle of whiskey in the other. She was practically naked.

"What the fuck?" McGrew said.

Amanda pretended not to notice. She climbed the steps and knocked on the front door. No one came. She knocked again, louder this time. Still no one came. Suddenly the old door sprang open and there she stood, without the blanket, without anything but her bottle. Her eyes were blackened from two-day-old mascara. Her face was swollen from tears.

"Leave me the hell alone!" she yelled. "This is my home and you can't come here like this!"

"Mrs. Conner," Amanda said after she found her voice, "we came to help."

"You came to laugh," she said. "You came like the others. They laughed at me. They laughed at him, and him dead. But he never did it. He never did nothing. He was my son. My son. Now you leave me the hell alone."

The door crashed closed. The dogs snarled and bayed and sprayed their slobber.

"Fuck," said McGrew.

This time Amanda barely heard him.

Back at the inn Amanda put in a call to the county sheriff's office in nearby Hamilton. The officer in charge of their sex offender registry hadn't had a request for information in the last two months. They spent the afternoon canvassing the nearby towns, from Old Forge all the way up to Blue Mountain, splitting up and asking merchants and waitresses if they'd seen a blond man with straight hair, maybe glasses, about two weeks ago, traveling alone. They were eyed with suspicion, even after they explained who they were. It seemed hopeless.

At six o'clock they stopped at the Burketown Diner for some food. Amanda carefully wiped off her fork and knife on a paper napkin, then ate her salad. When her grilled chicken sandwich arrived, she fished it out of its sea of mayonnaise and wiped it clean, too, before cutting it into small pieces. She looked up and noticed an older man in coveralls and a dusty John Deere cap staring at her. She smiled and he smiled back.

She went back to her food, trying not to notice the way McGrew was attacking two greasy-looking chili dogs smothered in jalapeños and onions. A paper boat of cheese fries and a root beer float stood by ready to follow them in.

"Not planning on taking another run, I see," she said.

McGrew licked his fingers and with his mouth full of dog said, "No, I'm going to sleep."

"Good," she said. "You're human."

McGrew smiled and shook his head.

"I'm okay," he said. "This is all I care about, that's all."

"This is it?" she asked.

"Yeah," he said. "Yeah, it is. I got a girl, you know, but nothing too serious really. I'm a cop. That's it. I want this guy.

"I've had some big cases, you know," McGrew said, straightening his back. "Big down on Long Island. I had this one case where this guy, he stabbed his wife's boyfriend, and I was the one who found the cigarette butts where he stood around waiting for her to leave so he could stab the guy . . . The fucking guy just stood there waiting . . . But this is different. This is like silver-screen material."

"Like Magnum PI?" she said.

"No, that's TV," he said. "I'm talking like the big screen. I'm talking like Bogey. Eastwood."

Back at the inn, Amanda phoned home. There was no answer. She called Parker's cell phone. He had the kids out for pizza and miniature golf. She started to remind him that it was a school night, but then shut her mouth. The kids got on and said they loved her. She loved them back. This wasn't so bad. They were happy. She was working. They'd all be together soon.

She stood by the window for a minute looking down at their pictures on the desk. Outside, the sun was going down. The water on Seventh Lake was still, like a pool of oil. It was growing cold.

Amanda sighed and changed into her running shorts. She pulled her sweatshirt on and descended the pine staircase into the lobby. It was empty. Outside, she stretched and then began her six miles down Route 28. It was a good workout. The strong fresh scent of mountain pine brought her no pleasure, but she did feel a growing sense of pride as she climbed first up and then down the long hills. She was growing stronger.

She needed it.

It was still dark the next morning when the phone rang in her room. It was McGrew.

"I got a call from Briggs. We have to go," he said.

"Go?" she asked. "What?"

She squinted and fumbled for the clock. It was five A.M.

"We've got a witness," he said.

"A witness?"

"A girl."

"A girl? Where?"

"Not here," McGrew said. "Pack your things. He killed another one. There's a girl in Vermont. She saw him."

CHAPTER 48

Jack wound his way up the tree-lined hill to Crestwood. He passed the spot where he'd seen Beth running so many months ago. He looked at the clock on the dashboard and heaved a sigh. He was early.

It had been almost six months, and finally Janet's doctor said it was all right to see her again. His hands sweated as he closed the car door. The air was still and heavy, the musty aroma of decaying autumn mixing with the scent of fresh-cut grass. A pair of orderlies in clean white uniforms strolled by, smoking cigarettes and chatting. From somewhere behind the building Jack could hear the excited squeals of a children's ball game. He stuffed his hands deep into the black leather jacket. The air had turned suddenly cool. A shudder danced up his spine.

At the steps leading into the institution he hesitated. A huge cheer, muted by the distance it had to travel, went up from someplace in back, drawing an involuntary smile from the corners of his mouth.

After a deep breath he mounted the front steps and passed through the doors. Inside, the lobby wasn't empty, as it was most afternoons during the week. A white-haired couple sat in the corner, side by side, reading old magazines and glancing nervously his way with glassy eyes before returning politely to their outdated reading materials. Jack hesitated, then rang the silver bell on the reception desk, feeling foolish at the sound while other people were with him in the room.

He looked back into the office to find himself the subject of Dr. Steinberg's powerful stare. After a moment, she blinked behind her glasses and pressed her lips tightly together as if to choke back any emotions. She opened the door with a curt but not unfriendly greeting and led Jack down the familiar back hall. When she finally came to a stop Jack recognized the door. It led into the same room he'd entered six months before. Dr. Steinberg reached out with her diminutive hand and grasped his forearm with surprising strength.

"Now, I don't want you to expect anything," she said. "If she remains calm in your presence—if—then you can talk quietly to her. Quietly."

The older woman opened the door and thrust him into the room. Jack couldn't help looking back at her anxious eyes, magnified by her glasses, peering intently at him. She made a whisking motion at him and he turned toward his daughter. She was sitting much the same as she'd been six months earlier, and Jack couldn't stop the dread from filling his stomach and weighing him down. Outside the window the colors were dimmer now; even the towering spruce trees seemed a muted green, weak and almost gray like the muted light from the sky.

Janet's skin had a bluish cast that was ghoulish. Her once golden hair had faded to a mousy brown. The circles under her young eyes had deepened and she had certainly lost more weight. The joints of her bones protruded grotesquely and still the welted scars burned angrily on her bare arms. Jack felt bile rushing up the back of his throat.

"Janet," he whispered involuntarily.

She turned her head his way and her big brown eyes widened with recognition while at the same time welling up with an immense sadness. Jack took a step closer.

CHAPTER 49

Twice during the trip Amanda advised McGrew to slow down on hairpin turns. Otherwise she was all for the breakneck speed as they raced through the twisting mountain roads, then down Route 87 to Troy and finally into Vermont. The cell phone reception was lousy, but Amanda was finally able to get through to have the agents from the Albany field office turn around and meet them in Bennington.

When they arrived, the nurse from the medical center was set up and ready to go. After a few courteous formalities with the chief of police, Amanda walked into the interview room with McGrew by her side. The nurse sat by herself, still in her blue scrubs, her long blond hair spilling free from its bun. She looked up and rubbed the weariness from her eyes. Amanda introduced herself as well as McGrew and then asked what happened.

"We were just talking," the nurse said, "when this crazy guy comes in yelling about his daughter not breathing. Well, we didn't know. We get some real nutty stuff late at night like that, it's not a big town or anything, but we do. So we jump up—"

"Did you see the man?" Amanda asked.

"I guess I did," she said. "They asked me to describe

him. I don't know if I really can. I mean, it happened fast."

"Would you recognize him if you saw him?" McGrew asked.

The nurse said, "I think so."

"Go on," Amanda said.

"So, Doug, Dr. Case, he catches the girl that this guy kind of just throws at him and he sees the tape on her mouth and he yells at me to go follow the guy and I did."

"And?"

"Well, all I saw was this black Town Car, shiny, racing around the corner. That's all I saw."

"It looked new?" McGrew asked.

"Yes."

"Many people have a car like that around here?" he asked.

"What do you mean?"

"I mean you don't see a lot of black Town Cars," McGrew said. "People around here drive mostly Jeeps and trucks and Volvos and outdoor woodsy things, right?"

"Kind of."

"I'm going to get on that," McGrew said. Amanda nodded and he left the room.

The nurse didn't know much more than that, but Amanda went through it a couple more times before she asked, "Would you be willing to try to identify this man in a lineup if we can find him?"

"A lineup?"

"Yes."

"Do I have to?"

"No," Amanda said. "I can't make you. But this man committed a very serious crime."

"He killed a guy," the nurse said.

"Yes."

"I heard the guy he killed was the one who kidnapped that girl," she said.

"We don't know exactly what happened," Amanda said. "But we think the man you saw killed Dante Pollard and others."

"Well," she said. "I guess I could try."

"It's very important," Amanda said, but she could see that the nurse doubted her. In the back of her mind she knew the most important witness would be the girl.

Amanda interviewed the doctor as well. He was against trying to pinpoint the man in a lineup. He didn't say so, but Amanda had the distinct impression that the doctor felt that their blond killer was justified.

Next, she went to the hospital. The teenage girl was with her parents and apparently doing well. The father was a Lutheran minister and very much in favor of having the girl do a lineup to help identify the blond-haired man despite the circumstances. The mother was less pleased with the prospect, but Amanda watched her wringing her hands and she knew who made the decisions.

If they could get a positive ID on the guy from a lineup, Amanda felt their chances were good for a conviction. When she got back to the police station, McGrew bolted out of an office down the hall and came her way. He was slapping a piece of paper with the backs of his fingers.

"Wait until you see this," he said. "I got on the computer and found all the rental car companies within a hundred miles that rent Town Cars. Then I got into their databases and started going through, searching for black Town Cars rented in the last week."

"And?"

"I cross-checked their driver's licenses for a male, blond hair, five eight to six feet," McGrew said. His crooked smile was blazing. "I got him. Guy's name is Jack Ruskin."

CHAPTER 50

"Daddy?" Janet said. Her voice was quiet and raspy.

Emotion filled Jack's throat. Tears blurred his vision, but still he saw that she was holding out her arms, opening them for him to come near. In a panic he looked back at Dr. Steinberg, who was still watching from the door. He sensed the doctor's amazement, and was relieved when she nodded and motioned for him to go ahead. Jack crossed the room and sat down next to Janet on the nondescript couch. Slowly he reached for her and held her to him. A stifled sob escaped him. Beneath the cotton hospital dress, her emaciated form was a frail jumble of angles.

He had to restrain himself from holding her too tightly. His fingers trembled as he stroked the hair on the back of her head. Tears spilled freely down his cheeks. The feeble hug she gave him sent an electric charge through his frame. And then, just as abruptly as she had emerged from her catatonic state, she was gone. Her arms dropped lifelessly to her sides and her eyes grew vacant. Jack struggled with the urge to squeeze her to him, to rip her from this place and run off with her, to reclaim her for his own. Instead he kissed her cool forehead and let her gently slump back into the couch.

He kissed her gently on the forehead again, then looked apprehensively toward the door for what he expected to be Dr. Steinberg's glare. But her expression was plainly mystified, and that might have explained the uncharacteristically gentle signal for him to come away. Jack rose, looking long and hard at his daughter before quietly leaving the room.

In the hallway she grasped both Jack's arms in her diminutive grip.

"That was marvelous," she whispered, as if not to disturb the inert girl on the other side of the door.

"Is she better?" Jack asked, realizing that his mind had jumped many months into the future. He was using the word in the sense of a total cure.

Dr. Steinberg looked up at him through her thick round glasses and blinked in surprise.

"I'm . . . I am surprised," she said. "She's made some progress, especially over the last two weeks. I thought there might be some indication of recognition, something in her eyes. But to have her say your name . . . to have her open her arms to you? That was . . ." The older woman shook her head.

"When can I see her again?" Jack asked anxiously.

"Come on," she said, "let's talk. We can sit in my office. I want you to understand how we got to this point. I want you to know what it's going to take to keep things going this way."

Jack followed her through a maze of hallways to a corner office that looked out over the fading remnants of the rose garden. He sat listening attentively as Dr. Steinberg recited for him the litany of treatments Janet had undergone and would continue to undergo. The drugs and the different psychotherapeutic methods meant little to him, but he knew they were essential to the healing process.

"I have to tell you that after your last visit, I thought we'd lost her."

Jack drove to the beach.

The sky, which had been bland and bleak only an hour before, was now darkening and seemed to reflect Jack's mood of boiling uncertainty and hope. A front was moving in quickly and the ocean, too, was roiling and capped with frothy white spray. The beach was abandoned and that was just what Jack wanted. He pulled his jacket close and hunched down over his shoes as he walked along on the edge of the wet sand. A seagull, its feathers ruffled by the wind, refused to fly but made way for Jack with a grating screech that barely registered in his brain.

Jack turned and headed back down the beach toward his car. Before he got there, a rent in the clouds opened the sky and a thick beam of sun lit the drab beach all around him. Jack looked up, pushed a tangle of hair from his face, and blinked.

On the way home he called Beth from his car. From the sound of her voice, he knew something bad had happened.

"Jack," she said. She was frantic. She was whispering. She was nearly hysterical. "Jack, the police are here, the FBI. I told them you weren't here, but they're waiting. They're in the driveway."

CHAPTER 51

Amanda and McGrew sat together in his car outside Ruskin's house.

McGrew looked at his watch and grinned. He was certain from the way the girlfriend acted that Jack Ruskin would be back soon. She was pretty, and it gave McGrew a newfound respect for his quarry Ruskin. He didn't mind waiting. He didn't have anything else to do but check an empty answering machine or eat Chinese by himself on the billionaire's deck. The crime scene tech never did call. Maybe she mixed up his number.

Women weren't on the top of his list anyway. His last real woman was a waitress from Denny's. They went home in the early-morning hours to be together. Afterward they shared a Marlboro Light. It was good. The next day he brought her a dozen roses wrapped in green tissue paper, brought them right to the restaurant. For some bizarre reason she didn't like that.

Women, he knew, had a hard time understanding his intensity. One day he'd find one who did understand, a woman who'd lay down and die for him. Until that time he'd have to wade through the chaff.

McGrew was feeling pretty good. No question, this was like a major Hollywood production. He was dogging the bad guy with a pretty damn good-looking redhead, racing through the mountains. Working through the night. Screeching his tires. Flying down here in a helicopter.

And behind the whole thing were his cunning and his connections. He was a fucking star. Amanda was practically blown away by what he did with tracking down the Town Car. She was still talking to the doctor when he was hot on the trail. It was like a scene you'd see Al Pacino playing, him battering the keyboard, bullying the rental car people, and cross-referencing things like a fucking computer genius.

After that was when he hit her with his really big idea.

"A helicopter," she said dully. "Right."

"I mean it," McGrew had said.

"Where in hell do you expect me to get a helicopter from?"

"I expect the Bureau has one around here somewhere. If not," he said, "I know a few people in the New York State police . . . If they got a call from a federal agent in a big interstate case . . .

"Okay," he said. "I'll make you a deal. You use your contacts to get us a federal subpoena for Ruskin so we can pop him into a lineup, and I'll get the copter."

They had been airborne, with the subpoena, by two o'clock.

McGrew was thinking about getting out to take a stroll and having himself a cigarette when a green Saab convertible rolled into the driveway. Without a word between them, McGrew and Amanda got out.

Ruskin—it was him—turned off the engine and got out. The girlfriend burst from the front door of the house and yelled his name.

"Mr. Ruskin," Amanda said, "I'm Special Agent Lee from the Federal Bureau of Investigation. You need to come with us."

"I'm Detective McGrew," McGrew said, leveling his gun at Jack, "Suffolk County homicide."

"Jack," the girlfriend said. She was eyeing McGrew's gun. "What's happening?"

"Everything's fine," Ruskin said, "just like I said. It's a misunderstanding. Everything's fine."

The girlfriend ran to him and Ruskin hugged her and kissed her forehead. He turned to Amanda and said, "My attorney will be here in a few minutes and we can go wherever you want. You're on notice, and she's a witness that I want my attorney present before you ask me anything."

McGrew pursed his lips. After an arrest in New York State, if the suspect asked for an attorney, anything he said to the police from that point on would be inadmissible as evidence in court.

"Please get in the car, Mr. Ruskin," Amanda said.

"You have to read me my rights first," Jack said. "If you're arresting me, you have to give me a Miranda warning."

"You're not under arrest, hotshot," McGrew said. He didn't bother to fight back a grin.

From her jacket, Amanda removed their federal subpoena and handed it to Jack.

"What's this?" he asked, peering at the document in the fading afternoon light.

"We're taking you to Vermont," Amanda said, "for a lineup. This subpoena gives us the power to transport you across state lines."

"By force if necessary," McGrew said.

Jack looked up from the paper to Amanda, to Mc-Grew's gun, and back to Amanda.

"My attorney," he said.

Amanda shook her head and said, "You don't need an attorney, Mr. Ruskin. You're not under arrest. You don't have the right to an attorney. This is a federal subpoena."

"Not yet," McGrew said. "Now get in."

Jack looked at his girlfriend. Her face was tight with anxiety, her mouth a perfect circle of disbelief.

"Everything's fine," he said. "Just wait for me. I'll be back and everything will be fine. It will all work out. Trust me."

CHAPTER 52

They were headed for a private airfield no more than fifteen minutes from Jack's home. The jackass named McGrew couldn't sit still. The skin on his scrawny neck burned red below his hairline. He was excited. The woman kept her eyes on the road and her mouth closed. They said almost nothing between them. It was the man who spoke when Jack finally collected himself enough to ask where he was being taken.

"We've got a couple of witnesses in Bennington who are gonna ID you for that Pollard guy you wasted," McGrew said, but only after turning around to face him.

Jack felt suddenly naked and it must have showed.

"Yeah," McGrew said, "we know about Pollard and all the rest. Let's see, there was Dayton and Cincinnati and Pittsburgh and Racquet Lake . . . but the one you did out in Suffolk County, Lawrence Brice? That was your big fuckup. See, that was when you came into McGrew's backyard and McGrew hasn't come across a homicide yet that he hasn't solved.

"Did I tell you that about me, Amanda?" he asked the FBI agent.

She merely glanced at him.

"You're probably gonna get the death penalty," Mc-Grew said. His manner was cheery.

Jack said no more, but it took all of his training to do so. Years ago he had marveled at the information criminal suspects would volunteer to police, even after they'd been given their Miranda warning stating not only that they had the right to remain silent, but that anything they did say would be used against them. Now, for the first time, he understood why more times than not those suspects spilled their guts. He felt for himself the inexorable compulsion to talk.

Jack was still contemplating that when they turned off the road and through a gate in the chain-link fence that protected the private airfield. A helicopter sat idly on the tarmac surrounded by a bevy of news trucks and a handful of cars. People with lights, cameras, and microphones sprang to life at the sight of the unmarked car.

"Just stop right here," McGrew said. He directed the FBI agent to a spot on the tarmac that would force them to walk through the throng of cameras on their way to the helicopter.

"What the hell is this?" Amanda asked.

"Oh, a little welcoming committee," McGrew said, his face dropping all signs of emotion.

"McGrew," she said, "what the hell?"

"I just thought . . ."

Jack saw Amanda's stare. She parked the car where he had indicated but followed at a distance as McGrew tugged Jack through the swarm. Jack buried his face in his arm under the glare of the lights. McGrew took him to the helicopter and loaded him in. Amanda followed and sat across from Jack with a straight face while Mc-Grew went back out to address the crowd.

After a murmur of questions, Jack heard McGrew say, "Right now he is merely being detained and transported under order of a federal judge. I'm sorry, but that's all the questions for now. Thank you."

Jack felt his stomach lurch as the helicopter rose and swung about before setting off.

CHAPTER 53

With an air of importance that belied his stature, the rotund officer assembled all of them in a line. Jack was second to last. His gut was knotted and he felt the urge to vomit as the line began to snake through a side door and into another room. He followed the others out onto a small stage and stopped. A small bank of lights shone brightly down on them from the ceiling. In front of the stage was a broad rectangular piece of glass.

Jack squinted but could only make out the vague shapes beyond the smoky glass. Five or six people sat there looking at him. They were all adults. Jack remembered the nurse and the doctor from the medical center. It could be either one. If he had to venture a guess, he would say the doctor. As a former prosecutor, he knew people didn't like to be witnesses to lineups. Most people didn't want to get involved. Many were afraid that a convicted violent criminal might want revenge.

McGrew's voice suddenly exploded from a speaker in the wall. It had a canned quality to it, but the arrogant bravado was unmistakable.

"Number five! Step forward and turn to the right."

Jack was numb. He looked down at his feet at the large number painted in red beneath his feet. He was number five. He did as he was told, forcing his eyes to stay straight ahead despite the desperate need to peer out through the glass.

"Turn to the left."

Jack did.

"Now turn and face the glass and please say 'she's not breathing' in a loud voice."

Jack did as he was told and was rewarded with nearly four minutes of silence. The other men shifted restlessly behind him, and behind the glass he could see the heads of the people conferring with one another.

"Number five, you can go back into the lineup."

Jack returned and stood sick on his feet while three other men in the lineup were put through different variations of his own performance. Then they came back to him. He was told to step forward and repeat his cry for help on the night he saved the girl.

"Louder than the last time, number five."

Jack was called back one more time before they were finally led back into the waiting room. He looked boldly around him now, disdainful of the suspicious looks that the men cast about among one another. He was determined not to look or act guilty. Even though he knew it wouldn't matter in a court of law whether he had appeared to be innocent or guilty, it mattered to him.

Twenty minutes later they were regrouped and led back into the lineup room. This time the assemblage behind the glass included a smaller shape. Jack felt the knot in his stomach give a violent twist. It had to be the girl. He recalled McGrew's boast of an eyewitness, but until now, he hadn't made the connection between the detective's words and the girl. It was unthinkable.

His sickness was suddenly replaced by sheer outrage. How could she do this? And more important, how could the parents of the child he saved allow her to do this? If only someone had done for him what he had done for the people behind that glass. He wanted to shout that at them, now, while they could hear him. He felt the words boiling in his chest, ready to burst out in a torrent of indignation.

Time took on a strange quality for Jack. In one way it seemed to stand still, and yet when he was led back to the waiting room and then finally to the interrogation room it seemed only a matter of seconds before the door opened again. Jack lifted his head up off the narrow table at which he sat. It was the woman named Amanda, but instead of being the preamble to a dramatic entrance for her partner, she merely turned and shut the door behind her.

"We appreciate your cooperation, Mr. Ruskin," she said. Her voice was soft and steady. "You can go home now."

Jack thought he would burst.

"What?" he asked, then added quickly, "—happened? What happened?"

Then he forced his brow into a scowl and said, "This whole thing is an outrage."

He knew he sounded ridiculous, but his lawyer's instincts had kicked in.

Amanda looked at him from behind a red strand of hair with her piercing blue eyes. She wore the weary expression of an athlete after a hard loss.

"We both know better than that, Mr. Ruskin," she

said, raising her chin. "But the witnesses were unable to identify you . . . or so they said."

Jack had to bite down hard on his tongue to keep his face from flooding with relief.

CHAPTER 54

Amanda and McGrew sat at an old plank table by the window. They were nestled with two other couples in the front room of a small Victorian house that had been turned into a restaurant. On the inside wall, sticks of apple wood snapped in the white marble fireplace.

"It's not even close to being over," McGrew said. He emptied the rest of his Budweiser into his glass. Beer foamed up and over the rim, then ran down the seam of the plank and dripped on Amanda's leg.

She shifted in her seat and looked at him through the smoke. What he said didn't even merit a response. She was stuck in Vermont with an idiot who smoked. She wanted to pay the check, get on her jogging clothes, and burn every bit of crap she'd heard today out of her mind.

"He'll do it again," she said, putting down the fork and waving the smoke from her eyes. "It's his nature. He wants these people so bad that it burns his heart. And we'll be watching."

McGrew smirked at her. She felt her face flush.

"What is that thing, anyway, McGrew?" she asked.

"What thing?" he said, taken aback, his eyebrows raised.

"That, that thing right here," she said, flicking her

finger at the patch of skin beneath her own lip but meaning his.

"This?" he said, stroking the little triangle of facial hair beneath his lower lip. "A lot of guys have these."

"Oh," she said.

"But Ruskin's smart," she said. "He'll wait."

"By then, we'll either be doing this as a hobby or working another case." McGrew examined the patch of hair in the mirror behind Amanda's head. She stifled a giggle. She'd gotten to him.

"You're the one who said it wasn't close to being over," she said.

"It's not," he said. "It's not because I say it's not. McGrew has connections and if you can't bring McGrew to the mountain, you just bring the mountain to McGrew."

Amanda looked at him.

"Do you always talk about yourself in the third person?"

"The what?"

"Third person. You know, first person is *I*. Second person is *you*. You talk about yourself as if it's not yourself. It's just very odd. I only thought athletes with subnormal IQs did that."

McGrew nodded, felt for the patch beneath his lip, stopping in midstride. He smiled. "McGrew understands."

"Well, tell McGrew it's getting late," she said. She stood up and took her coat off the back of her chair, then slapped a fifty down on the table. "I need to take a run."

"Wait," McGrew said. "Just listen."

Amanda was halfway to their hotel before she heard McGrew's huffing and puffing and frantic footsteps behind her on the sidewalk.

"Wait up," he said.

Amanda looked back at him.

"I'm going for a run, McGrew," she said, her breath filling the dark night between them with a silvery cloud that disappeared into the glow of the streetlight above.

"I know," he said, catching up. "I'll walk with you and tell you my plan. You'll love it and it'll cheer you up.

"You're right. Ruskin is smart," McGrew said, digging into his coat pockets. "And he won't do anything, unless we make him do something."

McGrew took a strong mint from his pocket and popped it into his mouth. Its cold clean smell filled the air.

"We make him do something," he said. "We can tempt him with the one thing he can't resist."

CHAPTER 55

When Jack got home, Beth's car was gone. He'd grown used to her black Jetta in his driveway. At first the small car looked strange in the big space vacated by his ex-wife's Mercedes sedan. He swallowed and tried to make himself go into the kitchen. The place felt empty. He dashed upstairs to the bedroom. His ex-wife's closet door was ajar. Gradually over the last several weeks Beth had begun to use it for her own things. It was now empty.

He turned on the television near the bed and knew why. His face was all over the nightly news. They had a blue-and-white graphic of all the places he'd traveled to, all the people he'd killed. They could never prove it. There was no blood, no fingerprints, no ballistics. He'd been too careful. He'd even dumped his Glock when he'd gotten Beth's call after his visit to the beach.

But Beth would know. She would have remembered Steffenhausers'.

The television caught his attention, but the news wasn't about him anymore. A local sports reporter was doing a feature: A girl, a high school senior who was one of Janet's teammates a few years ago, was being presented with a huge trophy: Long Island Athlete of the Week. Nice. Jack stared. That could have been his daughter. But Janet wasn't playing soccer. She wasn't getting ready to apply to college. She wasn't worried about her date for the homecoming dance.

His little girl was a shell with scars on her body and holes punched in her veins to feed her drugs. Jack smashed the button on the remote. It wouldn't turn off. He burst from his seat on the bed and threw the TV down off the shelf. The tube exploded with a heavy pop. Smoky gray glass was everywhere. Jack closed his eyes.

It was late. He went downstairs to the fridge and started drinking beer. The sky outside was already beginning to lighten by the time he fell asleep.

At ten-thirty a car horn did what the sunlight couldn't. Jack rolled off the couch and got some aspirin. Someone was knocking on his door.

Jack could hear the din before he opened it. He was still shocked at what he saw. It was like a little circus of crazies. In his driveway and on his lawn was a crowd of people, arguing. A big troll of a woman in a dark wool coat and a lime-green watch cap—the one who rang the bell—was berating him from his own front step.

"You're a murderer," she said. "You're a killer!"

A man in a suit with no tie pointed at Jack and yelled in the woman's ear, "He's a hero."

There were TV trucks on the street. Cameramen and reporters moved through the small crowd like popcorn vendors. Jack shut the door. He called the police. When he told the female sergeant who he was, her voice got funny. She said they'd send someone over.

Jack went upstairs to watch from his window. He put on the TV and found CNN. Within minutes they were talking about him. Jack let the curtain drop. He watched for a while, too numb to be horrified or even ashamed. He took a shower. When he got out, the police had arrived. They were putting up tape between the trees down by the sidewalk, pushing people off his grass.

Jack put on his best suit. He could only imagine what was going on in his office. He eased the car out of his garage, wary. Halfway down his driveway an egg struck his windshield. As if on cue, the TV cameramen ducked under the tape and began running toward him. A scuffle broke out. Jack sped up and broke out into the street, tearing around the corner, finding the highway and his breath.

He put on the radio. Howard Stern was talking about him.

"It's about time someone killed those perverts," Stern said. "They should all be killed. But don't mess with lesbians. They might abuse me."

Jack turned it off.

When he parked in the garage beneath his office, he noticed that the attendants were looking at him. He thought one of them pointed. Jack put his head down and picked up his pace. The people in the elevator didn't pay him any mind. Maybe he'd imagined the parking attendants' reaction. When he got off the elevator in his office, though, he knew by the receptionist's face that he hadn't. She grabbed the phone and brought it fumbling to her ear. Her eyes went down.

Jack plowed through the halls, briefcase clutched to his chest, eyes on the carpet until he was safe within his own office. Pat, his secretary, straightened her neck, her eyes wide, her mouth hanging open. Jack shut the door and sat down. His fingers were trembling. The Maalox came out of his briefcase and he took a good slug. He tried to log onto his computer. A small bell chimed. Access denied.

"What the fuck?" he said.

Pat was knocking at his door.

"Come in," he said.

She did, but only just inside the door. She made a couple of attempts to look at him. He stared back at her, searching. Finally she gave up and looked at the floor.

"Mr. Wells wants to see you," she said.

"Tell him I'm right here," Jack said.

Pat hesitated. No one said that to Arthur Wells.

"Tell him that," Jack said.

Pat nodded and left. Jack started putting some pictures in his briefcase, one of him and Janet at Disney World, one of her alone, hands in the air after scoring a goal. Wells didn't knock. He shut the door behind him and sat down scowling. In his hand was a manila folder.

"Why in hell haven't you returned my calls?" Wells asked.

"I thought it best to talk in person, Arthur," he said.

"The partners are very concerned."

Jack pressed his lips tight and nodded. "I can't get into my computer," he said.

"Everything any of us does belongs to the firm."

"You remember anything about law school, Arthur?" Jack asked.

"What?"

"Law school," Jack said, "you know, books and study groups and legal memos. Yale."

Wells looked at him like he was crazy.

"Ever take criminal law?" Jack said. "We all took that.

Remember 'innocent until proven guilty'? That's a funny concept, isn't it?"

"The partners of this firm have a fiduciary responsibility," Wells said.

"Oh, fiduciary. Just fuck up a man's life."

"You did that on your own," Wells said. His chin was up. He was sitting on the edge of the chair. He took an envelope out of his breast pocket and slapped it down on the desk between them.

"That's a check for two million dollars," he said. He took a sheet of paper out of the folder and put that on the desk, too, along with his own gold pen. "This is your resignation from the firm."

Jack looked at him with disgust. He did a quick calculation in his mind. Last year he had earned nearly twice as much as he ever had before, $670,000 with his bonuses. This year it would be closer to a million. As the chair of a thriving and lucrative practice group, he could expect the same kind of money for the rest of his days as an attorney, so long as he continued to perform. Even if this scandal cost him some business down the road, in the position he was in, $750,000 would be a layup. Based on that theory, one could make a cogent argument that Jack's partnership was worth at least six million dollars.

"Six million? That's insane," Wells said. His face turned red. "You can just stay and rot on the vine."

Jack sensed a bluff. He was a blight on the otherwise unblemished face of a very old, very dignified, very profitable law firm. A blight could be removed, but it cost money and it was worth money. To terminate Jack without cause would guarantee embroilment in a lengthy suit that the firm would most likely lose. Even so, Jack knew they would never give him six million. But when Wells, after huffing and fuming, said he could sell the partnership on three million just to make the whole thing go away, Jack knew the number was really four. He said so.

"You sign that," Wells said. "I'll go to accounting right now. I want this over with."

Jack signed the resignation without looking at it. He fished through his desk for some other small things, putting them into his briefcase as well. When Wells returned, he picked the paper off Jack's desk and studied it. Then he handed Jack another check. Jack took it and went to shake the managing partner's hand. Wells put his hand at his side and took a step back. Jack felt his face grow hot.

There was a police car on the street next to his driveway. Otherwise only the tape and the trampled grass remained. Jack shut the door and looked at the cop car to see if they were coming for him. They weren't. He checked his messages. Wells, irate. His lawyer. No police. No Beth.

Jack went upstairs and packed his clothes.

CHAPTER 56

Amanda drove through the barbed-wire gates of the Hempstead Correctional Facility with McGrew by her side. He was fidgeting again with the tuft of beard beneath his lip and looking hard at the approaching guardhouse. As Amanda pulled to a stop, McGrew leaned across the wheel and thrust their papers out the open window at the young guard—a blimp of a man with blond eyebrows and a thatch of short unruly hair. He scowled importantly at them after perusing the court order and asking to see their identification before he would wave them on.

Tupp was waiting for them in a small holding cell. He wore an ill-fitting green jumpsuit. The muddy color of his eyes seemed to have leaked into their whites, contaminating them like smoke stains. His kinky russet hair had receded halfway to the crown of his head, and the pink furrowed expanse was highlighted by an absence of eyebrows.

Even sitting, she could see that Tupp was at least six feet tall. Although his torso was short and pear-shaped, his legs were disproportionately long. He had them straight out in front of him, crossed. His hands were jammed down deep in his pockets. Amanda's eyes went to their motion. Tupp didn't bother to hide what he was doing. In fact, by the subtle expression on his face, he seemed to like that she had noticed. There was a strange smell in the air. Amanda wanted to vomit.

She and McGrew sat down in two chairs facing him. She wished there were something between them, a table, anything. His hands fluttered. McGrew began to speak, impervious, introducing the two of them. After briefly praising his uncle's political clout, he proposed the deal. Tupp would live in a small saltbox cottage in the country out on the end of Long Island for the remainder of his sentence. He'd be under house arrest. He'd have to wear a bracelet. But he'd have the run of the place.

"Some people don't like the food here," Tupp said. He wore a coy smile. His voice was high pitched, lilting, and squeaky. A fat blue fly buzzed off the ceiling and landed on his shoulder. His eyes flicked between them. "But they have vanilla ice cream, and that's my favorite . . . Besides, I've only got three more months."

Amanda heard a scream inside her head to just get the hell out of there.

"Your sentence is four years," Amanda said, trying to sound gruff.

"But I've been good," he said. His eyes had glowed when she spoke to him. "I'm a good boy and I know how it works."

McGrew was chuckling like the whole thing was good for a laugh. He looked mirthfully at Amanda, then turned to Tupp. McGrew's face dropped. So did his voice.

"Listen, fuckshit," he said. "Didn't you listen to me about who my uncle is? They can find a bag of cocaine in your cell by four o'clock, then you can eat vanilla ice cream out of your cellmate's ass for the next ten years."

Tupp swallowed and shook the fly off his shoulder. He took his hands out of his pockets and crossed them in front of his chest. His head drooped.

"I didn't say I wouldn't," he said.

The fly buzzed toward McGrew. He snatched it out of the air, shook it, and threw it down on the concrete floor with a little splat.

"Good," he said. He was grinning at Amanda.

CHAPTER 57

A cold rain whipped Long Island. McGrew had a fire going in the massive grate of the pink granite fireplace in the great room of the beachfront mansion. The wood popped and hissed, tossing embers up against an ornate brass screen. McGrew was hunched over the surface of a teak Oriental desk, delicately tapping the keys of his computer.

Amanda sat on a broad crushed-velvet couch, resisting the temptation to sink back into the luxurious layers of pillows and upholstery. Instead she leaned into the room with her hands on the edge of her seat and her knees pressed tightly together.

They weren't far from the small inland cottage where Tupp sat watching his own TV, wearing his electronic bracelet. McGrew had recommended the site because of its remote location. Tucked in a grass clearing bordered by pines, the two-bedroom dwelling was accessible by only a single stony drive. There were no neighboring homes in sight, and its isolation would enable them to easily keep watch on the perimeter if Ruskin made his move.

Tupp was the hook. Now McGrew wanted her to help with the bait.

"There!" he said, pushing himself back from the desk and staring pointedly at Amanda. "Now you tell me this isn't just the way a woman would write it."

Amanda rose from her seat and peered over his shoulder.

"It's not," she said. Her hands were on her hips.

"How can you say that?"

"You say 'sex offender.' A woman wouldn't say that," she said, pointing at the screen. "Not someone who'd been through something like that."

McGrew moved off the chair and Amanda sat down and started typing. A little while later she pushed back her chair.

"There," she said, tapping the screen with the back of her fingernails. "Look."

Dear Mr. Ruskin,

I can't tell you who I am, but I share the pain I know you, your daughter, and your entire family have felt. I was also the victim of a terrible crime. I now work in the district attorney's office in Suffolk County. I don't want to add to your misery, but I have to make you aware of something that makes me sick.

Eugene Tupp is being set free.

This was brought to my attention by a coworker who has no idea what happened to me or how I feel. Apparently, our so-called system of justice has seen fit to let him out at the earliest possible moment because of "good behavior" in jail. When I asked where someone that dangerous was going to be living, I was told Fire Lane 22 off Long Town Road outside Quogue, but that I shouldn't worry, they knew he was leaving the country for South America, where his mother was from.

This is true. I have attached a copy of the one-way American Airlines itinerary for Eugene Tupp. I know that your life is in shambles right now, but I also knew you'd want this information.

Mr. Ruskin, please believe me that every person who has ever been the victim of a crime like this thanks you from the bottom of her heart. I only wish there were more people like you.

"I like it," McGrew said, stroking the triangle of hair beneath his lip. "I really like it."

"I just don't know," Amanda said. She crossed her arms in front of her. "It smells."

"Ruskin is a psycho," McGrew said. "He's going to see this and blow a gasket. Think about everything he's done. Shit, he's blowing away perverts he doesn't even know. What do you think he's going to do when he thinks about Tupp getting out and disappearing for good?"

"He might," she said. She unfolded her arms.

"We don't have anything to lose," McGrew said. "My bank with my uncle is empty after this. My captain told me, FBI or not, I've got clearance to run a twenty-four-hour stakeout for two weeks and no more. After that I'm back in the ranks."

"That'll be the end for me, too, then," she said. She frowned. "I'm only in this because of your—because of you."

"You can say my uncle," McGrew said. He gave her that crooked smile. "I use him like I use everything. I won't stop, you can bet on that. But I'll be working this thing during off-duty hours."

"You're serious, aren't you?"

McGrew shrugged. "Yeah. That's what I do. I'm a homicide cop to the bone, one-third tough, another third cunning, and one-half crazy . . ."

"Is that from some movie?" she asked.

"No," he said. "Just my movie."

"Oh."

"Hey," he said, rubbing his hands together, "I was thinking that you and me should take the night shift. That's when he'll do it, at night. We'll have to go nocturnal for a couple weeks. You ever go nocturnal?"

"McGrew," she said, pushing the strand of hair from her eyes, "I've got two kids."

She said it kindly.

"But right now," she said, getting up from her chair, "I could use a little sleep."

"How about a drink?" he said.

"I just had two Saratoga waters," she said making her way into the front hall. "That's my limit."

McGrew shot up out of his chair and grinned. "Not what I was talking about. Come on, just a small one. We don't have to start the real work until tomorrow night. Show me you're human."

Amanda was putting on her coat. "McGrew, I'm going to my hotel."

"You want to eat something?" he asked, following her to the front door. "You've got to eat."

"Room service," she said, stepping out onto the front step. "Look McGrew. I'm tired. You're doing a really good job with this thing. Send the e-mail and get some sleep yourself."

"I think I'll . . . this place has like a massive marble Jacuzzi," he said. He laughed and rubbed the back of his head. "I can barely sleep unless I have a Jacuzzi and a couple beers. So you think of me when you get back to that Holiday Inn, just living here like a billionaire."

"You're living right, McGrew," she said.

"Well," he said, "see you tomorrow. Tomorrow it all begins. Tomorrow could be the big scene."

"Good night, McGrew."

CHAPTER 58

Jack stopped for the second time along Route 80. He was outside Des Moines, Iowa. He didn't want to get all the way across the country before he contacted Beth. She'd been on his mind a lot. He knew that some people might not understand what he'd done, but that's not what he was going to ask of her. He was going to ask her to forgive him. Part of him felt like he could stop it all, if she would come back. Part of him didn't know if he could ever stop.

Either way, he had to try, so he pulled off the road that would take him all the way from New York to San Francisco, where he planned to go as far up the 101 as he had to in order to find the right place. What that place was he wasn't quite sure. He knew he needed to get away from New York, far away. He'd fly back to visit Janet. Maybe one day she could come to him. Maybe one day she'd be all better.

There was a Red Roof Inn just off the exit and that was good enough for Jack. Mark Kane was the name on the fake driver's license he still had from when he presented himself to Tidwell in Pittsburgh. He used it now. The young woman at the front desk was pretty with long brown hair. She wore a gray suit and a white blouse. He pushed a hundred-dollar bill across the desk and she looked up at him. Jack held his breath.

When she didn't avert her eyes, or show any sign of recognition, he exhaled. Maybe it was the name, or the baseball cap, or the beard, even though it had only been three days since his last shave. Or maybe he was already far enough away. He took the keycard from her and returned her smile, then found room 112. He tossed his overnight bag on the bed closest to the door and set up his computer at the desk.

He was going to e-mail Beth. He was going to ask her to come back. He needed to see her, or at least talk to her. They had come too far for her not to let him plead his case. She hadn't answered her phone, and when he went by her apartment, her car was gone. She might be home, an upstate dairy farm. Wherever she was, she would get her e-mail.

He had to be careful, though. He had to avoid saying anything that could be used against him. A prosecutor would love to get his hands on an e-mail where Jack made any reference at all to the killings. He would have to be vague, but at the same time let her know that things would be different. He felt he could do that. If she could forgive him, then he could meet her halfway. He could change. At least he felt that way right now.

He had AOL for personal use at home and with his junk-mail filter, it didn't surprise him to see only three e-mails waiting for him. None was from Beth, but one jumped out at him. The sender was from Anonymity.com, the same service he had used to send word to Arthur Campion, the father of Tom Conner's victim.

Jack felt his heart begin to race. Beth wouldn't bother

to use Anonymity. There would be no reason. He opened the e-mail and read about Tupp.

Light-headed, he staggered into the bathroom and filled the sink with cold water. He dipped his face into it and splashed the water up over the back of his neck. His hands shook and his chest heaved with short frantic breaths. He blew a spray of water against the mirror and looked at himself, then dipped his face again.

He dried off and tried to regulate his breathing, forcing himself to inhale deeply, exhale slow. When he could think straight, he shut down his computer without writing his e-mail to Beth. He left his keycard at the desk without bothering to ask the girl for his money back. He couldn't get back in his car soon enough. He drove into the night, checking his rearview mirror. A nondescript car had pulled out of the hotel parking lot after he did and gone his way. Someone might easily be following him. Sometime after three thirty-seven, he fell asleep behind the wheel. The Saab careened off the road.

CHAPTER 59

The horrible vibrating sound of pavement grooves blasted him awake. He swerved back onto the road and almost lost control. He pulled off at the next exit and shut off the car in the parking lot of an all-night gas station. The seat went back far enough for him to feel some comfort and he dropped off with thoughts of a shotgun spinning in his head.

It was just past eight when the air horn of a tractor-trailer sounded outside his car.

"Asshole," Jack said, rubbing his eyes and looking for the reason the big purple truck had sounded its horn. There was a camper blocking the diesel pump. Jack filled up, used the bathroom, and got a large coffee before getting back on the road. He had plenty of time to think, so when he hit Route 81 south of Scranton and headed north, it was for good reason.

The small city of Binghamton was just over the New York State line. He wanted to buy a gun well away from New York City, at a place where shotguns weren't uncommon. With the Mark Kane New York driver's license, he knew he could buy such a gun without many hassles. He had no idea what would happen in Pennsylvania, and the diversion would have taken less than two hours if it hadn't begun to snow. The farther north he got, though, the thicker it was.

Just before he hit Binghamton there was a Wal-Mart close enough to the highway that Jack could even see it through the snow. In his rearview mirror there was no one. He wasn't going to be careless, but the absence of anyone behind him in this heavy snow made him think that his early suspicions about being followed were pure paranoia. He got off at the exit and found his way to the store. The parking lot was nearly empty, and the cars that were there already wore a thick layer of snow.

Jack stuffed his wallet into his jacket pocket and tramped across the lot. He slipped inside unnoticed. There would only be one person who could remember him. She turned out to be a disinterested middle-aged woman, a poorly bleached blonde with a small tattoo on her neck. She was wreathed in the stench of stale cigarette smoke.

The woman fiddled with her own key chain and gazed at her cheap watch while Jack perused the glass cabinet of guns behind her on the wall. He cleared his throat and pointed to a short-barreled stainless-steel twelve-gauge that had a black synthetic pistol grip instead of the usual shoulder stock. He hefted the gun and slid the pump action back and forth with a slick metallic sound.

"Home defense," he muttered as he pointed to a box of hollowpoint slugs. "I'll take six of those boxes."

The woman seemed not to care what he wanted. She examined some crud that had lodged itself beneath a fingernail while she waited for a response on the FBI hot line as to whether a man named Mark Kane had ever committed a felony. The answer came back negative.

Buying a shotgun didn't require anything more than that and cold cash. Jack filled out a simple form in the name of Kane, then counted out five hundred-dollar bills to pay for the weapon. He couldn't have asked for a better person to sell him the gun. She wouldn't be able to choose him out of a lineup of Sumo wrestlers. That would be if someone ever found her in the first place, which was seriously doubtful.

Jack felt the awful sickness begin to return as he walked through the empty aisles to the front of the store. Outside, the snowy wind moaned in pain. He found Route 17 and went east. At Roscoe the snow began to turn wet. By the time Jack reached the George Washington Bridge, he was speeding along amid a caravan of lit-up tractor-trailers through a steady rain.

By ten-thirty he was back in his own home. He was going to strike and he was going to strike fast. This had to be perfect, more perfect than all the rest. He would be a suspect, a prime suspect, *the* prime suspect when Eugene Tupp was found dead. It meant that unlike any other murder he had committed, Jack would need an alibi, anything, even if it wasn't a very good one. His mind jumped fifteen years back in time when he was an assistant D.A. Even the biggest cases turned on the smallest details.

The time codes on phone calls, faxes, and e-mails were evidence that juries found just as compelling as fingerprints on a bloody murder weapon. And—as Jack knew only too well—if a piece of evidence could be used effectively in a prosecution, the counterpart to that evidence could be used just as effectively in a criminal defense. Jack set up his computer and built a bank of bogus e-mails. He plugged his computer into a simple timer

device so it would be sending e-mails at the time he
might be killing Tupp. Alone, it wasn't enough to exon-
erate him, but it could help.

That done, he changed into a fresh set of jet-black
clothes. By midnight he had driven three times past Fire
Lane 22 on Long Town Road and seen nothing to make
him suspicious. He parked the Saab a quarter mile away
in some pine trees. He was exhausted. His stomach was
twisted into writhing knots. But he was also determined
to end it all. With the smell of death on him, he loaded up
his new weapon and melted into the dark wet night.

CHAPTER 60

The sound of rain pattering against the hood of her poncho lulled Amanda toward sleep. She snapped her head from side to side abruptly, fighting off the fatigue. She got up off her foldaway canvas chair and began to move around. Slow and quiet, she patrolled the rear perimeter just inside the trees that encircled the back of the gray saltbox cottage. The shifting blue light of the television in the front living room could be seen through the kitchen window in the back of the small dwelling.

McGrew was watching the front.

Amanda shifted under the poncho. Rain swept down on the back of a gusty wind. Despite the poncho's hood, her face and hair were soaked. The rest of her was warm, anyway, and that kept her comfortable enough that she had to fight the sleep. The thought of Jack Ruskin venturing out on a night like tonight seemed absurd.

Amanda stopped and leaned against the rough trunk of a massive spruce. She retracted her head down inside her poncho amid a pattering of rain and pressed the light on her watch. It read just after two A.M. Two more hours to go, and they would be the toughest, but she agreed with McGrew. If Ruskin attacked, it would be in the dark. It might be crazy, but it also might work. It was only two weeks, and if it did work . . . well, she could just see Hanover's face.

Amanda sighed heavily. She didn't know if she could really go two weeks straight on this thing. Part of her felt she'd burst if she didn't get home sometime to see her family. If she were gone more than two weeks straight, even the souvenirs would have a tough time thawing out the kids. She couldn't even think about Parker. On the other hand, she knew McGrew wasn't going to take it well if she took off, but he'd have to understand. She felt that nagging voice inside her head, telling her she couldn't do two things and do them both well.

She was tired. That was the real problem. It would be easier the second day. Night stakeouts always were. She thought about calling McGrew on the handheld radio. But listening to him ramble would make her even sleepier.

After a few minutes, her mind began to drift. She found her chair and sat down. They'd sent the e-mail just yesterday. Ruskin wouldn't be here tonight. As she floated off, she was comforted by that thought. Tonight was just a formality. Her chin slumped down against her chest. She was completely unaware of the shape, darker than the night itself, moving stealthily from tree to tree through the woods. At regular intervals, the form would stop and peer intently at her spot in the trees. It was the shape of a man. He was coming her way.

CHAPTER 61

Jack stepped softly over broken branches, taking great care with every move he made. He was no woodsman, but the rain-soaked earth made it easy to be quiet as long as he was careful. When something did break, the sound was muffled by the hiss of rain teeming down on the pine woods. His eyes were wide from adrenaline and his painstaking concentration in the darkness. Cupped in his hand was a small penlight, which provided just a bit of light for him to see his way. Now that he was almost through the woods, the cool glow from the cottage shed just enough light for him to make out the dark silhouettes of the trees. That's when he saw something unusual propped up against one of the trunks. It was a person beneath a dark green poncho. Someone watching. Someone waiting.

He froze. The figure didn't move, either, and he wondered as he crept closer if the watcher wasn't asleep. He circled the motionless form with plenty of cover between the two of them until he could just make out the profile of her face in the dim light. It was her. A trap.

The discordant tone of the e-mail rang out clear in his mind. He'd been too upset to listen to it before, but it had been there. They knew he killed the others, just as Beth knew, but they had no proof. Now they were trying to get their proof.

The sight of the female FBI agent enraged him. How could a woman be part of a scheme like this? They were helping set Eugene Tupp free. Didn't they know it was only a matter of time before he destroyed another young girl? Another family? The answer was that they did know. Apparently they didn't care.

He could understand the egomaniacal homicide cop. But the woman? A woman who went along with something this contemptible ought to be . . . Jack slipped the sling of the short-barreled shotgun off his shoulder. Directing the deadly weapon at Amanda's inert form, a wild thought from some dark corner of his mind goaded him into feeling for the trigger.

He was struck dumb by the image of the hollowpoint slug ripping through the poncho in a dark spray of blood. He could hear the eruption of hot powder and lead. Jack's head, dizzy from exhaustion, stress, and a slew of raw emotions began to swim. The gun blast would flush out whoever else was waiting for him.

His sixth sense told him that McGrew was somewhere close by. A gun blast would bring him out, along with whoever else was there. If there was anyone else. Maybe McGrew and the woman were it. He could dispose of them both in this dark lonely place. They set Tupp *free*. Then it would be just him and Tupp . . . and for Tupp Jack had something special.

He clenched his chattering teeth and squeezed the cold smooth curve of the gun's trigger. He winced in anticipation of the gunshot and felt the hot rush of angry tears coursing inexplicably down his face.

CHAPTER 62

Jack stifled a gagging sound in his throat and released the pressure on the trigger, gasping in horror at what he had almost done. He tried to console himself. He'd never taken the safety off. But the feel of the trigger and the wave of deadly destruction that had rushed over him was like the feeling he had when he had once peered over the edge of the rail atop the Empire State Building. It was that insanely urgent desire to jump. It was dizzying.

He staggered back in among the trees. He had to think. He couldn't lose control. It was a puzzle, that was all, a mind-bending riddle. There had to be a way. He was an intelligent man, not brilliant, but smarter than most, and if he bent his will to it he believed he could find a way without collateral damage or being totally self-destructive. He looked up at the flickering light that bled through the back of the cottage. His mind locked up.

Besides a bloody shootout that left everyone dead, a missing murder weapon, and a sufficient alibi, Jack had no notion of how he could kill Tupp and also escape. His wild idea to kill Amanda and whoever else was hiding around the cabin's perimeter wasn't all that absurd. It was wrong, but from the point of pure execution, it was probably as sound as any plan there was.

But Jack would never do that.

He began to move through the darkness again, deeper into the trees and then circling toward the front of the cabin. A more thorough reconnoitering might give him a better idea. A crazy idea might not be the right one, but it could give rise to something practical. He had to get in and get out. He didn't want anyone to die except Tupp, but he didn't want to get caught. What he needed was something that would lure the police away.

Cautiously, Jack prowled through the damp woods. He smelled McGrew's cigarette even before he saw the tiny orange ember glowing like a secret beacon in the dark rain. He gave him wide berth, keeping a careful eye on the detective. He came to the darkened driveway and dashed across the open space. On the other side he found McGrew's car.

It appeared to be just the two of them. Jack stalked through the woods to the edge of the clearing, plotting in his mind just where it was he'd seen Amanda and locating McGrew by the faint glow of his cigarette. He looked at the house. It was a good two hundred feet away from the edge of the woods.

Through the picture window in the front of the cottage, he could see the back of Tupp's head, planted in an easy chair, watching the television. At the sight of his wild tufts of hair, Jack felt an insatiable urge to bolt across the lawn that separated the cottage from the trees and empty his gun in through the window. For a moment it seemed like a feasible plan. But after the first nervous surge of adrenaline, he realized that it was just as likely he might fail. He would almost certainly be caught. He

needed something better, at the very least a better means
of escape.

It was while he trudged back through the woods to his
car that Jack solved the puzzle. It was simple, but it
would work.

CHAPTER 63

By midmorning the wet weather had moved up the Atlantic coast, leaving a pale innocent sky in its wake. Sunlight poured through the cold windowpane into Jack's bedroom, warming it beyond comfort and waking him. At dawn, he'd taken a sleeping pill. It was well past noon. He got up and rubbed the drug-induced sleep from his eyes then looked outside, squinting at the brightness.

He took a fast shower and sat down to quickly compose another series of alibi e-mails for the night. That done, he dressed for the day in dark clothes, a black Yankees cap, and black shoes with flat rubber soles. He stuffed a ski mask into his coat pocket along with a pair of gloves before laying them all inside his trunk. He also packed a duffel bag with the shotgun, two sets of fresh clothes and shoes, an empty mesh bag, and a ten-pound dumbbell that he would use to sink his bloody clothes to the bottom of an ocean inlet.

Less than two hours later, with the help of a map, he began to scour the roads in the area surrounding Tupp's cottage. Inland from the beachfront homes it was a rural area. He had to find a place where he could abandon one vehicle and exchange it for another. If he was going to be successful, the vehicle he used couldn't be traced back to him. That kind of evidence could convict him, even if his face was covered by a dark ski mask.

He was looking for a shopping center that was open all night, or a main street that would have late-night traffic, people coming and going from the bars. Nothing looked quite right. There was a movie theater next to some shops with a small parking garage, but it was nearly twelve miles away in Riverhead, too far for what Jack needed. Driving from one small town to another, he came across a nature center that wasn't more than three miles from Tupp's cottage. On a hunch he pulled into the long paved driveway, which led to a visitor center overlooking a marsh. Despite the brightness of the day, it was cool enough so that only a handful of other cars were there.

Inside the dark brown hexagonal center, Jack found some maps in a rack by the door. Most of the trails wandered through the marsh on their way to the nearby bay, but there was also a set of trails that looped through an adjacent woods. The border of those woods butted up to what looked like a power line. Jack's blood began to rise. That might be the place. He set off on foot down the path to where only a small row of pine trees separated the loop from the power line. Jack broke through the trees and out into the open. As he'd guessed, there was a gravel access road that ran along the edge of the metal towers. He marked the spot in his mind and returned to the center.

Back on the main road he passed an unmarked police cruiser heading the other way, in the direction of Tupp's cottage. He slumped down in the front seat and quickly angled his head so that the brim of his hat obscured his face. The cops, two stone-faced men staring straight ahead, paid him no attention. Nevertheless, Jack decided to abandon any further reconnaissance and make do with what he'd already found. He quickly located the gravel access road of the power line and pulled in. It was a rough ride to the spot where the nature trail met the edge of the woods, but even with last night's rain, the stony road was dry enough that Jack never felt like he might get stuck.

Jack tucked his car into some brush in the woods on the opposite side of the power line from the nature trail. He got out and took off his jacket. From his trunk he removed a dark nylon sweat suit and pulled it over his wool pants and sweater before setting off. When he was finished, he would shed them both; that way, if he succeeded, not a single fiber found in the car he was going to steal would match those in his own vehicle.

He stopped and looked around, wondering if he could find his way back to the car in the middle of the night. When he reached the pine trees by the nature trail he turned, looked back, and then pushed the alarm on his key chain. The Saab gave a yelp from its hiding spot and its headlights flashed on and off three times. Easy. He looked up at the metal towers that stood like robotic sentries along the line of the woods as far as the eye could see. He could hear the low hum of power as it surged through the drooping wires above. A low-flying flock of geese honked suddenly overhead in the cobalt sky, startling Jack. He puckered up his mouth and set off into the lengthening shadows of the woods.

At the pay phone outside the center Jack called a cab from Hampton Bays. He explained that his car had broken down. He needed a ride back to the western end of the island. The dispatcher told him it would be thirty minutes before she could get someone there. Jack looked at his watch. The sun was already an orange ball ready to dip into the horizon. He used the time to retrace the steps he would take that night and memorize the paths that would get him to his car in the dark.

There were two possible routes. One he would take if there was no one in sight—a direct route to the power lines. The other was a more circuitous route that led into the marsh, but circled back to the woods. That he would use if someone was following him close enough to see him running. He hoped then that they would presume he was heading for the bay to escape by means of a well-placed canoe or rowboat.

By the time his half hour was up, dusk had fallen and Jack felt confident in his plan.

CHAPTER 64

A battered white station wagon with an orange taxi light pulled into the center just as a family was loading up their car with cameras and bicycles. Jack watched from the shadows under the eaves of the building, waiting until the cab had pulled slowly past him and the people. It was important for him not to be identified. He emerged from his spot, skirted the glare of a lamp pole, and slid into the gloom of the cab with his face obscured by the brim of his hat. Immediately he launched into the brief story of a tow truck that had come and gone and a driver who refused to allow him to ride along back to the garage. He lowered his voice and did his best at a British accent.

The cab driver, an aging heavyset man with a fishing cap, said, "Some people are just assholes."

Jack sank back into the seat.

"I'm going to shut my eyes for a few minutes," he said, trying to sound weary. "My wife's coming in on a seven-thirty flight. I'm meeting her at the shopping center in Port Washington, The Miracle Mile. You know where it is?"

"Yeah, my sister-in-law goes to that place."

"You can just take me there. Wake me when we get close, will you?" Jack asked.

"No problem," the driver said.

"Thanks." Jack pulled down his hat even farther and tilted his head toward the floor. As they drove he went over his plan, his mind spinning like a gyroscope on a string. He fought the nausea that had returned and silently cursed himself for forgetting his Maalox. At the shopping center he thrust a hundred-dollar bill into the front seat and hopped out of the car. "Keep the change," he said.

He heard the driver's appreciative thanks as he shut the door and disappeared into the stream of people coming and going. A block away on the other side of the street was La Maison, the restaurant where he and Beth had bucked the snooty maître d' months before. It was during his drive home in the early-morning hours from Tupp's cottage that Jack had come up with his idea for obtaining a vehicle that would not link him to the crime he was about to commit.

He had remembered the young valet who'd left the keys to his car above the visor. It was quite likely the standard procedure. The lot where the cars were kept was sealed off except for a chain blocking a driveway leading into the delivery area behind the shopping center. Even if the valets didn't leave the keys above the visors of the cars they parked, Jack knew he was likely to have a chance to nab a set of keys from the valet station sometime during the confusion of a busy Saturday night.

Five minutes later he was tucked in a dark corner of the valet lot. The next car that got parked told him he was right about the keys. The kid stuck them right up in the visor and ran off. Near the chained-off driveway in the back of the lot was a crimson Land Cruiser, perfect for what Jack needed.

There were three kids working as valets. It was a busy night. Jack took the ski mask from his pocket and pulled it carefully down over his head, knowing that the DNA from even a single hair left behind in the SUV could ruin everything. He slipped on his leather gloves and waited until two of the kids were jogging back to the front of the restaurant while the third was pulling out with someone's car.

Jack jumped into the Land Cruiser, grabbed the keys, and fired up the engine. He glanced around quickly, backed out, got up a head of steam, and rammed through the chained-off exit. The snap and tear of metal as the chain broke and then whipped against the side of the SUV sent a bolt of panic through him, but he never slowed down. The Land Cruiser careened through the back of the shopping center, streaking past empty loading docks and massive silent Dumpsters. He screeched out from behind the shopping center on the other side and quickly melted into the busy traffic. Driving as calmly as he could, Jack got to the expressway and headed back out to the eastern end of the island for the third time in less than twenty-four hours. He would arrive just past midnight. This time the reconnaissance was over.

CHAPTER 65

McGrew sniffed in, detecting only the barest hint of moldy pine needles. He wiped his runny nose on the sleeve of his jacket. He was coming down with a cold. Most cops he knew despised the grind of a stakeout, but McGrew got along okay. He used the time to highlight the scenes of the past few days and chronicle the ones yet to come, composing cagey lines that would define his character for the audience in his mind. In this way, to himself, the existence of David McGrew always seemed bigger than life.

One thing he could clearly imagine was the furtive shape of Jack Ruskin, sneaking out of the darkness into the starlight, making his way up to the front door of the cottage, McGrew waiting for the sound of a gunshot before he opened fire himself. That would be a perfect action scene, blood everywhere, the smell of powder, the feel of warm metal as McGrew jammed his pistol back into the holster underneath his arm.

McGrew pulled his pistol out of its holster and aimed it through the dim light of the stars in the direction of the cottage. He found the back of Tupp's head in his vision, sitting in his usual spot in front of the television, its light flickering endlessly. McGrew drew a bead on the television. That would be a funny thing, blasting the scumbag's television out from under him. McGrew liked the idea that Ruskin might actually kill Tupp before being gunned down himself. That would be like a double play.

McGrew replaced his gun and rose from his folding chair to stretch. He peered through the dark toward the thick trees at the back of the house where he knew Amanda sat. He lit up a cigarette and began to fret. Would Ruskin go for Tupp? McGrew felt like he had to, but the uncertainty made him feel he might explode. He drew long and hard on his cigarette, filling his lungs with the calming smoke.

The rattling sound of gravel and tires had barely registered with McGrew before the dark shape of the Land Cruiser rocketed out from the driveway behind the blue-white glare of headlights. McGrew was momentarily frozen in disbelief. This wasn't how he had imagined it. The SUV had already lurched to a halt in front of the cottage before McGrew began to move. He was running toward the SUV at the same time as he struggled to free his gun from underneath his arm.

The night was torn apart by the explosion of the shotgun blasts and the shattering of glass. Orange tongues of flame flicked out of the SUV in rapid succession amid the pandemonium. As if in a dream or moving underwater, McGrew's body moved slower than his brain. The sluggish heavy movement of his limbs enraged him. By the time he had his gun ready, the Land Cruiser had already shot forward and away. McGrew ripped off three quick shots, but his mind hadn't calmed enough to focus on the target. He was throwing slugs into the vehicle at random, but he didn't stop until the gun was empty.

The SUV continued on as if nothing had happened, even though McGrew had heard the heavy thud of his bullets striking their mark. A quick glance told him the front room of the cottage had been obliterated. The television was dark. There was no sign of Tupp. McGrew raced in the direction of the road where his own car was hidden just off the driveway, his mind feverish with rage. He heard Amanda's cry from behind him, but all he could do was wave her on without looking back and shout, "Come on!"

McGrew burst through the brush with his cruiser and out onto the gravel drive, nearly striking Amanda. She had her gun out and he jammed on his brakes, sending up a shower of stones.

"Get in!" he yelled.

She whipped open the door and threw herself down on the front seat beside him.

McGrew didn't wait for the door to close before he smashed the accelerator to the floor. The police cruiser leapt forward and chewed up the drive. McGrew never slowed to look. He shot out onto the pavement and spun in the direction he'd seen the Land Cruiser's taillights disappear. On the open road he quickly got well up over a hundred. The Land Cruiser was surprisingly not yet out of sight.

"I may have hit him," he said.

Amanda looked at him hard and McGrew glanced briefly at himself in the mirror. He looked good. He realized Amanda was saying something to him.

"What?" he asked over the roar of the engine and the excitement.

"I said, 'We need to call for help!' "

McGrew shook his head. "We don't need no help on this one. This one belongs to me."

Amanda's mouth fell open. She started to say something, but then stopped.

"He's going into that park," McGrew said. "There's no way out. He's trapped."

"If he runs you're going to want a helicopter," Amanda said. She was calm, but McGrew saw her brace herself as the car shot up over a rise and lifted off the ground.

"It'll take time for them to get here," she said.

McGrew shot her a begrudging glance. She was right. He had visions of pinning Ruskin down and shooting it out, but if he ran—and McGrew was vaguely aware of the trails that permeated the park—then a helicopter would be essential. He might even need dogs. The last thing he wanted was for Ruskin to get away. A helicopter would take maybe half an hour anyway. That would give McGrew the time he needed to either run Ruskin to ground, or help in the event that he escaped into the backwoods.

McGrew picked up the handset of the police radio in his car and called in for the county helicopter as well as a couple of K-9 units. When he replaced the handset Amanda rewarded him with a nod of approval before they squealed around the turn that led into the nature center. There, parked right in front of the hexagonal building, was the Land Cruiser with its driver's-side door wide open. There was no sign of Ruskin.

McGrew screeched to a stop and jumped out, gun in hand. Amanda did the same. After scouring the shadows around the center, McGrew stopped, puffing in front of a large wooden relief map of the trails.

"The water," McGrew said.

"A boat?" Amanda said.

McGrew nodded then went to his car. Amanda followed him and watched as he pulled a flashlight and his handheld radio out of the front seat. Without saying anything to her, he set off back toward the marsh.

"Wait," Amanda said. "We should wait for backup. This is insane. McGrew!"

"You wait," he said without bothering to turn his head.

"McGrew! I'm not just walking into something!" she yelled desperately. "You're crazy! We'll have the helicopter in a few minutes. You don't know what's out there, he might be just waiting. He'll see your light! McGrew!"

McGrew stopped and turned back toward Amanda. He lit his face the way children do on Halloween, the flashlight shining up from beneath his chin.

"It's good to know you care," he said, smiling crookedly. Then he flicked off the light and disappeared down the path.

CHAPTER 66

Jack ran through the darkness, stumbling and falling not once but five times before he reached his own car, bruised and gasping for breath from his scramble through the woods. Underneath the mask his face was wet with sweat. The loud chirp of his car alarm and the flash of lights disrupting the stillness of the woods nearly choked him with panic. He dashed across the field beneath the power lines and winced as he was forced to actually arm and disarm the car again in order to find it in the dark tangle of foliage.

He laid the shotgun on the ground and methodically began to go through the routine he'd rehearsed in his mind over and over again, popping the trunk, stripping off his sweat suit, and stuffing it into a plastic garbage bag. He tied off the bag, put it back into the trunk, and then slid into his down jacket from earlier in the day. The trail of fibers was something he had considered from a prosecutor's point of view. He knew the mistakes other killers had made, and he knew that with care and planning he could avoid them. Once the bag of clothes and the gun were gone, nothing could connect him to the Land Cruiser and the crime of shooting up Tupp's cottage. But Jack still had one more change of clothes to make before the night was through. He removed a box of shells from the trunk and reloaded the shotgun.

He laid the gun on the passenger's seat, got into the Saab, took off jolting down the gravelly access road and then raced back down the rural highway in the direction of the cottage. He didn't know how much time he would have, or even if his ruse had worked. It was possible either McGrew or Amanda had stayed behind with Tupp.

If he saw anyone or anything, he would just take off. Jack was betting against it. It was also possible that reinforcements or an ambulance had already arrived, but he was betting against that as well. This far away from a large town, the chances were that even if they had called right away, any kind of help was a good half hour away. That gave Jack fifteen minutes. He pressed harder on the gas.

On the way back to Tupp's cottage he saw no other cars. His heart began to sprint as he pulled down into the driveway for the second time. He drove right up to the cottage and put the car in park with the engine running. The front room was still dark, although there was a light on somewhere in back, either the kitchen or the bedroom, that cast a malicious yellow glow. Jack opened the front door.

"Eugene!" he yelled. "Eugene. It's all right, you can come out."

Jack froze. Besides his own ragged breathing, and the hammering of his heart, he heard nothing. Tiptoeing, with the shotgun gripped tightly in both hands and leveled off in front of him, he stepped into the main room amid the broken glass. Jack knelt down and grimly examined the dark swatch of blood on the threadbare carpet. A tear in the stuffing of the reclining chair in which Tupp had sat told the rest of the story. Tupp was hit.

Following the crimson trail, Jack stepped carefully into the kitchen. The light came from above the range, an old yellow bulb. A jagged stripe of blood crossed right through the middle of the gray linoleum floor. One of two metal kitchen chairs had been overturned and lay across his path. Two bloody handprints and numerous marks like broad crimson brushstrokes marred the front of the old white refrigerator where Tupp had obviously tried to pick himself up off the floor. From the slippery stains and the even wider swatch that led to the next room, Jack presumed Tupp had failed.

Careful not to slip and fall in the bloody trail, Jack continued softly across the kitchen, his flat rubber shoes as silent as a cat. He put one hand on the knob of the bedroom door. The other grasped the pistol grip of the shotgun slung from his shoulder.

"Eugene!" he yelled. "It's all right. I'm a police officer. Everything's okay. He's gone. You're safe, Eugene. It's over."

Jack thought he heard a pitiful moan and a soft stirring from within. A red warning light flashed briefly in his mind. Did Tupp have a weapon of his own? But Jack knew he didn't have time to wait. Gun or no gun, he had to act. The police or an ambulance would soon be there. He threw open the door and tightened his grip on the shotgun, squinting into the darkness. Only the dull column of yellow light from the kitchen illuminated the room.

As his eyes adjusted, Jack could make out the crumpled form of Tupp propped up against the wall beside the tangle of covers that had been his bed. Blood gurgled audibly in his lungs and he clutched at the bleeding hole in his chest. The slug had punched clean through. The pitiful whimpering that escaped Eugene Tupp was laced with fear and suffering.

Jack was disappointed and surprised that the thought of Tupp's last twenty minutes of exquisite pain, huddled in agony on a dirty kitchen floor, brought him no satisfaction. Under the staggering sense of horror at the sight of what he'd done, his finger strayed from its trigger. He thought of Janet. He should be elated by every ounce of Tupp's suffering, but he wasn't. His stomach churned instead. His unpleasant reverie was broken by another sound.

He should never have hesitated. The metallic click of a gun safety was as unmistakable as a child's scream and even as he felt for the trigger of his own gun, Jack felt himself wincing involuntarily, anticipating the impact of a bullet.

CHAPTER 67

The closer Amanda got to the cottage, the more she reprimanded herself for racing off with McGrew. She was so distressed that she didn't even tell him she was going back. It had been instinctive to take off after the fleeing Land Cruiser, but irresponsible. Neither had given any thought to the human being they'd used as bait. Amanda wondered if it had been the heat of the moment or a subconscious categorization of Tupp as something less than human. Probably it was both.

When she emerged through the trees and saw the Saab, she understood immediately what had happened, how Ruskin had lured them away. She should have known. Not only had each of the murders he'd committed been devoid of evidence, but the fate of his victims had never been left to chance. Not one of the bodies had suffered less than eight shots—each of which by itself would have scored a kill. It didn't make sense that he would now have done a sloppy kind of drive-by shooting. It was too uncertain a tactic for a victim who to Jack Ruskin must be infinitely more important than all the rest.

She slid to a stop on the grass beside the Saab and jumped out of McGrew's cruiser. She slipped her gun from its holster and caught a deep breath. The last time she had drawn her gun she had been able to do nothing more than watch as her partner was murdered. It was only years of training that pushed her on through the front door of the cottage. She heard nothing, but she could feel Jack Ruskin's presence. She saw the blood trail that led to the dimly lit kitchen.

She stepped carefully, quietly, ready at any moment for Ruskin to jump out from the next room with his gun blazing.

"Eugene!"

Amanda nearly shrieked. She recognized Ruskin's voice.

"Eugene. It's all right. I'm a police officer. Everything's okay. He's gone. You're safe, Eugene. It's over."

Amanda tried to control the slight tremble that seemed to be spreading from the barrel of her gun, down her hands, and through her body all the way to her knees. Her mouth had gone dry, and the stale smell of the hot dogs that Tupp had cooked on a frying pan for his dinner seemed suddenly overpowering. She rounded the corner. At the other end of the kitchen was the black masked figure of Ruskin. His shotgun was aimed into the bedroom. Amanda took a deep silent breath. At the same time, she settled her weight over her feet, took aim, and clicked off her gun's safety.

"Stop!" she heard herself yell.

CHAPTER 68

Jack whipped his head around and the sight astounded him.

It was her. That strand of red hair had fallen across one eye, but the other held him fixed in an immovable gaze.

"Put the gun down, Mr. Ruskin," she said slowly and quietly, a real professional. "Just stay calm and put the gun down."

A wave of hopelessness washed over Jack. He staggered, but instantly regained his feet and adjusted the shotgun's barrel, leveling it carefully at Tupp.

"It doesn't have to end like this," Amanda said, stepping slowly toward him. Her voice was beginning now to quaver.

Jack felt a sound escape him from deep inside.

"Do you know what he did?" Jack said, his voice breaking off in a high-pitched squeak. His eyes welled up with tears that spilled over their brims only to be soaked up by the woolen mask.

"Do you know what he did to her?" he cried out in pain.

Amanda nodded that she did know. She shut her lips tight and her chin rumpled.

"Then you know," Jack said through his teeth. His face

twisted. Rage bloomed in his brain like a bloody cloud.
"Why . . . I . . . am going to do . . . this!"

Jack turned his attention from the agent back to Tupp
and pulled the trigger. The blast from the gun was deaf-
ening in the small space and filled it with the pungent
aroma of gunpowder. The hollowpoint lead slug hit Tupp
in the face, rocking him back, erupting in a fountain of
purple gore. His feet began to kick wildly against the
floor as if he could somehow struggle free from the certain grip of death.

Jack turned his head and looked into Amanda's face
from behind his mask. Her mouth hung open in disbelief.
Her hands trembled more visibly now than before, the
gun barrel wagging.

Jack spun slowly around, the smoking gun still heavy
in his hand, and reached for the back door.

"Stop . . . I'll shoot," she said, but her voice sounded
plaintive and lacked conviction.

Jack looked at her wearily.

"That's okay," he said. "I understand."

Without waiting for her response, Jack opened the
door with complete indifference and stepped easily out
into the night. The stars glowed brightly from above in
the cold clear air. His breath, issuing from the mouth hole
in his mask, filled the stillness around him in great gray
puffs. In the distance the sound of a helicopter droned. Inside the cottage a cell phone went off. After his first few
steps Jack began to jog. He rounded the corner of the cottage and saw the police cruiser with its door open, beside
his Saab. His car was still running and Jack got in
quickly.

CHAPTER 69

At dark he came out. Mosquitoes bumped off his face as he rode through the woods. A nice trail for children to walk to school.

He liked watching them from the woods. He was growing comfortable with the neighborhood. The people were nice. They smiled and waved. He smiled back, keeping his mouth closed. He was saving his real smile.

The black Schwinn bumped over a wooden bridge. The smell of stagnant water filled his nose. He shot through the green area at the end of the block, dressed all in black, speeding like a mink.

The sidewalk was littered with fallen leaves. Red and brown and dead. Many still clung to the trees overhead. They rattled in the small breeze. It was turning cool.

He rode past the house. The black truck sat like a stupid dog in the driveway. Yellow squares of light seeped from the downstairs windows. He looked at his watch. Not bedtime yet.

He rode around the block. Around and around he went, his tongue skipping over the pointed tips of the two sharpened teeth, the wind filling his mouth, mosquitoes bouncing off his helmet, his glasses.

Then something different. He stopped on the sidewalk

and looked. The lights had shifted to the upstairs. Bedtime. It was the little girl. She was wearing the pink nightdress. The pretty one with the white frill.

He watched from the darkness, invisible. Smiling.

Then the night exploded with light.

He hit the sidewalk hard, splitting his helmet. The bike crashed down. He screamed, a high pitched, blood-curdling scream.

Something hit him in the mouth, then the eye. Someone was on him, pounding him. He fought, scratching, biting, screaming.

They had his throat. They were choking him. Killing him.

Everything went black.

CHAPTER 70

Amanda's phone rang five times before she could bring herself to answer it. She expected McGrew. It was Parker.

"Parker?" she said, her spinning stomach dropping ten thousand feet at the sound of his voice. "What's wrong?"

"Everyone's okay," he said. She knew instantly by his tone that it wasn't.

"What's wrong?" she said, hysteria rising like a flood. Sensory overload. In front of her was a dead man. She stumbled outside into the moonlight.

"The kids are fine," he said, "and so am I, but I think you should come home. I . . . Mike Collins is here—"

"At the house?"

"—I think he can explain it better."

"Hello?"

"Mike?" she said. "What the hell is going on?"

"Everything's fine," he said. "I got him before anything happened."

"Got him? Who?"

"Charles Wheeler," he said. "The guy Hanover told you about. The guy I've been following. Oswald's partner."

"What the hell are you talking about?"

There was a long silence and then Collins said, "He didn't tell you?"

"No one told me anything."

"The guy you saw ducking out of Oswald's kitchen in Jackson is a guy named Charles Wheeler. They were cons together and when they got out, they were a couple. When I found the guy, he was living about ten minutes from your house. I told Hanover and he was supposed to tell you."

"My God."

"But it's okay," Collins said. "We caught him sneaking around your neighborhood about a half hour ago and I body-slammed the son-of-a-bitch and tossed his ass in jail. I came to check on your husband. We checked on the kids and talked to them. They're fine, but I guess Wheeler was with them in the park. He didn't do anything, just let them play with a couple of kittens. He said they could have them, but the kids didn't take them."

"Oh my God," Amanda said. She was shaking uncontrollably. She started for the car. "I'm coming. I'm coming."

CHAPTER 71

During the search of the marsh, a lieutenant asked Mc-Grew about Tupp. The two of them stood in front of the relief map outside the nature center. They had been divvying up the park among search teams with dogs.

"I have no idea," McGrew said.

"Did anyone call an ambulance?" the lieutenant asked. He was a short man with a crew cut whose dark blue uniform possessed every brass accoutrement known to law enforcement.

"I don't know," McGrew said. "Did you?"

"I didn't."

"I guess we should."

"I guess so," the lieutenant said with a sour frown.

McGrew made the call and found a patrolman to send back to the cottage. He was busy out in the marsh with a K-9 unit when the lieutenant radioed everyone in. He was calling it off.

McGrew snatched the radio off of his belt.

"What the hell?" he said over the airwaves. "You can't call this off."

"Detective," the lieutenant said. "Report to me immediately."

A pink ribbon of light lay across the horizon, brightening the purple sky. The stars were fading one by one, and the lusty smell of salt water floated in the chilly air. McGrew, angry and weary from his search, trudged back up the trail to their impromptu command center.

"Well," the lieutenant said, his eyes clear and sharp, almost accusatory. "You've got another murder on your hands."

"He got Tupp?"

"Got him good," the lieutenant said. "Right between the eyes."

"Between the eyes?" McGrew said. "How the hell . . ."

"He went back," the lieutenant said. "That's why I called it off. They found footprints in his blood. Whoever it was, he came back and finished him off while we were out here."

"It was Ruskin," McGrew said forcefully. "That's who it was."

The lieutenant considered him for a moment before saying, "Well, the chief wants to see you before you go harassing Ruskin again. I guess his lawyer already filed some suit."

"The chief? I've got to get back to that cottage. I've got to get this thing going."

"No. You don't," the lieutenant said. "The chief said he'll see you in his office in a half hour."

"I've got to see the fucking scene," McGrew said.

"That's an order, McGrew."

"My uncle—"

"The chief already spoke to your uncle," the lieutenant said, smiling now. "He's not happy. I guess you're kind

of out of favors, so you might want to bring your hat
when you see the chief."

"My hat?"

"Yeah, you know, go 'hat in hand.' Your ass is in
deep."

CHAPTER 72

Hanover's ears were hot. He'd seen the article in the *New York Post*, so he was expecting the call. What he didn't expect was that it would come from the director himself. Why couldn't anything ever go right for him? Things weren't even his fault.

He got up from his desk and straightened a chrome frame that held a photo of him next to the country singer George Jones before returning to his seat. He then picked up his phone, trembling, and said to his secretary, "Get Mike Collins in here."

On his way in, Collins paused briefly, filling the doorway.

"Sit down," Hanover said.

"I have to talk to you," Collins said.

"I said sit down."

Collins sat, glowering.

"You were supposed to tell Amanda," Collins said.

"What the hell does that have to do with anything?" Hanover asked. He held up the *Post*. "Did you see this yet? I just got off the phone with the director. I'm getting blamed for what you did. Me!"

"I probably saved those kids' lives," Collins said.

"You dumb ass," Hanover said. "You've got nothing

on Wheeler. You even said so yourself sitting in this office. He had an assault charge fifteen years ago for God's sake. He was practically a kid. He's been clean ever since."

"Clean my ass," Collins said. "He's been cutting up little kids."

"Where the hell have you been?" Hanover asked. "You think you're J. Edgar Hoover? It's all conjecture. We don't even know if he was with Sanderson or Oswald or whoever. Shit. You embarrassed the entire Bureau. You attacked a man for riding his bicycle down the sidewalk and threw him in jail. They're going to have a press conference today. A goddamn press conference, him and his lawyer, post-nine-eleven intimidation tactics by the FBI and all that bullshit . . ."

Collins's angry scowl turned into a look of complete stupefaction.

"What?" he said. "That creep was stalking those kids. We can't put two and two together anymore? Is that where we're at now?"

Hanover stared at him.

"Don't talk so goddamn stupid," he said. "You're an FBI agent, goddamn it. You're on paid leave."

"On leave? And that psycho is still loose?" he said. "I know him better than anyone. I've been on this for months. How the hell can you expect anyone to just step in?"

"No one's stepping in," Hanover said, opening his drawer and removing some papers. "Mr. Wheeler is to be left alone. We're not going to embarrass ourselves any more over this . . ."

" 'Mr. Wheeler'?"

"I've got my orders and now you do, too," Hanover said, pretending to begin his study of the papers in front of him. "You stay away from him or you're finished."

"Finished? Ha! You're lucky, Ben. You're lucky I . . ."

"Are you threatening me?" Hanover's voice broke with excitement. "Was that a threat?"

Collins was on his feet, towering.

"You take it how you want," he said. "I don't give a fuck. But if anything happens to those kids, it's on you."

CHAPTER 73

Jack loaded up his Saab and then unloaded it again. He couldn't stand just waiting, but he didn't want to run. That would make things worse if he were arrested. If he ran, no judge would let him out on bail. If he was charged and things looked bad, he needed to get bail. He had the money to jump it and disappear. But that would be a whole other program. A last resort.

Jack turned on the TV, then turned it off. More than twenty-four hours had passed since he killed Tupp and still there was nothing. It was bizarre. The media he could understand. The police sometimes didn't release specific information for days when it suited their purposes. But what about McGrew? More important, what about the woman, Amanda Lee? He wondered if or when she'd come for him and what made her tick.

Jack went to the desk in his library and started up his computer. As a federal agent, any trial testimony, former cases, or task forces she had been a part of would be in newspapers around the country. He could find that information using LexisNexis. Accessing the service through AOL, he was able to get on and use the firm's general billing information to conduct a search.

He typed in *Amanda Lee* and *FBI* and waited. The first

thing up was a news article from the *Washington Post*. It was dated today. Jack clicked on it. He sucked in his breath. His face grew dark as he began to read.

Va. man claims to be harassed by FBI agent
Agent claims the man was stalking a colleague's children.

By a *Washington Post* Staff Writer
Wednesday, October 17, 2002; Page B1
A man accused of stalking an FBI agent at her Manassas home was released by a county judge Wednesday. The judge says the man had committed no crime.

Charles Wheeler, a self-described artist, said at his appearance before County Judge Ladale Lloyd that FBI agent Mike Collins threw him from his bicycle and beat him the day before, causing the apparent welts on his face and hands. He said he was just riding his "black Schwinn" bicycle through the suburban neighborhood.

However, Wheeler's arrest report from the incident stated that he's a known pedophile who was allegedly stalking a colleague of Collins. Louisiana Department of Corrections files show Wheeler was convicted in 1988 of an assault stemming from an incident in New Orleans. Further details were not known late Wednesday.

"I'm 110 percent innocent of anything," Wheeler said in court. "I was just riding my bike, like I always do, and these guys just jumped out of the bushes and started beating me up for no reason."

The arrest report stated Wheeler targeted Collins' colleague Amanda Lee and her children because Lee had killed Wheeler's former cellmate. Department of Corrections files do show that Wheeler bunked with Hubble Sanderson while at Angola prison. They were later separated for what prison records called "deviant behavior."

Sanderson was killed in a shootout with the FBI last spring outside Atlanta, Georgia. A suspected serial killer, Sanderson stabbed and killed FBI Agent Marco Rivolaggio during his apprehension before being shot by Lee.

"As with all cases, the FBI will investigate the allegations," said FBI spokesperson Melinda Norris.

Jack kept going. He found the articles on what had happened to Amanda and her partner in Jackson. He cross-searched for Hubble Sanderson, the man the FBI called Oswald. He was a serial killer. A pervert who preyed on kids.

Jack closed the file, got off the Net and then into the northern Virginia phone directory. In the town of Manassas, he found "Lee, Parker & Amanda." MapQuest gave him directions from the train station in D.C. He knew how he could repay Amanda and make sure she never testified against him. Now all he needed was a gun.

CHAPTER 74

It was broad daylight and Jack worried, but he shouldn't have. Drugs were available 24/7 in Upper Manhattan. Once you got north of Central Park, things started to go down. Jack went up Lenox Avenue almost to the Harlem River before turning off onto a mean-looking side street. The very next corner showed him what he wanted: two kids in ridiculously baggy jeans and oversize NBA jerseys beneath heavy leather coats and awkward caps. They stood on the corner. Chains of gold hung from the tall skinny one's neck. The round one backed crablike into a doorway as Jack's Saab rolled to a stop. He put down the passenger's window.

"You a cop, man? No, you ain't no cop."

The tall skinny one in the purple Lakers jersey swaggered up to the car. The round one shifted his small dark eyes nervously. He edged his hand toward the bulky shape beneath his red Hawks shirt.

"I got rocks and I got bags," the skinny one said. "What you want?"

"I've got a thousand bucks," Jack said, holding up the money fanned out for him to see. "I'm looking for a gun."

"Man, we ain't selling no guns," he said. "You crazy?"

"How about his gun?" Jack said. He nodded toward the round one. The kid couldn't be more than fifteen.

"Shit, that gun's worth 'bout two thousand dollars," Lakers said.

"Let me see it," Jack said.

Lakers motioned with his chin for Hawks to come over. Hawks slid up to the car and whipped a big nickel-plated Colt .45 out of his pants, pointing it at Jack. His hand was stone still.

"Okay," Jack said. He swallowed. "Two thousand. You put the gun down on the seat."

Lakers whipped out a Glock. Pointing it at Jack, he said, "Go ahead, Chino."

Hawks dropped the gun.

"I'll get the money, okay?" Jack said. He reached slowly into his pant pocket and took out his wallet. He emptied it, added the bills to the ones he'd already fanned out, then handed them across the seat. Hawks snatched it up.

"Come back an' see us again," Lakers said. He lowered the Glock.

Jack exhaled and drove away. At the next light he stuffed the big .45 into his briefcase.

He drove downtown and found a parking garage near Grand Central Station. In his trunk was an envelope fat with cash. He loaded up his briefcase and his wallet, then pulled a Yankees cap down low on his head. He looked at himself in the side mirror. He had on an old tortoiseshell pair of glasses and his beard wasn't half bad. No one said a word to him. No one whispered or pointed. Fifteen minutes later he was on the express train for D.C.

CHAPTER 75

Amanda stared out the kitchen window past the swing set, past the sandbox and the bike Teddy left on the lawn. She was looking at the trees. There were houses like hers on either side, each neighbor marking their property with lines of shrubs and more trees. Through the woods out back were more homes, homes she could only see in the wintertime. She liked the fall foliage, red and orange hardwoods mixing with the green undergrowth. But now she only saw it as shelter for the enemy. She held the phone tightly.

"He's an asshole," Collins said, summing up his feelings on their boss. "I don't know what to tell you, Amanda. I don't know if you can go over his head . . . if they'll even listen. The director is really bent on this. Believe me, I know."

"But you think Wheeler will come back, Mike?"

"I know he will. I don't give a shit about Hanover. Listen, I told Parker I'd hang around, but he said no. I want you to know that. He told me he'd handle it. I don't know. I got the Manassas cops to send a patrol car over to keep an eye on the school anyway. This guy will be back."

"Why?" she said, twisting the phone cord around her finger. "Why do you say that?"

"I know this creep," he said. "I've been studying him. He's smart, but he's also arrogant. He knows he jammed me up. He and that asshole judge knew just the right buttons to push high up. I'm worried about you and your family . . ."

"I mean," Amanda said, "I just have to sit here and wait for him to do something?"

"No one's going to touch this guy until he does something," Collins said. "He's safer than the pope."

Amanda thanked Collins for everything he'd done and hung up. She went into the living room where Parker was playing Super Mario. She had sent the kids to school again, not wanting to alarm them. When she found out about Wheeler's being set free, she called and alerted the principal. He told her there was already a patrol car outside and assured her that they would keep a special watch.

"What's up?" Parker asked.

Amanda told him the story and then asked, "Why did you send Mike Collins away?"

Parker turned off his video game and stood up. He went to her and held her.

"Hey, I can take care of my own family," he said. "You don't have to be an FBI agent to do that. But if he's right about this guy, then I say we should go away for a while."

"Go?" she asked, separating herself.

"To my brother's hunting cabin," he said. The place they'd been that summer. It was only forty minutes away, but it was deep in the woods near Shenandoah National Park. It was built on a flat spot above a deep ravine near a thundering waterfall.

Parker's face was beginning to flush, the way it always

did when he talked about his brother's place. His voice was invigorated. "We can go there and stay there and wait until this blows over. I'll call him."

"Blows over?" she said. "How long are you thinking to stay?"

Parker shrugged and said, "Who knows. We'll just stay. It'll be great, really. You can get the kids' schoolwork or something. I can do some hunting. We can be a family . . ."

"This isn't . . ." she said, then stopped. "No. This is good. They'll be safe. You'll take the kids and keep them there . . . You'll keep everything as normal as you can, Parker. You have to try to do that. I don't want them upset."

"Me? Where will you be?"

Amanda pressed her lips tightly together and pushed the strand of hair free from her eyes.

"I've seen what Wheeler is capable of. He's sick. Mike Collins says he won't go away. He says he's coming after me. Well . . . we'll let him come. And when he does . . . I'll be waiting for him."

CHAPTER 76

The Humvee was the perfect vehicle for going to the cabin. Parker pulled out onto the main road leading from their suburban development riding high. He punched the gas pedal and the big machine roared. The kids were strapped in and bouncing along with their hands holding tight to the sides of the seats. Both his guns were resting in the custom rack behind the seats, glistening with gun oil. Their gear was expertly loaded up in the back. Teddy sat up front next to Parker with his Washington Redskins blanket and a favorite pillow. Glenda sat in the back, clutching Big Bird and sneaking her pinkie into the corner of her mouth.

"Glenda," Parker said, casting her a frown in the rearview mirror. The finger shot out. "You gonna swim in the waterfall?"

"It's too cold, Daddy," she said, her voice like the chirp of a small bird.

"Well," he said, "not if we get a good sunny day it won't be."

"Can I shoot Marty's BB gun?" Teddy asked, looking anxiously at his father. Marty was his cousin and the proud owner of a Daisy single-pump. Amanda said no guns for Teddy until he was twelve. When no one was around, Parker would sometimes let Teddy tote the Daisy around in the woods near the cabin.

"Yeah," Parker said. "I don't see why not."

Teddy grinned broadly, clenched his fist and pumped it in the air. *"Yess."*

"What do you want to do, honey, if you don't swim?" Parker asked into the rearview mirror.

Glenda shrugged and bounced almost out of her seat when they hit a bump. She frowned.

"That's what the seat belts are for," Parker said, chuckling at the look on her face. Sometimes she was so much like Amanda.

"Can we have a fire tonight?" Teddy asked.

"Not outside," Parker said. "But in the fireplace, okay."

"Yeah," Glenda said. "Can I light it?"

"Can I?" Teddy chimed in.

"Glenda asked first," Parker said.

"Aww."

"You can help."

"But I go first, right?" Glenda asked.

"Yes," Parker said. "You go first, but Teddy can help."

As they headed west, the hills around them began to grow in size. The sky was cloudy but crisp and dry, and the autumn foliage blanketing the countryside was fiery orange, speckled in places with dark green pines. They took Route 66 all the way to the Riverton exit and then headed south. When they got to the dirt road that led to the cabin, Parker reached down and put the Hummer into four-wheel drive.

"Hang on," he said, smiling. It was like an adventure.

The twisting road ran through a canopy of colorful

hardwoods and climbed steadily upward until they came to the cabin. It was perched on a knoll in a stand of silver beech. A small brook ran past the back of the cabin, singing its endless babbling song. In the background the nearby waterfall hissed like a monstrous snake. The rich smell of fallen leaves riding on the fresh easterly breeze was intoxicating to Parker. He took a deep breath.

"Can we see the waterfalls?" Glenda asked.

"Sure."

Parker held Glenda's hand. They followed Teddy around to the back of the cabin and down a carefully groomed gravel path that led them straight through the beech trees to a small rocky bluff that overlooked the precipitous falls. The water cascaded a good hundred feet to the bottom and left a small shimmering mist in its wake.

"Stay back from the edge, Teddy," Parker said. He always said it, even though his brother had bordered the bluff's edge with boulders and the kids knew better than to go beyond them. The sight of the swimming hole and the rocky stream below was dizzying.

It was a sight that even the kids found fascinating.

Hugging one of the big boulders, Teddy peered up over the edge. "When can I go down that rope, Dad?" he asked.

"Never."

"Well why?" he asked. "Why is it there then?"

"Because my brother is a . . ." Parker said. He took a deep breath. "This isn't our place Teddy, it's Uncle Bob's place. He likes to do crazy things sometimes, but we're not doing them."

"Like 'You don't jump off a bridge just 'cause your friend does,' right, Dad?" Glenda said.

"Or shimmy down a rope and drop into a swimming hole," Parker said. "That's right, honey. You hear that, boy? Don't you ever."

Parker looked at his watch. If he was going to get out in the woods, they needed to get going. He led them back to the cabin and unloaded the vehicle. By the time he had finished, Teddy already had the Daisy in hand and was lining up the stock of recyclable cans for target practice on a big moss-covered rock by the brook. Glenda went straight to work unpacking their clothes and putting them in a drawer the way Amanda would have if she were there. When they were settled in, Parker threw a can of beans in a pan and fried up some hot dogs. It was a little early for dinner, but the mountain air made them all hungry and the kids even used the ends of their hot dog rolls to wipe up the juice from the beans.

They sat at one end of a long rough wooden table that was the only delineation between the great room with its stone fireplace and the kitchen area. There was one bedroom off the great room and two more up a narrow set of stairs. Teddy emitted a loud belch, expressing his happiness with the meal and the soda their father had let them drink instead of milk.

"You're the best, Dad," the boy said.

"Hey," Parker said, "I'm in my element here. We're in the hunt camp now."

"When's Mommy coming?" Glenda asked.

"Oh, you know Mom," Parker said. "She'll be here as soon as she can. She's got some important work."

" 'Cause this is an unexpended family vacation, right?" Glenda asked.

"That's what it is, a little unexpected, but fun," Parker

said, pushing back from the table. "Now, I want you two to clean up here—"

"Awww."

"You want to have a fire don't you?" he asked. "And marshmallows?"

"Marshmallows?"

"Uh-huh, I've got some in my bag. I was hiding them," he said, "but if you don't want to help clean up . . ."

"No, we will," Teddy said. Glenda nodded.

"Okay," Parker said, rising and taking his camouflage coat down off a peg by the door. "I'm going out to see if I can take a nice buck before dark. You guys just get cleaned up and crumple up some paper for the fire. I'll build it when I get back. I don't have to tell you not to touch the matches and Teddy, you don't use that Daisy unless I'm here. Okay?"

"Okay, Dad," he said.

Parker nodded. He kissed them on the tops of their heads and took his rifle from where it rested leaning against the wall by the coats next to his beloved turkey gun.

"I'll be back just after dark," he said. "You stay in the cabin now. Okay?"

On the porch Parker inhaled deeply again. He took the grunt call from his pocket and tested it out. He loaded three shells into his gun and checked the safety. Then he zipped up his coat and started back up the driveway, past his glorious black machine. He walked for nearly a quarter mile, conscious of the wind and dreaming of a scent-lock suit that would enable him to hunt without worrying about the direction of the wind. The thought of a scent-lock suit made him smile.

He came to the bend in the road that was marked by a small footpath. The path only went about fifty feet before ending at the foot of a sixteen-foot ladder leading up into a box treestand. Parker climbed up and sat down on the wooden seat with his back to the trunk of the massive beech. Below to his right, and halfway down a shallow ravine, he could make out the intersection of two well-used deer trails, two muddy lines snaking through the woods in the ocean of fallen leaves. To his left, he had a clear view up the driveway before it went into the bend. Sometimes deer would walk right down the drive.

Parker brought the rifle up to his shoulder and looked through the scope. If he saw a deer, that would be a nice bonus, but the wind wasn't quite right for this stand. He was here as a scout. If that son-of-a-bitch Wheeler some-how found them, then he would be there to greet him with his .243. Amanda wasn't the only one capable of protecting the family. She should know that.

And as the breeze drifted through the trees, pulling random leaves free from their purchase and sending them spinning to the mat below, Parker daydreamed about that. He could see that scumbag pervert with his little black beard trying to come down this path, and him putting a bullet right between his eyes. Parker had never killed anyone or even thought of it before, but fuck this guy. These were his kids, and this was his element.

He rested the rifle in the corner and leaned forward with his forearms on the edge of the stand to listen. If Wheeler came, Parker would definitely kill him.

CHAPTER 77

Amanda put the lights on upstairs only. Downstairs, everything remained dark, even the porch light. The thought of what Wheeler was capable of made her eyes water. She had always pushed her work into a separate corner of her mind. The evil was out there. She'd seen the horrifying corpses, but it had always been in another place. She never imagined it could come to her home, threaten her family. But now that it had, she wasn't going to go to slaughter like some dumb animal. She knew how to save herself. She walked the inside perimeter, checking locks and windows with her P40 in hand. She wanted everything open.

The front room of the house, across the foyer from their dining room, was a formal sitting room they never used. She walked across the thick gold carpet and ran her hand over the thickly woven upholstery of a large over-stuffed chair tucked in the corner. It still smelled faintly new, hinting of plastic. Amanda sat down and pushed herself back into the chair, wiggling until she was comfortable. With her back to the corner, she felt safe. It was also the perfect vantage point.

Through the picture window, she could see across the front lawn all the way to the street. There was a smaller window on the wall to her right that let her look out onto the side yard. If she turned her head the other way, she could look back through another opening to the living room and the sliding glass doors that went out back. Immediately in front of her was the foyer. She could watch the front door and the stairway that led to their bedrooms. If Wheeler wanted to get at them, he'd have to cross her path of fire—and she'd have plenty of time to see him coming.

She knew the laws. An intruder in someone's house at night could be shot and killed, and that's what she intended to do as soon as he set a single foot inside her home. She wasn't going to have Wheeler thrown in jail. He was a monster, dangerous, determined, and stoppable in only one way. Even if he were sentenced to a jail term for breaking and entering, he'd be out in a few months and right back after her. No, he had to be dealt with aggressively, but still within the confines of the law, and she knew how to do that.

She checked her weapon, took a breath, and began what she knew might be a long wait.

It wasn't.

She saw a car go past that she didn't recognize. It was slowing down. It disappeared from her sight behind a tall thick wall of lilacs and a cluster of twelve-foot blue spruce. Her palms grew damp and the knuckles wrapped around the grip of her pistol began to ache from the pressure. She focused on breathing, controlling herself. Then she saw his shadow appear from behind the black dense mass of lilacs. Only the faintest glow of moonlight shone through the clouds overhead, but it was enough for her to see his moving shape.

He was walking up the sidewalk. When he got to the driveway, he looked up and down the street before starting for the house. She could see by the tilt of his head that he was focused on the upstairs windows. Then she lost him from sight. Her heart nearly stopped. She tried to swallow. Her mouth was too dry. She listened. The doorbell rang suddenly and the sound made her jump. She stifled a cry.

Had he cut the phone line?

She sat still, determined not to give her position away. The bell rang again, and then again. He didn't stop. She thought she'd go mad. He was trying to flush her out. She rose from the chair. She needed him to be *inside* the house. Then she could kill him. She had to kill him, or sooner or later he'd get her children.

Without making a sound, she inched her way across the room. The ringing stopped when she reached the foyer. She froze. He knocked, loud. She raised the gun and held it chest high at the door. If he would just open it, open it and step in.

Her hands began to shake. She leaned against the wall to steady herself, bracing her elbow. The knocking stopped. The door handle began to turn. It squeaked, stopped, and turned some more.

CHAPTER 78

Slowly, the front door began to open. Amanda backed up. Her hands were shaking badly now. She needed more support. She couldn't get Marco out of her mind. She thought of the last man that she'd pointed a gun at, Jack Ruskin. She hadn't been able to hold steady, hadn't been able to pull the trigger. But she had to pull it now.

She knelt on the blue carpet and braced both hands against the molding between the foyer and the sitting room. The touch of dim yellow light spilling down the stairway from above made all the difference. The door swung the rest of the way open and there he stood, on the threshold. One more step and he was a dead man. He froze.

"Agent Lee?"

Amanda felt her hands drop. Her mouth followed. She stood up, still trembling.

"I almost killed you," she said.

There was a silent pause as both of them absorbed the scene.

Ruskin finally said, "You're waiting for him, aren't you?"

"I have no idea what you're talking about."

"You're going to kill him."

"I . . . You have no right," Amanda said. "What do you want? Why are you here?"

"I came to help you," he said. The two of them stood there, facing each other in the near darkness. She made no effort to turn the lights on.

"How can you help me?" she said. The bitterness remained.

Ruskin just looked at her.

"I'm not you," she said. "I'm not like you."

"I read about you," he said. "I know what you've been through, the things you've seen. I can't believe you even did what you did with Tupp, letting him out."

"He was getting out anyway," she said. "I don't have to explain this to you. You're a criminal."

Jack stepped toward her. He took a gentle hold of her upper arm.

"I want to help you," he said. "Let me."

Amanda looked up at him. Even in the faintest light she could see the clear blue of his eyes, luminescent amid his scraggly growth of beard and his dark cap and clothes. The phone rang.

Without a word, Amanda turned her back on him. She went down the hall and into the kitchen. The phone was on the desk.

"Hello?" she said in a hushed voice.

"Mommy?"

"Teddy, honey," she said, panic surging through her frame, "where's Daddy? What's wrong?"

"I don't know, Mommy," he said. He started to cry. "He said he'd be back and don't worry, Mommy, but he said he'd be back at dark and it's been dark, Mommy. Glenda's scared."

"Teddy, listen to me," she said, her voice rising. "You get your sister and you get into the basement. Get inside the crawl space where Uncle Bob keeps the peaches. Go, Teddy. Go and hide. Don't come out until Mommy gets there. Don't come out! And don't make a sound, honey. No matter what, don't make a sound."

CHAPTER 79

Wheeler was driving down the four-lane road, heading toward the park, when he braked to a stop. The big black Hummer was going the opposite way. It was like a fucking beacon. He whipped the Tahoe around but kept his distance. A fucking beacon. It was easy. Where was he going with them?

That fat-ass thought he could run and hide, hide the children. The bitch deserved to die, but first she should suffer, the way he did. Life with Hubble was like a symphony, perfect, clear, and climactic. And then she killed him.

When he got hold of those brats, he was going to do what Hubble would have done.

An angry little noise leaked out of his throat. He pricked the inside of his mouth with one of his sharpened teeth. The black vehicle got off the highway. He followed it down a rural road, keeping well back. It was so big and stupid and shiny he could let it slip from sight from time to time and then pick it back up easily. He almost lost it when it turned down the dirt road, but as he topped a rise, the glint off its back end caught his eye moving through the trees. He rolled slowly past the dirt road and then kept going.

The road went another half mile before the next turnoff. He turned around and went back, pulling off the road at the crest of a hill where he could see the driveway. He took his backpack from the backseat and began to examine its contents: rope, duct tape, some rags, a Baby Ruth bar, a bottle of water, a flashlight, and a survival knife. He took the knife out of its sheath. The serrated edge was sharp enough to cut bone. He dragged the blade lightly over his arm and watched the black nubs of hair topple and gather along the silver edge.

When the sun finally dropped behind the distant mountains, it turned suddenly chilly. He removed his sunglasses and looked at the purple ring around his eye in the rearview mirror. He put on a black North Face jacket, then started the truck. He drove down the hill and a little way into the driveway with the headlights off before stopping between two thick trees. This way, the fat bastard couldn't escape.

He got out, shouldered the pack, and set off carefully up the drive. The going wasn't easy, especially in the fading light. Rocks and mud made for tough footing. He trudged on, wary.

He rounded a bend and stopped. Something was wrong. He could feel it. By the time the gunshot registered in his brain, he was already halfway to the ground. It felt like someone had hit him in the arm with a baseball bat. He toppled off the road into a shallow ditch lined with deep ferns. He lay still. A whooping war cry came from not too far away, breaking the silence of the woods.

He opened his eyes without stirring. Another whoop went up and he saw where it had come from. The fat bastard was climbing down out of a tree with his rifle in one hand. When fatty disappeared from sight, he crawled behind a tree and wrestled frantically with the backpack. His left arm felt numb, but his hand worked enough to help his right find the knife. He drew it from its sheath and held it by his side, crouching and peering around the bole of the tree. It was almost dark.

Sticks snapped and leaves rattled. Fatty came breaking through the underbrush like a buffalo, out onto the dirt road. The fat shit jogged toward the ferns and stumbled over a rock, falling to the ground, the rifle clattering on the stones.

CHAPTER 80

Wheeler sprang from behind his tree like a panther, striking knife-first. A thudding filled the air as the knife pumped up and down, into his fat carcass like the needle of a sewing machine. A mist of blood filled the air, specking his face and hands. He pumped and he pumped and he pumped.

Fatty came to life, tossing him aside, sending an unbelievable shock of pain up his arm. By the time he could collect himself, the fat bastard had crawled away into the brush. He was rattling around in there, moaning, helpless.

Wheeler rose slowly to his feet and staggered back to his truck. He examined the gunshot wound. The bullet had gone clean through his forearm, and it felt like it had broken the bone. That fat fuck! He took one of the rags that were supposed to go into a child's mouth and wrapped it around his arm before binding it down tight with the tape.

In four-wheel drive he set off up the dirt driveway. When he got to where he'd been shot, he stopped to listen. The fat bastard was still moaning out there, but it didn't sound like he would be giving Wheeler any more trouble. He grinned and went on. When he got to the cabin it was dark, but the lights were on. Welcome.

Still grinning to himself, he got out of the truck with the backpack in hand. He wasn't going to kill them here. That would be too easy. He wanted the bitch to know he had them. He might send pieces. He skipped up the front steps and knocked on the door.

"Children," he said, calling out cheerily, "it's Uncle Charlieee. Children? Be good now, and open up the door. Uncle Charlie is here. He has kitties for you . . ."

He stopped and listened to the sound of his voice echo through the woods. The waterfalls hissed in the background.

"I said I'm here to get you!" he screamed, and then laughed at the echo.

"Open," he said, kicking the door, "up."

He kicked and kicked, his anger building, and then the door broke. He searched through the first floor, calling out to them, talking nice, sometimes screaming. Nothing there. He went up the narrow stairs and rifled through the bedrooms and their closets. Nothing. But he knew they were there. He could feel them. He could smell them.

"Bad, bad, children," he said, raising his voice above the clump of his feet on the plywood stairs. "Bad children to hide. If you come out, Uncle Charlie will be nice."

He found the door to the cellar.

"If you come out now," he said, calling down into the darkness.

He found the light and flicked it on.

"But if you don't," he screamed as he started down the stairs, "then Uncle Charlie is going to hurt you! That's what he's going to do you little fucks and you asked for it now! You made me! Now he's going to hurt you!"

CHAPTER 81

They rode into the darkness in total silence. Amanda worked her phone, dialing Parker's number again and again. It went right over to voice mail and she knew he didn't have the phone on. But she kept trying. It was all she could do. She didn't want to ring the cabin. She didn't want the children to come out.

How could Wheeler have found them? Maybe he hadn't. Maybe Parker was just being Parker. Maybe he hit a deer and was tracking it. Maybe he lost track of time. Maybe he was just being the jackass he'd always been.

"Your husband took the children to hide?" Ruskin said, breaking the silence.

"Yes," Amanda said.

Ruskin nodded. "I never had the chance to do that with Janet. My daughter. Do you know what happened to her?"

Amanda bit her lip. She didn't want this.

"I really don't want to talk to you," she said.

"She was gone for ten days," he said. He was staring out at the road.

The Subaru's hood swallowed the road's white-painted dashes whole. Amanda tightened her grip on the wheel and gave it more gas.

"They never stop, you know," he said, turning his head her way.

She looked straight ahead at the road.

"No," he said. "They just keep doing it until they're dead. Those are the rules. I didn't make them. I wrote a letter once to a father whose little girl was taken from him and killed. I signed it 'The Fifth Angel.' Do you know why?"

Amanda glanced at him quickly and then back at the road. She shook her head in disgust. When she looked again, he was still staring.

"I don't care," she said.

"It's the fifth angel of the apocalypse," he said. "I'm not very religious. I'm spiritual, but not really religious, but after all this, sometimes I think about things like that, you know?

"Anyway, this man I wrote to, his daughter was killed by that Tom Conner," he said. "And for some reason, I wanted to sign the letter that I sent him. I wanted him to know I killed Conner. I did it for him and for all the rest. I did it for all the fathers and the mothers I don't even know. I only wish someone did it for me . . .

"Anyway," he said, "I found this Bible and I looked in Revelation. I didn't know what I was looking for exactly, but I knew there was something there, something I'd heard of. The fifth angel is the one who pours out the fifth vial of the apocalypse. He pours it out on the throne of Satan and then Satan and his followers gnaw their tongues for pain. That's what it says.

"I think when I found Tupp in that cottage, shot

through the lungs, and he saw me there, that's what he was doing," Ruskin said. "I think he was gnawing his tongue. He deserved that, didn't he? It's different when it's your own kids . . . isn't it?"

Amanda pressed her lips together tightly. Her chin wrinkled and tears began to well in her eyes.

After a silence she said, "Why are you telling me this?"

Ruskin cleared his throat. He spoke quietly, gently.

"No matter how hard you rationalize it," he said, "no matter how much they deserve it, it does something to you . . . to kill someone. It changes you."

Amanda glanced at him again. His blue eyes glistened.

"I don't want you to have to do that," he said. "I don't want anyone to have to do that . . . I'll do it for you."

"Here it is," she said, forgetting everything he said at the sight of the dirt road. "Hang on."

The closer she got, the faster she went. A panicked shriek escaped from inside her when she saw the unfamiliar truck. Rocks slammed the undercarriage. Jack held on.

Amanda smashed right into the back of the white Tahoe and they both jumped out, Jack with his shiny .45, Amanda with her flat black USP 40. Light tumbled out the broken front door of the cabin.

"You go in the front, I'll take the back," Ruskin said to her. "Don't shoot me." Without waiting for a reply, he darted toward the side of the cabin.

CHAPTER 82

Wheeler had looked in every dark damp corner the cellar had, behind every broken piece of furniture, underneath every moldy rug. There was only one place they could be.

Behind the stairs was a hole in the cobblestone foundation. The pitch-black fissure bled slime down the wall. It smelled of raw damp earth. Old fruit jars reflected light from the bare bulb that hung in the middle of the cellar. They stared back at him like broken teeth.

He moved slowly toward the opening, dropping his backpack and ducking to get under the stairs. Cobwebs, draped with filth, licked his face. He sputtered and spit and wiped his face clean.

"Little fucks," he said in a singsong manner. "Uncle Charlie is here."

He could see now that the jars had been moved. He was still. He could hear her. A sniffle. His heart raced. He lifted a jar and tossed it to the side, shattering its contents across the stone floor. The rich juicy smell of peaches filled the damp air. His nostrils flared at the hint of alcohol.

He reached into the darkness, giggling now, giddy with delight—

SNAP!

Something stung his eye. He reeled back with a shriek, screaming and pawing at the pain. Blood and juice from his eye dribbled down his cheek and into his raging mouth, infuriating him further.

He pushed back the pain and darted for the hole.

SNAP!

It bit into his forehead this time, burning with pain, but this time, he kept digging. He felt the cold tube of a cheap gun barrel and yanked on it hard, snatching it from the hole and throwing it out into the cellar. A BB gun. The boy was screaming now, screaming from fright. The girl cried. The excitement of it all was truly heady. His pain only made it more . . . more climactic.

He got his hands on the boy, kicking and punching and screaming he dragged him toward the mouth of the hole, pulling him out onto the cellar floor. They wrestled momentarily and he felt a wave of dizziness wash over him when the boy kicked his broken arm. But then he righted himself and he *beat* him. He beat him and beat him and beat him until he was still.

She was still crying. Crying in the dark like an unborn baby and he liked that. He crawled into the black hole and got her out. She didn't even try to fight him, sweet thing. He found his tape and wrapped her with care, stuffing her mouth with the other rag, taping it tight. Her eyes shone wide and bright, sparkling with delicious tears.

He cradled her in his arms and ascended the stairs. That's when he heard the crash and saw the flash of sparks as another car smashed into his truck.

There was a back door and he dashed for it. The shivering little bundle under his arm began to squirm, but he held her tight.

CHAPTER 83

Jack saw the dark shape melt into the woods. He heard the *scritch-scritch* of gravel beneath its feet. He started after it, cautious, silent, keeping just off the edge of the path. He became suddenly aware of the water. With each step the hissing intensified. He felt a cool mist on his face, drifting through the dark trees. He shivered. The woods opened and Jack saw him, clearly illuminated against the broad backdrop of white spray.

Wheeler was puzzling over where to go, looking and pacing the ledge as if it were a cage. Under his arm was a bundle—no, it was a child, a little girl.

Jack felt the familiar hatred and disgust churning within his gut. He steadied his gun. He held on. But Wheeler was moving and Jack wasn't a good enough shot to pick him off. Without thinking, Jack stepped into the opening.

"Stop!" he screamed, hoping the sudden sound might make him drop the girl. "Put the girl down."

The Colt .45 was leveled at Wheeler's head but he immediately held the child up in front of his chin.

"You stop," Wheeler said. He was grinning. He hopped nimbly up onto one of the boulders balanced on the edge of the bluff.

Jack sensed the vastness of the abyss beyond. The nasty hiss of the falls came from a long way down.

"Drop the gun," Wheeler said, "or I'll throw her off."

Bile shot up from the pit of his stomach and Jack swallowed fast. He stepped back and dropped the gun.

"Now come out here," Wheeler said, grinning. "Come out here on these rocks. I'll do it!"

Jack moved slowly.

"Get up there," Wheeler said, his voice pitched with anger. Bloody spit flew from his mouth. He nodded his head toward the rocks on the opposite end of the ledge.

Jack stepped carefully up onto the biggest rock. He felt his shoe slipping on the wet stone. He looked down and sensed a flash in front of him. His heart leapt. Had the girl gone over?

No, it was Wheeler, jumping down and snatching his gun from the ground. He was laughing now, laughing at Jack, cackling insanely. He aimed the big shiny .45 at Jack and Jack closed his eyes.

The mist washed over him. The hissing became a whisper, filling his mind, dreamlike, carrying him away. When it came, the crack of the gunshot seemed distant. It was another world. Another place.

CHAPTER 84

Tears streaked down Amanda's face. She raced upstairs, saw the mess in the bedrooms, and began to cry. The kids were already gone. She dashed back down and that's when she noticed the open cellar door and the light it belched up from down below. She took the steps two at a time and nearly fell. Her eyes tore across the dreary space, dissecting each shadow, each heap, in nanoseconds. Then she saw Teddy under the stairs.

"Noooo!" she cried.

She threw herself beneath the stairs and scooped him up, cradling him, cooing and crying.

"No, no, no," she said, shaking her head, refusing to believe he was gone.

In a trance she stumbled, carrying him up the stairs and laid him on the kitchen table amid the bread crumbs.

"Teddy!" she screamed. "No!"

She pressed her ear to his chest. Nothing.

She measured up his sternum with her fingers and laid her palms against his chest. With five quick thrusts she tried to set his heart to beating. She pinched his nose and filled his lungs, twice. She pumped again, then blew, then listened. Teddy choked and gagged, vomiting hot dogs, beans, and phlegm. He inhaled dramatically, opened his eyes, and began crying. Amanda cried out with joy, then she heard the distant shout.

Glenda.

She laid her battered son on the couch and covered him with a blanket, then bolted from the cabin. The shout came from the falls. She sprinted down the gravel path. A voice cried out in her head. Amanda had no gun. She'd dropped it on the cellar floor. She had to go back, but she couldn't. There was no time. She didn't need a gun. She could kill him with her hands.

There he was, standing with Ruskin's pistol in his hand, his back to her, the shiny weapon gleaming in the glow of the falls. Wheeler was laughing. Instinctively, Amanda threw herself at him with all her force, knocking him to the ground. The gun went off. She clawed his face, tearing into his eyes. He shrieked and swung the gun at her head.

Amanda saw stars. She felt herself dropping to the ground. She sensed him rising. She reached up and grabbed his groin, clenching her fingers with every ounce of hatred she ever knew. She yanked down hard, twisting at the same time, and he came down with a shrill cry. The gun clattered on the flat top of a boulder. He struck her again, violently, and tore free, diving for the gun.

She felt a stone the size of a grapefruit beneath her. She grabbed it and went after him. He had the gun. She swung the stone with all her might, smashing his jaw, shattering teeth. The gun went off again. She swung again, connecting with his skull. She swung again and he lay still. She staggered back. Ruskin lay facedown on the ledge. A pool of blood crept out across the rock from beneath his golden hair.

Amanda heard a muffled hysterical cry. She turned to her daughter, saw her eyes, wide with fear, and spun back around. Wheeler had risen from the boulder. He stood over them, menacing, his face a bloody pulp. With a primal shriek, Amanda shot forward and struck him in the chest. His broken face discharged a tattered scream as he plummeted a hundred feet to the rocks below.

Amanda dropped down on her knees beside her daughter. They cried together as she released her from her sticky bonds. They cried and they kissed and they hugged each other. Then she heard something more. She looked up. Behind her stood Jack Ruskin, glasses broken, blood dripping freely from his nose.

He smiled.

EPILOGUE

Jack looked around at the inside of his jail cell. He was alone.

"Ruskin," the guard outside his cell said. "It's time."

Jack got up off the bunk, listening to the unique sound of its squeaking springs for the last time. The smell of ammonia, without the lemons, filled his nose. He wouldn't miss that, either . . .

It could have been much worse. He could have ended up on death row, or in a maximum-security prison for life. Here, he had been able to see the sun and the sky through a window. He had been able to use his computer, e-mail, read books, exercise. His cellmate for the past year was an accountant who had been convicted of grand larceny.

He could still see clearly the look of triumph on McGrew's face when the jury foreman read the verdict. Guilty.

But then that smile was wiped clean. Jack was found guilty of assault. On the other counts—attempted murder, second-degree murder, and first-degree murder—the jury found him innocent. Eight women on that jury, that was the key. That and the fact that Amanda Lee had refused to testify. Jack recalled her, sitting there with her husband, both of them stone-faced.

"I guess you got someone waiting for you," the guard said.

He opened the door at the end of the hall. They passed through a guard station.

"See you, Jack," the guard behind the glass said.

"Hope not," Jack said.

The guard nodded.

The first guard opened another door, and there she was. She stood up but didn't move toward him.

"Bye, Jack," the guard said. "Good luck."

Jack heard the door close behind him.

"You came," he said.

"I said I would."

Jack sighed. Her hair was down. She wore jeans and a black leather coat. She looked the same. She looked good.

"It's hard, you know, to know what will happen," he said. "E-mail is one thing. I didn't know if you'd ever really be able to understand."

"I *don't* understand," Beth said. "I told you that. I'll never understand."

"But you're here."

"I said I forgive you, Jack," she said. "That's different. I forgive you and I love you, but I don't understand. I can't."

"I know," he said.

The two of them rode together, holding hands. The warm feel of her fingers made Jack's eyes well up with happiness. He kept breathing deep.

When they reached Crestwood, it was almost dark.

The great green trees were frosted with snow and still it drifted quietly down from the sky. A gentle breeze hinted of the ocean nearby. Jack walked up the stone steps, his footprints invisible in the golden light that shone from within the old stone mansion. Even though the place was closed, the door was open. Jack went in.

There was no one in the waiting room and no one behind the desk. He looked at himself in the mirror on the wall, wondering how he would appear to her. His beard was neat now, and he'd cut his hair short.

There was a noise on the other side of the big doors, footsteps, small and quiet. The ornate brass handle turned and Dr. Steinberg's face appeared in the opening.

"Come on," she said. She spoke softly, saving her animation for the movement of her small knotty hands as she waved him in.

Jack followed her down the long hall and into a cozy wood-paneled room that also looked out over the snow-white lawn. In a red leather chair, staring into the flickering light of a fire, was Janet.

Jack caught his breath. She looked . . . better. Not all better, but better.

"Hi, Daddy," she said softly, looking at him, sadly, but looking.

"I love you, honey," he said. He hugged her, gently at first, and then gradually tighter. She hugged him back and he began to cry. When he stopped, he took a staggering breath and, sitting on the arm of her chair, removed a newspaper article from his pocket. He handed it to her.

She looked inquisitively at him. He glanced nervously at the doorway, but Dr. Steinberg was gone.

"Read it," he said.

She read. Her fingers began to tremble. Jack saw a tear drop from her face and splat against the newsprint. He felt sick, but when she looked up at him, he saw the look of relief.

"You don't ever have to worry," he said. "He's gone."

Janet bit her lip and nodded. She hugged him again and he kissed the top of her blond head until Dr. Steinberg appeared in the door with an urgent whisper that he had to go.

"I love you, Janet," he said. "I have to go, but I'll be back. I'll always come back.

"And then, one day soon"—he glanced briefly at Dr. Steinberg—"maybe you'll come to me."

Jack let himself out the front door. The clouds gave way to a bright slice of moonlight. The snowflakes drifted down. He retraced his steps to the Saab. Its rear end sagged under the weight of all the things inside. He got in. On the way down the long lonely road, Beth reached over. Jack kept his eyes on the road ahead, but he grasped her hand as if he would never let go.

More
Tim Green!

Please turn this page
for a
preview of

THE FIRST 48

available
wherever books are sold.

PROLOGUE

His name was nobody. Nobody Jones. Nobody Smith. His passport and cruise ship ticket said Mott, a name he'd found on a bottle of apple juice. You could do such things without much effort when you knew the right people, and you had the money. Official documents and tickets were only what you told people you were. He liked being Mr. Nobody. Especially Nobody on a vacation.

On the third day, they'd cruised out of San Juan and headed over to Grand Cayman. He spent most of his time on deck by the pool, watching the women slather themselves with suntan oil and drink funny little drinks with umbrellas. There was nothing like this in Ukraine. This was like Mars.

But now he had a feel for it all. He knew the ship. He knew the people, their habits, and the way they talked to each other. There was a group of twentysomething men who sat around a glass table under the eaves of the bar playing a drinking game they called quarters. He had practiced in his cabin, bouncing his own quarter off of the small bathroom vanity and into his drinking glass.

There was an empty chair. He bought two pitchers of beer at the bar, and, standing there in his flowered shirt and khaki shorts, he asked if he could play.

They looked at him, grinning, red-faced from too much sun and too much drink. Two laughed out loud. One grin turned into a frown.

"Sure," someone said.

He plopped the pitchers down in the middle of the others. Beer sloshed up over the lip of one and spilled into the swill that already lathered the tabletop. He sat down and adjusted his straw hat. He stroked his thick mustache and the game began again. Quarters bounced off the glass. Some went awry, finding the deck. Many plunked into the drinking glass full of beer, and they shone brightly from the bottom amidst the swirl of bubbles and golden liquid.

You had to point with your elbow, or you were the one who had to drink. He learned fast, though, and soon his own dark hairy elbow was flashing around the table. There were groans and a few cheerful curses. He flagged a waitress for four more pitchers, then lost his turn on purpose so as not to hog the game.

The laughter grew hot like the sun-baked wood beneath his feet. They began to call him the Russian Bear. He had to roll back a sneer. He was a Soviet from Ukraine. He'd told them that. Hadn't he shown them the CCCP lapel pin stuck to the collar of his shirt? Leave it to a handful of American jackasses not to know the difference.

It was his turn again. He reached into his pocket and fingered the little wax bead until it broke. Then he worked the quarter and sent glasses of beer all around the table.

It was half an hour before a tall thin man with bad skin and a shock of short blond hair popped up out of his seat, turned, and vomited in the general direction of the pool spattering three rows of deck chairs. Screams erupted and two of the people in deck chairs got sick as well.

The Soviet stroked his wiry mustache and left the table in the midst of the uproarious howls of his new friends. He climbed the stairs to the deck that overlooked the bar and pool. There was a chair by the railing with no one in it. He removed the soggy towel from its back and sat down to watch. Within a half an hour, two more young men lurched to their feet, also sick. The game broke up and he went to the casino.

The next day the ship stopped at Cozumel. The Soviet was in the casino again when the fat lady next to him at the blackjack table turned green, clutched her stomach, and hustled for the bathroom. Later, a farmer from Ohio lost his ham sandwich at the roulette wheel, and the casino shut down amid the twittering laughter.

That night less than half the vacationers showed up for dinner. People stared accusingly at one another, and if someone coughed, heads turned and hands gripped the table's edge. The waiters in their cheap tuxedos shot nervous glances at one another and spoke in subdued tones about the three-layer chocolate cake. The Soviet drank a good deal of the tart cork-tainted Chardonnay and grinned around at the others who sat at the half-empty table picking at their food.

On deck at 2 A.M. a helicopter sputtered secretly down out of the dark sky. Medivac. Two gurneys were hurried out across the deck. In the flashing lights of the helicopter, he could see the wincing faces. Tubes in their noses. IV bottles swinging above them. Nobody knew that they probably wouldn't make it. Word spread fast. By 6 A.M., there was an angry crowd outside the bridge demanding that the ship return immediately to port.

Later that day as they were pulling into Miami, a line snaked in front of the ship's hospital all the way out onto the deck. People covered their faces with T-shirts and makeshift masks. A dozen people were trampled by the crowd pushing to get down the stairs and off the ship. The Soviet waited patiently, then tugged the wrinkles out of his flowered shirt and marched ashore with his leather briefcase, trying not to smile at other people's misfortune. Who could blame him for that? After all, it had been a very fine vacation.

CHAPTER 1

Tom Redmon didn't need to hear more, but he knew the couple needed to talk. Beneath the desk, he clenched and unclenched his hand, squeezing the tennis ball, trying to be patient. Finally, they finished. The mother was sniffing and dabbing her eyes with a napkin from McDonald's. He looked past them and out through the old glass to a bright locust tree, wavy and distorted.

In his office, the paneling of one wall sagged under the weight of diplomas. A 1996 calendar of a German castle high on a mountaintop hung by a pushpin. In a wood frame was a cheap print of Van Gogh's *View of Montmartre with Windmills*. Tom loosened his tie and unbuttoned his collar. Size nineteen. If he could, he'd take off his coat.

The couple was young. Their little girl sat between them, her eyes hollow, her head bald and white. When she smiled, her teeth shone gray with great gaps between them. The father worked at the power plant, stoking coal. The mother stayed at home. There were four other kids, too. None of them were sick. Yet.

Tom slapped his hand on the desk, and said, "We'll sue them."

"Who?" the father asked.

"Everyone," Tom said, standing. "GE. The state of New York. The city of Ithaca. The Power Authority. The EPA and the DEC."

"Everyone?"

"I mean it," Tom said. "I've done it before. I just sued the New York State Dormitory Authority and won.

"These big corporations. These colossal government entities. They need to be taken down, and that's what I do, Mr. Helmer. Don't you worry, Mrs. Helmer. They'll pay."

"I just want her to be okay," she said through the napkin.

"We all do," Tom said.

He patted the little girl on the shoulder. She smiled up at him.

"I'll have the papers ready for you to sign by the beginning of next week," Tom said. "Say Tuesday. How's ten?"

He opened the door, and his secretary looked up from her romance novel. She was sixty. Yellow hair. Cat glasses and chewing gum.

"Tuesday at ten for the Helmers, Sarah," he said. "We'll start on the papers first thing tomorrow morning."

He showed them out and turned to Sarah, his secretary. She sat staring blankly at him.

"The property management company called again," she said.

"That's the problem," he said, smiling. "When one man owned this building, a favor here and there wasn't forgotten. Now it's a nameless faceless LLP that you can't appease, and you can't kill."

"We are two months late."

"Let them evict me," he said. He winked and grinned

and took off his blazer and lost the tie. "Take the rest of the day Sarah. Get some sun."

"You've got Mr. Potter scheduled for three-thirty."

"Cancel it."

"Tom, they will evict you."

"Cancel it. This Helmer case could be the big one."

"We've had a lot of big ones, Tom," she said. "They never pay. The small stuff is what pays."

"We got the janitor."

"That's one. They settled because their witness died, remember? Mr. Potter will pay a retainer up front. I told him that on the phone and he agreed."

"Sarah," he said. "I know you care, and I appreciate that. But I'm sick and tired of DUIs and shoplifters and aggravated assaults. I'm tired of drug dealers, pickpockets, drunks, crackheads, motorcycle gangs, and dregs. These are the people I used to put in jail."

"You're a defense lawyer, Tom. You need money to file that suit. You need an index number. You need an investigator," she said. She was standing now with her hands on her thick hips. "You already owe Mike Tubbs six thousand dollars."

"He sent a bill?"

"Of course not," she said, pressing her lips tight.

Tom flattened the tennis ball and rubbed his chin.

"Then reschedule Potter for Thursday and go get some sun," he said. "It's beautiful out there. And do me a favor, will you? Dial up Mike Tubbs and tell him I'll meet him at Friendly's at three-thirty, sharp."

"Of course," Sarah said.

CHAPTER 2

At Friendly's Ice Cream, Tom edged past a sunburned crowd of summer tourists wearing visors, shorts, and golf shirts where an empty booth waited for him in the back. The waitress set down two sweaty glasses of water just as Mike Tubbs stumbled in, jostling the tourists. Thirty years old. Flirting with the three-hundred-pound mark. A head of thinning hair with small, matching, ginger mustache and goatee. Extremely capable.

The broad forehead beneath his fine hair was beaded with sweat. A streamer of toilet paper rode in on the bottom of his sneaker.

"Sorry I'm late," Mike said as he wedged his way into the vinyl booth.

Tom took the younger man's meaty hand and shook it.

"A good investigator," Tom said, "respects time."

Mike smiled, but his cheeks went pink.

"Sorry, I . . ."

"Two chocolate Fribbles," Tom said to the waitress.

"Could you make mine light on the chocolate?" Mike said, raising an inquiring finger toward the waitress.

She scrunched up her face.

"You just make it with vanilla ice cream," Mike said.

The waitress looked confused.

"Forget it," Mike said. "It's okay."

"Okay," she said.

"And miss," Tom said.

"Yes, sir?" she said, barely forcing a smile.

"You better take this now," he said, handing her his American Express card.

"This one's on me," he said to Mike with a wink.

"Hey, you don't have to do that," Mike said.

Tom raised his hand, signaling an end to any debate.

"Now," Tom said, "you and I have some things to discuss . . ."

Mike looked down at his hands and pattered his fingers against the tabletop.

Tom smiled and leaned back into the booth feeling a cold blast of air-conditioning on his face.

Over Mike's shoulder, he noticed a man who had just entered the restaurant wearing a three-quarter-length Army coat. His eyes were small and shifty. His face was dirty with stubble. His dark hair long. Tom squinted and started to slide out of the booth.

"Tom?" Mike said, turning to look over his shoulder.

"Shh," Tom said. His hand was on the tabletop, his butt on the edge of the booth, his feet tucked up under his knees.

"Who would wear an Army coat in the middle of summer?" Tom said in a low hiss.

"I don't . . . know," Mike said.

The man looked around and marched up to the cash register. His hands were jammed in his coat pockets. He spoke to the cashier. A young girl with a paper hat whose face went suddenly pale. Her mouth, pink with lipstick, formed a perfect O.

"The price of greatness is responsibility," Tom said under his breath, his eyes on the man.

"Churchill?"

"Yes," Tom said. He was on the move.

"Tom?" Mike said, from somewhere behind him.

Tom was halfway there. When he hit the cluster of tourists, he shoved them aside.

"Hey," someone said. Irate.

The girl was nodding to the man now. Frightened. Teary-eyed. She reached into the cash register, saw Tom, and hesitated. The man looked over his shoulder and spun around with his hand clenching something inside the jacket pocket. Tom was in his stance. He uttered a cry.

The man's hands darted from his pockets. In one was a dark heavy object.

A woman screamed.

Tom shot in. He chopped one hand, then the other. The object fell to the floor. The man lunged. Tom had his arm. He pivoted and tossed the man over his hip to the floor.

When the man hit, his breath left him in a great gust. Tom was on him instantly. One hand expertly clamped to his throat. The other pinning the wrist that had held the weapon.

"I've got him!" Tom yelled. "Everyone back! I've got him!"

Someone was crying.

The robber's eyes rolled into his head. Tom looked up. The cashier. Her pink face was crinkled. Mascara streamed down her cheeks.

"It's all right, young lady," Tom said. "It's all right. Someone call the police."

The girl cried harder.

Mike was there, bending over. He had the weapon.

"Tom," he said, putting a hand on Tom's shoulder. He held something in front of Tom's face.

"Come on, Tom," Mike said in an urgent whisper. "Let him up. It's a wallet."

A uniformed policeman burst in through the front door with his gun drawn. More people screamed. The herd of tourists broke past the hostess's stand for the rear of the restaurant.

"Freeze!" the cop yelled.

"I've got your man," Tom said. "He was trying to rob her."

The girl behind the cash register, still bawling, said, "He wasn't. He wasn't. That's my dad."

The store manager popped up from behind the counter. He put his arm around the girl and patted her back. He glared at Tom.

"What?" Tom said.

"Mr. Redmon," the cop said. "What the hell did you do this time?"

"I . . ."

"It's my fault," Mike said. "I'm sorry. I told him it was a robbery. Tom is a martial arts expert."

"Jujitsu," Tom said, getting up and dusting his hands. "I'm terribly sorry. It's a martial art with roots in feudal Japan, a period lasting from the eleventh to the sixteenth centuries of near-constant civil war."

"Jesus," the cop said, holstering his gun and kneeling down beside the fallen man. He began to chaff his wrists.

"I'm very sorry," Mike said. He pulled a fat wad of money from the front pocket of his pants and stripped off a hundred-dollar bill. He slapped it down on the counter. "This is all my fault. Come on, Tom. I'm sorry."

Mike led him out by the arm.

"Holy shit," Mike said.

"Hey, my credit card," Tom said, turning to go back.

"Tom," Mike said. "Later. Please."

"Who the hell wears an Army coat in the middle of summer?" Tom asked, shaking his head.

"Please," Mike said, tugging at his arm, looking frantically around, his cheeks burning with color, "let's just get out of here."

"Now you're not going to cover my back?" Tom said, shaking free. "When I was a cop, a partner covered your back."

"How can you say that?"

"How can I not?"

"You . . . I . . ." Mike's face bunched up. "Who helped you dig up that federal judge's wife to see if she died of natural causes? Who was that?"

"I'm not talking about that kind of stuff," Tom said, getting into his old Ford truck. "That was a mistake. I just have discipline. I've trained myself to react."

"I've got discipline, too," Mike said, raising his chin. His nostrils widened.

"In what, Mike?"

"Fiscal discipline," Mike said. His lips were smashed together tight.

Tom's face went slack. He opened his mouth, then stopped to catch his breath.

"Is that what this is about? Money?" Tom said. He looked hard at Mike. "And I'm buying you a Fribble?"

Mike threw his hands up in the air.

"I knew about your doubts. Ellen said something to me . . ."

"Ellen?" Mike said, his face losing tension. "What?"

"She . . ." Tom clamped his mouth shut. He had slipped. How could he tell anyone that sometimes she was still there? There and gone. Sometimes whispering. Sometimes it was just her laughter. He wondered himself.

"I've got to go," he said, closing the door.

"Tom . . ."

Tom backed out of his spot and got onto the road.

Halfway to the marina, he pulled into the convenience store and bought a six-pack of Labatt Blue beer. Next door he picked up a small brown bottle of Knob Creek. His heart pounded in his chest just watching the deep brown liquor swish in the thick glass.

The summer in upstate New York brought with it a rich carpet of trees. But even the sweep of broad green maple leaves and the whispering blades of the huge locust trees couldn't entirely conceal the crumbling gray concrete, the sagging metal roofs, and the corrugated walls washed in rust.

Like so many small upstate New York cities, Ithaca was pockmarked with structures that had long outlived their usefulness. The worst of these buildings butted right up against a lush green park that capped the south end of Cayuga Lake. Tom drove through the worst of them, graffitied brick, plywood for windows, kicking up gray dust in the heat.

The marina lay nestled in the midst of this eyesore. Tom's boat was a once-proud twenty-one-foot Regal with an open bow. *The Rockin' Auitie*. Previously owned by the spinster from L.A. who spent her summers on a lake home up in Aurora.

The hull had been battered up one side and down the other by nearly twenty years of minor accidents. The windshield wiper had no blade. The prop was gouged and bent. Its red racing stripe had faded to a drab dirty pink. It rested between two sailboats, sleek and white, with their long sweeping lines. Tom didn't know how to sail; that was for people who grew up with money.

He was the son of a cop who was the son of a cop. Their combined experience on the lake could be traced to a couple of fishing poles and a bag of ketchup and bologna sandwiches on board a battered aluminum skiff. In his mind, he could still hear the wheezy seven-horse Johnson outboard motor and smell the oil that bled from every seam. It had been the sole constituent of the Redmon family fleet.

Tom popped open the first of the Labatt Blues. He dropped down in a cushioned seat and leaned back, cutting off the wax around the whiskey bottle's neck. When he tilted his head a certain way, that first bit of whiskey heating the inside of him, he almost felt like she *was* there.

Had it really been ten years?

"You know the secret everyone wants to forget," she said. *"It's why you are who you are."*

He looked at her foggy shape, his cheeks feeling wet.

"You know there's evil in this world," she said. *"True evil. And it's only a matter of time before it enters your life again."*

He nodded.

And he drank.

GRIPPING READING FROM
NEW YORK TIMES
BESTSELLING AUTHOR
TIM GREEN

☐ **DARK SIDE OF THE GAME:**
MY LIFE IN THE NFL
(0-446-60520-4)

☐ **THE RED ZONE**
(0-446-60756-8)

☐ **OUTLAWS**
(0-446-60635-9)

☐ **TITANS**
(0-446-60636-7)

☐ **RUFFIANS**
(0-446-60637-5)

☐ **DOUBLE REVERSE**
(0-446-60849-1)

AT BOOKSTORES EVERYWHERE FROM WARNER BOOKS

1123a

VISIT US ONLINE @
WWW.TWBOOKMARK.COM

AT THE TIME WARNER BOOKMARK WEB SITE YOU'LL FIND:

- CHAPTER EXCERPTS FROM SELECTED NEW RELEASES

- ORIGINAL AUTHOR AND EDITOR ARTICLES

- AUDIO EXCERPTS

- BESTSELLER NEWS

- ELECTRONIC NEWSLETTERS

- AUTHOR TOUR INFORMATION

- CONTESTS, QUIZZES, AND POLLS

- FUN, QUIRKY RECOMMENDATION CENTER

- PLUS MUCH MORE!

Bookmark AOL Time Warner Book Group @ www.twbookmark.com